Quiet Man

Also from Kristen Ashley

Rock Chick Series:
Rock Chick
Rock Chick Rescue
Rock Chick Redemption
Rock Chick Renegade
Rock Chick Revenge
Rock Chick Reckoning
Rock Chick Regret
Rock Chick Revolution
Rock Chick Reawakening, a 1001 Dark Nights Novella
Rock Chick Reborn

The 'Burg Series:
For You
At Peace
Golden Trail
Games of the Heart
The Promise
Hold On

The Chaos Series:
Own the Wind
Fire Inside
Ride Steady
Walk Through Fire
Rough Ride, a 1001 Dark Nights Novella
Wild Like the Wind
Free

The Colorado Mountain Series:
The Gamble
Sweet Dreams
Lady Luck
Breathe
Jagged
Kaleidoscope
Bounty

Quiet Man
A Dream Man Novella
By Kristen Ashley

1001 Dark Nights

EVIL EYE
CONCEPTS

Quiet Man
A Dream Man Novella
By Kristen Ashley

1001 Dark Nights

Copyright 2019 Kristen Ashley
ISBN: 978-1-970077-24-7

Foreword: Copyright 2014 M. J. Rose

Published by Evil Eye Concepts, Incorporated

Acknowledgments from the Author

One thousand and one thanks to Liz Berry and MJ Rose for creating an outlet for authors to work together to share their creations and bask in the sisterhood. Not to mention, gratitude must be extended to my darlings Liz and MJ for being such *fabulous* shopping enablers.

Thanks also to their team for all their hard work in prettying these babies up and getting them out there.

And last, much love to Lottie and Mo and much gratitude to them for letting me tell their story. I loved spending time with you two, and I can't wait for more!

Rock On!

Sign up for the 1001 Dark Nights Newsletter
and be entered to win a Tiffany Key necklace.

There's a contest every month!

Go to www.1001DarkNights.com to subscribe.

As a bonus, all subscribers can download
FIVE FREE exclusive books!

One Thousand and One Dark Nights

Once upon a time, in the future…

*I was a student fascinated with stories and learning.
I studied philosophy, poetry, history, the occult, and
the art and science of love and magic. I had a vast
library at my father's home and collected thousands
of volumes of fantastic tales.*

*I learned all about ancient races and bygone
times. About myths and legends and dreams of all
people through the millennium. And the more I read
the stronger my imagination grew until I discovered
that I was able to travel into the stories… to actually
become part of them.*

*I wish I could say that I listened to my teacher
and respected my gift, as I ought to have. If I had, I
would not be telling you this tale now.
But I was foolhardy and confused, showing off
with bravery.*

*One afternoon, curious about the myth of the
Arabian Nights, I traveled back to ancient Persia to
see for myself if it was true that every day Shahryar
(Persian: شهريار, "king") married a new virgin, and then
sent yesterday's wife to be beheaded. It was written
and I had read, that by the time he met Scheherazade,
the vizier's daughter, he'd killed one thousand
women.*

Something went wrong with my efforts. I arrived in the midst of the story and somehow exchanged places with Scheherazade – a phenomena that had never occurred before and that still to this day, I cannot explain.

Now I am trapped in that ancient past. I have taken on Scheherazade's life and the only way I can protect myself and stay alive is to do what she did to protect herself and stay alive.

Every night the King calls for me and listens as I spin tales. And when the evening ends and dawn breaks, I stop at a point that leaves him breathless and yearning for more. And so the King spares my life for one more day, so that he might hear the rest of my dark tale.

As soon as I finish a story... I begin a new one... like the one that you, dear reader, have before you now.

Chapter One

Smithie

"I'm getting a breast reduction."

Smithie took his attention from the piece of paper he held in his hand, looked across his desk and all the way across his office to the woman striding through the room.

The woman who was the subject of the words written on the paper in his hand.

His throat was tight.

"I'm going natural," she finished her announcement.

Charlotte McAlister.

Lottie.

Known far and pretty damned wide as Lottie Mac.

Lottie Mac, Queen of the Corvette Calendar.

Though Smithie just called her Mac.

He'd been wrong. She wasn't done finishing her announcement.

Mac stopped at the front of his desk and proclaimed, "And you can't talk me out of it."

It took Smithie a minute to force his mouth to regain the ability of speech.

"I don't care what you do to your body. It's not my body. I don't know why you think I'd have a say in it."

Lottie gawked at him.

He got this.

He was a strip club owner and she was a stripper. His premier stripper. He had velvet ropes to contain the people who lined up, wanting to watch her dance. It wasn't a stretch she'd think he'd have a problem with her getting rid of her implants.

Forcibly pulling his mind from the paper in his hand, he turned it over and laid it on the desk, giving his full attention to Mac.

And what she was saying.

Mostly, *why* she was probably saying it.

Before he could dig into that with her, she kept speaking.

"I interviewed seven plastic surgeons in the Denver area. I've chosen one. I'm doing it next month."

"Why?" Smithie asked.

"Why?" Mac asked back.

"Not heard a thing about you doin' this, now you're not only doin' it, you did all the research into it," he pointed out. "So what's the deal and what's the rush?"

He knew both.

He just wanted to have the conversation.

"There's no rush," Mac lied.

When these women would learn that they couldn't get away with lying to him, he did not know. He was in a variety of relationships with several women of his own, had kids with them, and he'd run a strip club for decades. He could spot a lie before the person even spoke the words.

Hell, his bouncers were the worst culprits. They thought they had that, "you're a man and I'm a man" thing going on when no man was any kind of man if he lied through his teeth.

"Mac," he stated warningly.

She didn't answer his question.

She said, "People will still come watch me dance."

"I know people will watch you dance. Had Joaquim do a head count coupla months ago for a few nights. Thirty-five percent of the people through the door were female. They say ten percent of the population is gay. So we can assume ten percent of that were lesbians who might have another reason they're here to see you. But that means twenty-five percent of those females were here just to get a drink, but mostly to watch you dance. And you're probably the only time a man can get away with saying he comes to a strip club to take in the talent of a dancer's moves. You got big tits, you got regular tits, it's not gonna affect your line at the rope. So let's stop with the bullshit. Now, tell me *why*?"

Mac lifted her chin and stated, "I'm also looking into sperm donors."

There it was.

Smithie sat back in his chair.

"Mac—" he began.

"I'm not getting any younger, Smithie," she snapped.

As noted, he was in a relationship with several women. They knew about each other. Mostly, they shared because he was a lot to take and they didn't mind the break.

But often, it was a juggling act and he was the juggler.

One thing he learned that helped him not drop a ball was never to field it when a woman lobbed that at him.

Though, he didn't field it right then not just because of that.

"It's your sister," he noted.

She shook her head. "It isn't my sister."

"How many has she pushed out for Eddie so far?" Smithie asked a question the answer to which he already knew.

"Jet doesn't make babies *for Eddie*," Mac shot back.

Smithie sighed.

"I'm just ready," she stated.

"You are not ready," he returned.

Her face turned from confrontational to pissed.

"You think I haven't thought about this for a long time?"

"I think, when you decide to bring a kid in the world, once you think you've thought about it long enough, you should think even longer about it. Then you should talk to people in your life about it. Then you should think on what *they* say about it. And only when you're super, double, *extra* sure do you do it."

"I've got the money—"

Smithie shook his head. "It isn't the money, Mac. But even if you think you got the money, you don't got the money. It's not about the food in their bellies or the roof over their heads. It isn't about keepin' up with all the latest phones and kicks. It isn't even about saving for college tuition. It's all the shit times in life that are gonna rise up and bite you in the ass that you didn't count on. They're your kid. They're gonna roll with the punches. But are you ready to say you're in the spot you're good to make them do that if that shit happens?"

Mac said nothing, looked to the side, then took a step that way and sat her ass down in one of the two chairs in front of his desk.

She was not ready.

At all.

She was something else.

And Smithie needed to get to the bottom of it and not to save her fantastic tits.

To save her from jumping too soon into something for which she was not ready.

He leaned forward in his chair and dropped his voice.

"There's gonna be a mean kid in class that gets in their face. There's gonna be a health situation that's probably the croup or a flu that you're not gonna understand and it's gonna scare you shitless. Girls'll get their hearts broken by an asshole. Boys need to learn not to *be* assholes. You gotta have it together, Mac. No one can be fully prepared for being a parent. But you gotta *know* you're as ready as you'll ever be."

She held his eyes and said, "I'm ready, Smithie."

"You're watchin' your sister and her man make babies and you're so in love with your nephews you can't see straight so you're feelin' the time tick by and doin' that, the itch is comin' on to one you can't help but scratch," he returned.

"This has nothing to do with Jet and Eddie," she returned.

"Okay, then, how often does Jet go out with those Rock Chicks? Answer me that, Mac. How often?"

"She sees her crew all the time," Mac told him.

"Right, and she can do that because her husband is home, lookin' after their boys."

She got his point.

This was why she shut her mouth before opening it and saying, "Or Blanca looks after them."

"Blanca looks after them when Jet and Eddie are out together. Unless he's workin', no one looks after his boys but him if their momma ain't around to do it."

Mac turned her head and studied the wall.

It wasn't that interesting.

But she kept doing it.

"Mac, look at me," he ordered.

She did, that stubborn lift in her chin.

Smithie took his voice to soft. "You're gonna find him, darlin'."

She got his point on that too.

"I don't need a man," she bit out.

"No. But you want one and you're gonna find him. You just need to be patient."

She was losing patience sitting right there. "This is not about finding a man, Smithie."

"How many of the Rock Chicks don't got a warm body in their bed?" he pushed.

"I can get a man whenever I want."

She absolutely could do that.

She wasn't beautiful. But she was pretty. Crazy pretty.

Her sister, Jet, had the quiet, shy, girl-next-door vibe going for her.

Mac couldn't be more different.

She lived life large and loud. She was sexy, but not brash, instead ballsy. She had an opinion, she stated it. She loved you, she showed it. You were toxic, she scraped you off. She identified a goal, she worked to it.

If she wanted it, she got it.

Except a man.

She was a serial dater, not because she liked to play the field, but because most men were motherfuckers and she had zero tolerance for that.

Not that she should.

She just didn't.

As far as Smithie was concerned, that Rock Chick posse had lucked out. Found the best men there were in Denver. Claimed them (or got claimed, whatever). Game over.

Then again, Lee Nightingale had essentially vetted them for his woman's friends, so he'd already taken the guesswork out of it.

"Havin' a kid is a lot easier when you got someone to help," he pointed out.

"*Havin'* a kid is all on the woman," she retorted.

"Okay then, smart girl, *raisin'* a kid is a lot easier, you got someone to help," he revised, and before she could get anything out of her mouth, he went on, "and you can't argue that. You had a single parent home and who raised you?"

That mouth closed.

"Your sister 'cause your mom was working," he answered for her. "Now what's your sister got?" He again answered for her. "Pointin' out the obvious, I didn't wanna hear this shit, but I heard it when you bitches were gabbin', and from the first, if he wasn't workin' a case, Eddie got up with Jet for every feeding. Every *damned one*. Went and got his boy and brought him to his wife. Took him back and laid him down. Same with the next one that came along. And so on. Jet didn't even have to get out of bed."

He had a point to make but he took that too far and he knew it when her chin wobbled before she got control of it.

"Mac—"

"I want a baby," she whispered.

He believed her.

She also wanted an Eddie.

"Give it time," he whispered back.

She threw up both hands. "How much?"

"As much as it takes."

"Sadly, I can't Mick Jagger this sitch and make a baby when I'm seventy."

Jagger shouldn't even be doing that shit.

"Honey, you're still in your thirties," he reminded her.

"They're all gone," she declared.

Now he had no idea what the woman was talking about.

"Who?" he asked.

She bopped forward on her seat with agitation. "*Them*. The good ones. The Hot Bunch. The only ones left are Roam and Sniff and they're too young for me. Not to mention, if Shirleen thought I'd even spoke their names in a conversation like this, she'd cut me."

She was not wrong.

Shirleen was Roam and Sniff's foster momma, though in her mind, there was no "foster" about it and it wouldn't matter one bit that Roam and Sniff were both long since of age and men in their own right.

She would cut her.

Mac was also not wrong that the Rock Chicks had snagged all there was of the Hot Bunch.

Maybe Lee was hiring.

"Mac, darlin', just give it time," he urged. "And in the meantime, spoil your nephews. Because when you find a man and you start makin' your own babies, you won't have the time for them you have now, but you'll love it that you had the time you have now. You dig?"

She gave it a beat before she puckered her lips and blew out a breath.

Then she said, "I'm still going natural."

She dug.

Crisis averted (or at least this one, he corralled strippers, bouncers, bartenders and waitresses, they were all young and fit and prone to do stupid shit, so it seemed his entire life was averting disasters).

This one over (for now), Smithie rolled a hand at her, turning his eyes to his desk. "Do whatever you want with your tits. Just give me some notice. I gotta prepare the staff to adjust to half the amount of asses in seats, I don't got my headliner."

"Smithie," she called.

He turned his eyes back to her.

She was now grinning.

And she had a new declaration.

"You're the shit."

"I know that seein' as I put up with your crazy ass. Now get out. I'm not up here twiddling my thumbs. I got shit to do."

She kept grinning as she rose from the chair and sashayed her tight ass to his door.

"Close that behind you," he ordered.

She didn't close it behind her.

She turned at it and looked to him.

"I'm giving it a year."

Something else Mac was.

Decisive.

"I'll take it," he replied. "Now get out."

She shot him a white smile that miraculously his retinas had built up a tolerance to so they weren't burned out, then she moseyed out the door.

Thankfully, she shut it behind her.

Smithie stared hard at it while considering hefting his bulk over to lock it.

He wasn't going to take the time.

Instead, he picked up the paper, turned it over and read it again.

It stated, plainly, he was fucked.

More alarmingly, it stated, chillingly, Mac was in danger.

This was a problem more than it was already a colossal motherfucking problem.

Any other one of his girls, he'd pick up the phone to Lee Nightingale, the man behind Nightingale Investigations, the commander of the baddest badass motherfuckers in Denver. He'd hand over this letter and he'd get this problem solved.

But Mac was Charlotte McAlister, Jet McAlister Chavez's little sister. Jet was married to Eddie Chavez. Eddie was Lee's best friend. And Jet worked for Indy, Lee's wife, the Queen of the Rock Chicks, and thus Jet Chavez was a bona fide Rock Chick.

Mac might not be a card-carrying member of the Rock Chicks, mostly because she had a job where she worked nights, the time those crazy bitches instigated the most fucked-up of their varying antics. Though they weren't averse to mornings and afternoons. It was just that the stungunnings, kidnappings and the like mostly took place at night, and Mac was busy then.

She was still a Rock Chick, or at least she was by association.

Considering the Rock Chick link and the blood ties to Jet, if Lee knew Mac was in danger, he'd tear the town apart to put a stop to it.

And Eddie…

Now Eddie, Smithie didn't even want to think about it. The man was a cop. The shit Lee and his boys did with flair and a flagrant disregard to just about anything, Eddie could not do.

But Eddie wouldn't blink at doing whatever he had to do to make his sister-in-law safe.

And the man had mouths to feed.

So yeah.

This was a problem even more than it already was a colossal motherfucking problem because Smithie couldn't call Lee.

Which meant Smithie had to find a different set of badasses to deal with it.

His first call would normally be the Chaos Motorcycle Club. Mac wasn't one of theirs, neither was Smithie, but they had ties to Lee, they could keep a secret, and they didn't dick around when it came to women and their safety.

But they'd just come out of a war, and like any war, that had been some serious fucked-up shit.

They needed a breather.

Lee, and Chaos, also had ties to…

"Well, hell," Smithie muttered, the words on the letter blurring, the sick feeling in the back of his throat easing.

He dropped the letter and picked up his cell.

If you couldn't call a badass…

Then it was far from second best to call a commando.

* * * *

"Let me see it."

Smithie lifted his eyes from his laptop on which he was doing the club's accounts to the tall, built, black-haired man prowling through the door.

Behind him strode a man that even gave Smithie, who this didn't happen to often, a tingle of, "Holy fuck, don't let me meet that guy in an alley."

"Well, hey there, motherfucker," Smithie greeted the man in the lead. A man known as Hawk. "And by the way, come on in."

Hawk Delgado had made it to the front of Smithie's desk.

He stopped there and held out his hand.

"Smithie, let me see the letter."

Seeing as the man was wearing a tight black T-shirt over black cargos and black cargo boots, looking like he was about to invade Somalia, and more, *could*, but he was in an office over a strip club in Denver, Smithie dug the letter out from under a bunch of stuff on his desk and handed it to Hawk.

The hulk behind Hawk edged closer and read over his boss's shoulder.

While reading it, Hawk's face only tightened a little.

The face of the man behind him went from scary to *Jesus fucking shit*.

"I read it to you over the phone," Smithie reminded him.

He didn't have to, and Hawk didn't have to remind Smithie that he was a busy guy, but Smithie had phoned and Elvira, Hawk's assistant, had picked up. He'd read the letter to her and she hadn't messed around with getting her boss on the line.

When Hawk heard it, Hawk got un-busy, called Smithie, then Smithie had read the letter to him.

So he'd made even more time to drop on by.

And there he was, tight-faced and clearly taking that letter as seriously as Smithie took it.

He finished reading and looked at Smithie.

"Before this one, you get any more of these?" Hawk asked.

Smithie shook his head. "Though I think one is enough, don't you?"

He handed the letter over his shoulder to the monster behind him.

"One is enough," Hawk agreed. "You got the envelope?"

Smithie dug out the envelope the letter came in and handed it over.

Hawk didn't even look at it. He gave it direct to the man behind him.

Then he asked, "You call the cops?"

"You know who Lottie Mac's sister is?"

Hawk's mouth tightened even further.

He also knew how gonzo Eddie Chavez would go if he knew someone had written that letter about Mac. And any cop who read that letter would go straight to Eddie.

"Charlotte McAlister know about that letter?" Hawk asked.

Now Smithie understood Hawk definitely knew who Mac's sister was.

He knew who Mac was. That letter didn't refer to Mac as anyone but Lottie Mac and "Charlotte McAlister" was not the name Smithie used on the marquee.

"I haven't shared..." he paused, "yet."

"She get an escort home?" Hawk kept at him.

"To her car at night." After he gave him that, Smithie shook his head again and wished he wasn't doing it. "Not home."

"Fuck," Hawk muttered.

"She will now," Smithie told him. "In fact, I got a guy sittin' on her house right now, which is where she is. She was here, but she took off and I put a man on her."

Hawk jerked his head to the man standing behind him. "He'll be relieved by Mo."

Well, all right.

Smithie could get on board with that beast being Mac's bodyguard.

Smithie stood. "I approve of your selection, Delgado, but what next?"

"We track that asshole down and put him out of commission," Hawk replied immediately.

And it didn't take long to slide right into the gray area with Hawk Delgado.

No, that wasn't it.

Lee could do gray and did. All the time.

When it came to Delgado, shit got downright murky.

"What would that entail?" Smithie asked.

"Do you care?" Hawk returned.

"Kinda, considering I'm payin' you for this shit," Smithie told him.

"Whatever it needs to entail," Hawk answered. "That letter," Hawk did another head jerk, "we'll need to make absolutely certain our message is received. Could be building a case to hand over to the cops. Could be something else."

Right. For now, he could deal with that.

"Mac needs protection," Smithie stated.

Hawk nodded his agreement. "And she'll have Mo. Twenty-four seven. We aren't Secret Servicing this shit, even if we are. He's on her, day and night. He sleeps on the floor by her bed if she doesn't have a chair or something in her bedroom. He goes to the grocery store with her. He stands outside the bathroom while she's showering. I'm thinking you can fill in the rest of that picture."

He could fill in the picture, but Smithie wasn't sure he was totally following.

"Secret Servicing this shit?"

"Secret Service passes off. They do shifts. There will be no pass off. Mo's hers for as long as it takes to find this guy."

Now Smithie wasn't sure he was liking what he was following.

"Is that smart?"

"I'm sure I can make a passable attempt at finding a decent stripper. Though I couldn't pick a headliner if she tapped me on the shoulder. So how 'bout you let me make the calls I gotta make 'cause you assume I know what I'm doin' like I would do for you if my business got caught up in yours. Something that's happening right now. But I'll let you do yours if you let me do mine."

"Gotcha," Smithie murmured.

"Your staff, on heightened alert. The dancers. The bouncers. The bartenders and the waitresses. I'll brief them, tell them what they're lookin' for, this being after we interview them to ascertain if they've already clocked someone of interest. You tell McAlister. She needs to know and make smart choices. I'll coach her on that."

Smithie flicked his gaze to Mo and back to Hawk. "Won't Mo coach her on that?"

"Mo's not a communicator."

This was not a surprise.

Hawk spoke on.

"Call her. Tell her she's got Mo. Tell her he's not on her house, he's gonna be *in* her house. Tell her she's gotta come in early. Tell her Mo'll be bringin' her in early. I'll be here when she gets here, and you and me'll share. I'll tell her what she needs to know. And we'll go from there."

Smithie nodded.

Without another word, both men turned as one to walk out the door.

Smithie watched them go.

After Mo disappeared out the door, Hawk stopped there and turned back.

"Secret Service is also trained to put themselves in the path of the bullet," Hawk said.

Shit.

"Right," Smithie whispered.

"For that man on the mark, it isn't about getting the target to safety. It's about taking the bullet *for* his mark. You with me?" Hawk asked.

That Mo guy was a leviathan, but he wasn't bulletproof.

Goddamned *shit.*

"I'm with you," Smithie confirmed, because he had no choice.

Hawk studied him before he noted, "You haven't asked me how much this is going to cost."

"That's because I don't care," Smithie told him.

They held eyes.

Hawk broke it by lifting his chin and exiting the room.

He shut the door behind him.

Slowly, Smithie sat in his chair.

He'd had trouble in the club from some assholes not long ago.

At the time, it had nearly broken him. He'd thought it had come in the form of a man's worst nightmare about what could happen to women he held in his heart.

He'd been wrong.

Chapter Two

As Often as I Could

Lottie

When the doorbell rang, I was already mildly freaking out.

When I looked through the peephole and saw nothing but a black compression shirt covering a muscled chest, I got even more freaked out.

I was barefoot. My peephole was nearly at eye level. Regardless, it magnified the area outside it.

And still, all I saw was chest.

Right…

How big *was* this guy?

"Who is it?" I shouted through the door.

"Mo!" was grunted back.

Okay, that was the name I was given.

"Squat down, I can't see your face!" I yelled, still looking through the peephole.

The chest moved, and a thick, ropy throat came into view before I got a face.

Whoa.

Smithie described my new bodyguard as "motherfucking huge, bald and ugly."

He got two things right.

The last was a matter of opinion. That fixed stare from silver eyes under a protruding brow and over a large nose that was framed by cut cheekbones with cavernous cheeks and a jaw so perfectly angled, it could be used in geometry class could be considered too brutish for some.

But not me.

This was going to be a problem.

"I'm opening up!" I bellowed, still staring at his face.

That face disappeared, and I got his throat and chest again as he straightened.

Yes, this was going to be a problem.

I unlocked and opened my door.

Then I immediately, and automatically, took a step back.

All right.

Whoa.

I could get a hint from the chest and what it might be attached to with what I'd seen of that throat, but this guy had to be six five, maybe taller.

And his height was only a part of why Smithie described him the way he did.

He wasn't "motherfucking huge."

He was *motherfucking huge.*

I was average height.

But slender.

My sister had ass.

My job was physical. It wasn't just the nightly dancing. It was the practice and constantly choreographing and adding new routines. I could probably eat a boatload, but I didn't because I was too busy to eat, and when I did, I'd learned long ago what all the experts said was what an expert would know from studying it. Eating good food gave me more energy, made me sleep better and put me in a better mood (most of the time).

So unless the occasion was special, I put good food in my mouth and didn't drink much outside water, flavored water, sparkling water, with the odd antioxidant vitamin drink thrown in.

So yeah, I was slender.

And two of me could make this guy.

Maybe three.

He moved forward.

I moved back.

His movements were unwieldy. Not clumsy—heavy and plodding.

It didn't matter this guy was a bull in a china shop.

He'd terrify small children.

Hell, he'd terrify grown men.

And that had nothing to do with the gun worn openly on his hip.

It had to do with what that compression shirt barely contained, not to mention the carved protrusion of the muscles of his biceps exposed by the short sleeves, the sinewy, richly veined lengths of his forearms and the trunks of his long legs covered in dark gray commando pants.

He shut the door behind him, twisted at the waist and I heard the lock click.

He twisted back to me.

"Hey," I forced out.

He dipped his chin.

"You're Mo," I stated unnecessarily.

"Yup," he agreed.

"Okay, so…"

I stood there, barefoot, in my tight tank that had ridden up to gather around my middle and as such exposed an inch of flat belly over my low-slung faded jeans, and I didn't know what to do.

He was looking me in the eye.

Right in the eye.

Not once did his gaze drift down.

Or up, to my hair.

I had great hair.

And great tits.

And, well, not to be conceited or anything, but considering a lot of folks came to watch me take my clothes off, it wasn't lost on me I had a good body. But I already knew that because I just did.

I was struggling with dealing with a man who not only looked like this but was also as big as this and was there for the purpose he was there.

But it was worse because I had no clue how to deal with a man who looked me right in the eye and appeared to have no interest in anything beyond that.

Except for the fact I was no longer freaked out, and considering Smithie had phoned to tell me I now had a bodyguard, though he'd shared he'd explain why later, my freakout might have been mild, but I'd still been freaking.

Now, instead, I was battling the urge to climb him like a tree.

I contained the urge and asked, "How freaked out should I be that Smithie put you on me?"

"Hawk'll get into that."

Well, there you go.

Freakout returned.

I mean…

Hawk Delgado?

Smithie hadn't mentioned Hawk Delgado.

Smithie had only mentioned I had a bodyguard, and ugly stuff had gone down at the club in the past. Ugly stuff that tore Smithie up. So I put it down to him being overcautious, something he was now on a normal basis.

Hawk Delgado was either reaching the extremes of overcautious or shit was serious.

And my guess was, Smithie didn't tell me about Hawk because he was parceling out the bad news.

Shit.

"Right. Hawk," I said. "Now how freaked out should I be that Smithie brought in a guy like Hawk Delgado for whatever is going on?"

This guy made no reply.

He just kept looking me in the eye.

"Mo—"

"Hawk'll get into that," he repeated.

I threw up a hand. "Listen, I'm sure this is no big thing. It isn't unusual to have guys fixate on me. It's happened before. They're typically harmless."

Mo had nothing to say to that either.

"Or Smithie has a word with him or sends in Joaquim or Jaylen and they back off. If they had the guts, they'd just approach me from the beginning."

Mo still didn't feel like replying.

"If Smithie's freaked and called in Hawk, that says to me I should be seriously freaked," I pointed out.

Again, no input from Mo, but it cut through my freakout that he might not be moving his mouth, but his eyes said, "Yes, you should be seriously freaked."

So I went from getting seriously freaked to *being* seriously *freaking* freaked.

"Ohmigod," I whispered, my hand drifting to my belly. "This is bad."

That was when it happened.

That exact moment was when my entire life changed.

His gaze moved down to my belly.

And his face went from harsh and impassive to wholly beautiful.

This was because it softened.

Whatever was happening, he hated it was happening.

Whatever had Smithie freaked, me freaked, Hawk Delgado (of all people) pulled in to deal with it, Mo didn't want it to be happening. He didn't want me to feel what I was feeling, what I would feel until this situation was brought to an end.

He hated I would be feeling that too.

He was there. He was going to get paid to protect me from it.

But it was not just a job to him.

It was more.

He did not know me, and I wasn't just a great pair of tits and a fantastic head of hair any guy with a dick would want to see go unharmed.

I was a person who was feeling something sucky and he was a person who didn't like people to feel sucky.

No.

He hated it.

That was the guy he was.

Yes, my entire life just changed.

"Mo," I called quietly.

His attention returned to my face.

"It's gonna be okay," I assured him.

That strong chin dipped again.

Okay.

Moving on.

"Do you want something to eat?" I asked.

"Tour," he grunted, but he did it not looking around.

He needed to know the lay of the land.

But now I had another problem.

I was nervous.

Actually nervous.

I didn't get nervous around guys.

Handsome. Confident. Built. Successful. Rich. It didn't matter to me.

Were they funny?

That mattered.

Were they smart?

That mattered too.

Did they have goals in life and weren't afraid to do the work to attain them?

That totally mattered.

Did they define me as a stripper in all that conveyed to the judgmental world who didn't get I really couldn't give that first fuck what people thought about what I did to make a (very good) living? Thus, they thought I was sleazy and easy and could get in my pants and then brag they tagged a stripper and not even remember my name?

That definitely mattered.

I couldn't remember the last time I was nervous around a guy.

In fact, I didn't think there *was* a time I'd been nervous around a guy.

But I had this insane desire to play with my hair, was worried I'd trip when I turned around to guide him into my house, and worst of all, I was suddenly completely focused on not doing anything that would make him think I was a dork, an idiot, or anything the slightest bit unattractive.

Shit.

I successfully made the pivot and moved him through the short foyer of my Denver Tudor into the living room and immediately regretted decorating in mostly white.

White with gray veins in the marble of the fireplace. Boxy white contemporary sofa (though it had big, colored throw pillows and warm but light-colored wood feet). White walls. White curtains (though they hung at the sides and the Roman shades were bamboo). Even the rug was mostly white with a gray geometric pattern. But the floors were oak (however, it was *white* oak, *gah!*).

Did Mo like fresh, clean and bright?

Did he have a problem with the salmon accents?

I mean, my armchair was salmon. Was that too feminine?

And if he sat on the sofa, would he bang his head on my standing lamp that arched over the side? (Thank God it was black.)

"Uh," I swept out a hand, making a mental note to adjust the arch of the lamp, and turned to him, "this is the living room."

He said nothing.

But he walked to the window closest to him and my blinds—which were only partially lowered because they looked good that way, giving the room a warmer feeling from the wood—came down because he made that so.

He then lumbered over to the other window and did the same.

"Okay, so no one looking in, right?" I guessed, feeling the room turn suddenly chilly, and not because the sun was no longer shining into it.

He turned and dipped his chin to me.

He then looked toward the open plan dining room and kitchen that fed from the living room and moved there.

I followed him.

The (white) dining room table had a turquoise block rug under it.

That was good.

But the kitchen had oversized, gleaming white subway tile all over the walls. Stark white counters. Though one side was white cupboards, the other side was black, and I had one below-counter, hunter green cupboard to throw in some contrast. The railing to the stairs that led down to the back door was white, but the door was black.

More bamboo shades, no curtains.

And the floor was tiled in a kickass black and white artisanal design and the light fixtures were gold.

The hunter green was *semi* manly.

Did men do white?

At all?

I realized when Mo made the rounds of the blinds in the dining room and kitchen that he didn't care about artisanal floors or my stemmed, wide but shallow wooden fruit bowl and whether or not that fruit bowl was feminine or mostly unisex.

Through his ministrations, the entire space was shrouded in darkness, so I flipped a light switch.

And he didn't care about the gold fixtures.

He was again looking at me.

"While this is going on, you should feel free to eat and drink what you want," I offered and opened the door to my fridge (white SMEG, dammit, SMEG was definitely girlie, wasn't it?). "You cover my ass, *mi casa* is definitely *su casa*."

His gaze flicked to the inside of the fridge and his face registered open approval I could not miss before it came back to me.

So, he ate healthy too.

And maybe he approved of my obsessive lining up of stuff and tidy placement and (perhaps OCD) usage of matching food storage containers.

If he did, this would be good.

I mean, it looked like a Container Store ad in there.

It was then it hit me he didn't say much.

But he definitely communicated.

And this was further demonstrated when he turned his attention to the foyer.

He was done in the kitchen, time to move on.

I didn't move on.

"I like light, bright space."

"Blinds closed," he declared.

His voice was very deep. Not rough. Not smooth.

Just right.

Shit!

"I mean, I like bright space so that explains all the white," I told him.

He didn't care even a little bit about all the white.

His attention went again to the foyer.

"And I'm tidy," I shared.

He looked to me.

Then immediately back to the foyer.

Okay then.

Time to move on.

I moved us on.

I took him along the short hall that contained the stairs to the study and TV room on the other side of the house (more closing of blinds).

After that, I took him up the stairs and into the guestroom, bathroom and my pole room where I practiced and choreographed (he didn't bother with the shades in the guestroom, but the pole room was closed off for sure).

We then went into my master.

I was pretty proud of my house. You know, me buying it. Me gutting it (or hiring someone who did that). Me decorating it. All on my own. No help. No man.

The little stripper that could.

And the master was the *masterpiece.*

The two-side slanted ceilings of a Tudor upper floor. The diamond-paned windows that featured the window seat. The shelving around all that filled with my beloved books (yeah, strippers read) and stereo. The clean-lined lighting. The cool rattan rugs. The creamy tones of the couches and bedclothes, all this mixed with some warm orange notes in the toss pillows, because I liked orange.

Mo had no opinion on the color orange or the fact it was clear I read a lot.

Mo assessed the fact my tall, but narrow windows (all four across, with two square on top) didn't have blinds and his mouth got tight.

"The bathroom has frosted windows," I shared helpfully. "And there aren't any windows in the walk-in closet."

The bed was against the back wall.

He turned and looked down at me. "Do not go near those windows or the couches."

My master was huge. I had a massive seating area for reasons that were mostly aesthetic, unless my nephews were up here messing around, which was usually right where they ran the minute they entered my house because it drove Jet crazy and my boys *and* me loved driving my big sister crazy.

Two couches faced each other over a coffee table made entirely of glass.

If I was in the mood, it gave me options for lounging and reading.

It gave Mo bad thoughts.

"I read a lot, Mo, and—"

"No window seat. No couches. Or we put up a sheet until this is over."

I pressed my lips together and sucked them between my teeth.

A sheet would totally mess with my masterpiece.

"And you're not in this room without clothes, ever," he went on.

I let go of my lips and nodded.

"Not even just underwear," he added.

That seemed OTT, considering.

"I strip for a living, Mo, and—"

"Not even just underwear."

Okay then.

I nodded.

"I sleep on the couch." And he tilted his head toward the couch.

Um…

Say *what?*

"I have a guestroom," I pointed out.

"I sleep on the couch."

"Won't one of Hawk's other guys—?"

"Just me."

Okay.

Wait.

What?

"You're not gonna…trade off or something?" I asked.

He shook his head.

Once.

I still got the negative.

"Well, uh…I don't want to be telling you your job, but…is that the way it's normally done?"

"Absolutely."

It was?

I clearly showed my surprise because after I did, the Quiet Man gave me more words.

"Military. You train with someone. You bunk with someone. You breathe their air all day every day, they mean something to you. You could hate their guts and you'd still form a bond. They're in it with you. They're family. There are men…and women…who might rush into danger just to save a life. But there's a big difference between instinct and already being in danger. Knowing your time could be up at any moment. And watching that grenade fall at your feet. Which is also at the feet of your brothers. Then throwing yourself on it knowing every man standing with you has the same exact thought to do the same exact thing because one might have to go, but that bond is so strong, you'll die not to make the other ones have to break it."

"You're gonna need to throw yourself on a grenade for me?" I whispered.

"I need you to trust that I'd throw myself on a grenade for you."

That was easy. I did that already. I mean, he was wearing cargo pants. And a gun.

And I could do it and he could sleep in the guestroom or have an afternoon off.

"I trust you, Mo," I promised.

"You have no idea the meaning of the word trust, Ms. McAlister."

"Lottie."

He tilted his chin up this time.

"So, you have to sleep in the same room with me?" I asked.

"Yes," he answered.

"But you'll be sleeping."

"I require four hours of sleep a night, ma'am. And from REM to battle ready requires two point five four seconds. I don't know what the time is to do that and get down the hall if you're facing a threat. I just know it's longer than two point five four seconds."

Two point five four.

Exact.

"You've timed it?" I queried disbelievingly.

"Yes."

Wow.

"When will you shower?"

"I don't waste time when I shower. It takes less than five minutes. So I'll shower with you in the bathroom with me and the door locked or I'll shower while you're dancing, when Smithie has his men on you. That is, if I feel the club is clear. If not, I shower with you in the room with me. Outside me taking away that choice, it'll be your choice."

He did not offer the choice of showering *while* I was showering in the same shower, which was a shame.

"Why don't we, um…just play that by ear," I suggested.

Back to dipping his chin.

"Do you need to go pack a bag or something?" I asked.

"It's in my truck," he answered.

"Okay," I muttered.

His deep voice went low. "This will be done soon and I'll be gone."

Now who was a freak?

I was.

Because I didn't know exactly what was going on, but I knew it was bad, and I still didn't want it to end because I knew exactly one solid thing about this guy, the fact he was called Mo, and I didn't want "this" to be done soon so he'd be gone.

"What's your full name?" I asked abruptly.

"Kim Seamus Morrison."

I stared at him. "Your name is Kim?"

"My mother's Norwegian."

Since I wasn't an expert in Norwegian names, that didn't explain it, except apparently Kim was a Norwegian dude's name.

"Your dad?" I pressed.

"Half Scottish. Half dick."

Oh man.

He rattled that off by rote.

I opened my mouth.

He shook his head.

"This doesn't get personal," he stated.

To hell with that.

To hell with nerves too.

There might come a time he'd shower with me in the bathroom with him.

Or better, with me in the shower too.

So yeah.

To hell with that.

I motioned to the couch, "We're bunking together. We're breathing the same air. You wanna train together, I'll show you the pole and you can spot me on the weight bench. You'd fall on a grenade for me. I'd say this was already personal."

He said nothing.

"Mo," I snapped. "Seriously. Who knows how long this is gonna take? You can't just hulk around silently with your gun on your belt, waiting for something to happen to me."

He again said not a word.

Which told me he could hulk around silently with his gun on his belt, waiting for something to happen to me.

Or more, waiting for it to happen so he could stop it.

"Okay, Rambo, how about I don't *want* you hulking around silently, waiting for something to happen to me," I amended.

More nothing from him.

I crossed my arms on my chest (and *still*, he didn't look in that direction).

I got paid for men to look at my tits, it was my way of life.

But never did I *want* a man to notice my tits as much as I wanted Mo to notice them.

"Right. I'll start," I offered. "I'm Charlotte McAlister. Not *ma'am*. Never *ma'am*. Lottie to family and friends. Which means Lottie to you. Lottie Mac to the world. Queen of the Corvette calendar and headliner at Smithie's strip club. You got a problem with me stripping?"

One head shake.

"You think I'm downtrodden and promoting the objectification of women?" I asked.

He looked around the room briefly.

This answered part one of my question.

He looked to me.

"Yes."

That answered part two.

But wait.

Whoa.

"Really?" I asked.

His mouth said nothing.

His face repeated, "Yes."

"I'm not, you know. I can do what I want with my body, including using it to make money," I stated.

"True," he muttered.

"And I'm a woman." I jerked my head his way. "You are very much not. So I think that's my call to make."

"Where does it go from there?" he asked.

"Where does what go from there?" I asked back.

"You take your clothes off for money. And then where does it go from there?"

I felt my eyes get squinty. "Where do you think it goes?"

A shrug of his massive shoulders which I was pretty sure wafted a breeze through the room.

I still got what he was saying.

"So me stripping means I'm in some way responsible for a man's bad behavior," I translated the shoulder shrug verbally. "Because, you know, me stripping means men can think of women on the whole as nothing but sex objects, if they want them to or not, and further on from that, they can *treat* them as sex objects, whether we want to be treated that way or not."

Mo didn't confirm.

His look did.

"That's bullshit," I told him.

He silently disagreed with me.

"And it's manthink," I informed him.

This made him look amused.

And again I wanted to climb him like a tree.

Those silver eyes dancing and his mouth quirking an eighth of an inch up at the ends?

Damn.

We totally had a problem here.

In fact, several of them.

But the one I wasn't going to get into right then was me thinking about how badly I wanted to treat *him* like a sex object.

"You know, men get drunk a lot," I pointed out. "Women do too. They get drunk alone, among only men, or only women, or mixed. It happens millions of times every day and every night. And does every one of those millions upon *millions* of men get drunk and then go out and perpetrate a sexual assault on a woman?"

His amusement vanished.

"No," I answered for him. "Because to do that, they have to have the monster in them. Bottom line. You either have it in you to do that, and thank God the vast majority don't, or you don't. It has not one thing to do with booze. Or drugs. Or what a woman wears. Or what she doesn't. Or how she behaves. She has absolutely no responsibility *at all* for a man harming her. A monster does that because he's a monster. He just hides it when he's sober. But when he's weakened, that monster comes out. And that's it. The end."

His big body shifted slightly, but he made no response.

Though I read in that it *was* his response.

He was with me.

"And the same with any kind of bad behavior a man commits," I continued. "If he harasses a woman. If he beats her. I'm sick and tired of men, and women for that matter, blaming women for the bad behavior of men. That said, there's something that helps to make this never ending. You know what perpetuates this kind of thing?"

He shook his head.

"Locker room talk and no man in that room having the balls to say, 'You know what, that shit does not make you sound cool. It makes you sound like a loser who can't get laid by a real woman. Knock it off,'" I told him. "When men allow men to talk shit about women, *that* reduces women to sex objects. It gives the impression all the men in that room are down with reducing women, and with that validation, some men carry on with that, the asshole ones, and they do things directly in an attempt to reduce women. And since it's men doing it, they have no clue what it's really doing. Reducing *them*."

Mo agreed with me.

He didn't say it.

I saw it.

Considering he communicated his response (his way), and even though I liked he had that response, I kept talking.

"Turn this around, what do you think of a woman who goes to a Chippendales show? Thunder Down Under? Is that about skanky guys who are probably addicted to drugs and have no other choice in how to make a living?" I asked.

"Skanky, maybe. The rest, no," he muttered.

I felt my lips twitch but kept at him.

"Though, women who go to those shows are thought of as randy or out-of-control bachelorettes with their bridesmaids or desperate. Why the contradiction?" I demanded.

"Men that watch strippers are considered randy or bachelor party dickheads or desperate," he returned.

Hmm…

"I do not let men objectify me, Mo. I don't drag them to the club to watch me dance. They come on their own. And you can look at it two ways, just as you could look at a woman watching men dance while taking their clothes off. I make a damn good living off a man who's totally down with appreciating the female body and he's at one with the fact he enjoys it, or it turns him on, and it ends right there. Or I make a damn good living off weak men who are weak because they're not strong enough to respect strong women, even if those women are strong women taking their clothes off. And I'm okay with both."

"You're you," he grunted.

"And what does that mean?" I asked.

"You're beautiful and together and confident and I hear you're talented. Most women who do what you do don't do it because they're proud of it. They do it because they're in a life where they don't want to. But they have to."

There was a lot there.

Primarily the fact he thought I was beautiful, together and confident.

Good job I didn't trip when pivoting to show him the living room.

But also, he had a point.

"Yeah," I agreed.

His expression registered surprise.

"I don't have an argument for that," I told him. "Though I will note that I didn't ask about how you felt regarding the career of stripping as a whole. Just me doing it."

For a second, his face blanked.

Then he let out a roar of laughter.

I was relatively sure my toss pillows wobbled.

And I was transfixed.

Totally transfixed.

I'd heard one thing that was more beautiful.

The laughter of my nephews.

But this was a close second.

I stayed transfixed for only a beat.

And then I dedicated my life to making him laugh as often as I could.

Thus I was smiling at him when he quit.

He didn't look in my eyes then.

He stared at my mouth.

Now we were getting somewhere.

"Are you hungry?" I asked.

He shook his head.

"Are you going to tell me about your military service?" I went on.

He shook his head.

"Are you going to tell me how your dad's a dick?" I kept at him.

He shook his head.

"We'll get there," I mumbled, beginning to head to the door, still mumbling. "I'm hungry. Time for dinner."

I walked out the door of my bedroom.

Kim Seamus "Mo" Morrison, my bodyguard and the most fascinating man I'd ever met, followed me.

Chapter Three

Start with Your Toes

Mo

She was on the stage, busting out a performance to Shakira's "Loca," and making Mo, for the first time since he started with Hawk, wish he had another job.

Honest to fuck, if he managed to get through the whole night, and all three of her feature sets (this was number two), without jumping off the stage and punching every motherfucker watching her in the throat, it'd be a miracle.

He got why she was the headliner.

He got why it was a packed house.

She was graceful. She knew how to dance. She was beautiful. She had an awesome outfit on (or was taking it off).

And she was sexy *AF*.

Christ.

He'd learned during the first set that he needed to watch the crowd, which was his goddamned job, and not her or he'd be standing in the shadows just offstage, unable to take his eyes off her at the same time fighting his dick getting hard.

Which was what every motherfucker out there was doing.

And why Mo wanted to punch them all in the throat.

Fuck.

If they didn't get this guy and soon, this was going to be torture.

Mo knew this without a doubt.

And he knew it wasn't just about her dancing.

It was also about her just being *her*.

But he was trying not to go there.

And failing.

Her house was the shit.

Her fridge was as neat as his (if he went grocery shopping, which was rare, he was too busy working and hanging with his buds and his family, but if he did, the inside of his fridge looked like hers, mostly, without the lining up of shit, but he'd start doing that the minute he got the shot).

Her barefoot, all that blonde hair tumbling down, in that tight tank and those jeans with her little ass he could palm in one hand, for fuck's sake.

That massive bed he'd give his left testicle to fuck her in.

The fact she could concede a point in a discussion without being a bitch about it.

Her huge, bright white smile.

And most of all, how she'd taken the news from Hawk and Smithie.

She read the letter. Hawk's call. Smithie had not liked it (and honestly, Mo didn't either), but Hawk wanted her to understand the seriousness of the situation.

Mo knew she'd been freaked.

Her face got a little pale, and that was it.

But he could smell it on her.

Then she listened to Smithie, and after, Hawk, total eye contact, short head nods, complete focus.

No interruptions.

No hysterics.

No backtalk.

Almost the same when he was going over things with her.

Sure, she balked at the shower gig. Sleeping in her room. He got that. It was an intimacy and invasion of privacy she wasn't ready for.

She still didn't give him shit and make him spend half an hour explaining precisely why he knew what he was doing, and she had to listen to him.

And she'd agreed not to bring in Eddie or Lee and his boys.

This, Mo knew, was to protect them. Those men had lived through a lot while claiming their women. Car bombings. Kidnappings. One of their women shot. Another one raped.

There'd been peace for a few years. They'd had weddings. Made babies.

It was all copasetic, or as much of that as it could be with Rock Chicks in the mix.

They'd go apeshit at that letter.

And Lottie knew it.

So she agreed immediately to protecting them by keeping them in the dark.

It was the smart call.

But for her, it was more the loving one.

Charlotte McAlister was a class act. Funny. Smart. Talented. Thoughtful. Together. Professional.

And sexy *AF*.

Yeah.

This job was totally going to be torture.

"Jorge, other side," Hawk said in his ear and Mo turned his head to look at his boss who was standing behind him. Mo was unconcerned and unsurprised Hawk got the drop on him. If the man wanted to, he moved like a ghost. "Need you a minute."

Mo only left his place to follow Hawk when he looked across the stage to see Hawk's second in command, Jorge, standing there.

Jorge was not watching Lottie, his attention was on the crowd.

This was good.

Mo trailed Hawk as he walked down the back hall past the dancers' dressing room to the end where there was a door to the back. Quieter there, but you could still hear the music.

Hawk stopped and turned.

Mo stopped and shifted slightly to the side so he wouldn't have to waste the nanosecond it'd take if he had to make a full turn to get back to Lottie if she needed him.

"You saw her first set," Hawk noted.

Mo nodded.

Hawk jerked up his chin.

Then he asked, "You gonna be able to do this?"

Hawk Delgado was not stupid.

And he knew his men.

"Fuck no."

His boss didn't look surprised, but he started to look impatient.

"Mo—"

"But I'll do it," he finished.

"It's just a job. Her job. Three sets. A couple songs. Then she sits back in the dressing room because Smithie doesn't want her mingling," Hawk told him something Smithie already briefed him on.

Smithie didn't want her mingling not because it made her seem elusive and exclusive.

He did it because he knew, like Mo knew, that a lot of men were assholes, those who weren't were whackjobs, and the ones who were neither of those were at home with their wives.

In other words, Smithie didn't want her in danger.

Where she was now.

Because she stripped.

"I'm on it," Mo stated.

"It's just her job, Mo. She's good at it. She's famous for it. But to her, it's how she pays her mortgage," Hawk told him.

He didn't need another lecture about stripping that day (or ever again).

But he was surprised Hawk would press this with him.

Mo had four older sisters.

Hawk knew Mo had four older sisters and a mother, all of whom Mo looked after since he had his first coherent thought, so no way he'd ever be down with a woman taking her clothes off for money.

That didn't matter.

It wasn't about it being *her* job.

It was about it being *his* job to protect her.

And he could do that.

"I'm on it, Hawk," he repeated.

Hawk gave him a look.

Mo just stared at him.

Hawk got his meaning and because he did, he shared, "Callin' in a favor with a friend at the FBI. That religious fanaticism shit, Lottie might not be the first for this asshole. Sent him a copy of the letter, he's gonna run it through their system to see if there's any language quirks that match."

Good.

Mo nodded.

"Postmark gives us nothing," Hawk carried on. "Doing an analysis on printer, toner, paper, envelope, stamp. Stamp was self-adhesive, so no DNA, also no print, which does not bode well. Could be some on the flap. Took prints off the letter. Got one of our friends at DPD to run 'em."

Lottie hadn't touched the actual letter, just a copy.

The actual letter would have his, Hawk's, Smithie's and maybe the perp's prints on it.

Mo hoped like hell if it did, the guy was in the system so this could all be over and quick for Lottie, but also for him.

"Jorge and I had a sit down with all the bouncers and bartenders on tonight. Tomorrow, we'll hit any who were off tonight. And the dancers," Hawk continued. "Askin' if anyone's seen someone that gives off a bad vibe, a regular that creeps them out, anyone who's said something that's off."

"Know the drill, Hawk," Mo reminded him. But he asked, "Anyone give you anything?"

"It's a strip club. Every second asshole out there gives off a bad vibe, creeps someone out or says something that's off."

Great.

"We'll get him and we'll get him quick, Mo," Hawk assured him.

Mo nodded again.

The music ended, the crowd went wild, and without an order from Hawk, or a word to him, Mo pivoted fully and strode swiftly down the hall.

He met Lottie coming off the stage, shrugging on a robe.

She barely glanced at him before she rushed across the hall to the dancers' dressing room.

"Man coming in!" she called as she pushed through the door.

He hesitated a beat, two, but that was all he gave it for the girls to get situated before he followed her.

He was fighting a sea of strippers heading the other way as he walked in.

"Got it covered, Mo," he heard Hawk call.

Mo glanced over his shoulder, lifted his chin at his boss, then looked away before the door closed him in on Lottie.

He'd been in there earlier as she got ready, sitting in front of one of those mirrors with the lights all around that you see in movies, makeup and hair shit scattered all over the shallow counter in front of it. She'd gotten dressed behind a screen, something that had surprised him, considering what she did for a living, but after watching her act the first time, he was grateful for it.

The other dancers had clearly been warned about his presence before they'd showed.

Some of them did the behind-the-screen thing, some of them did their thing right out in the open.

He didn't watch. He wasn't there for material to have a yank later.

But he was beginning to understand the difference between life and performance.

This was their space, and for some of them, they needed it safe.

Out there, it was a job for bills only.

Other than that, Mo hadn't bothered to take much else in because he didn't give a shit what a stripper's dressing room looked like.

He didn't take anything in then because Lottie was on him.

He automatically flexed his body solid when she put her little hands into his chest and shoved with all her might.

He didn't move an inch.

Before he could ask what the fuck, she was shouting at him.

"*Where were you?*"

Ah, hell.

He opened his mouth to say something, but she kept shouting.

"I did a turn, looked for you, *and you weren't there!*"

Right.

He could smell she was scared.

But now she was showing it.

Big mistake.

He never should have done that to her.

She should not be feeling what she was feeling.

Most of that was not on him.

But he shouldn't have left her.

No way.

And that was absolutely on him.

The worst part about it, he didn't feel bad because he freaked her, and he shouldn't have.

He felt bad because he freaked *Lottie*, and he didn't want her to feel that, or more of it.

He'd had so many bodyguard jobs, he couldn't count them.

He already knew this one was different. But the feeling he was feeling right then knowing he did something to spike her fear, he now knew this one was going to be even more of a challenge than he thought.

"Hawk needed to talk to me," he told her. "Jorge was on you. Other side of the stage."

"Could Hawk maybe talk to you *after* you tell me you have to take off so Hawk can talk to you?" she asked.

"Next time, we'll do that," he muttered.

"Jesus!" she yelled.

Then she did it.

Fuck him, his worst fear (for now).

She turned stiltedly, raked a hand through her hair, looked at the floor, started pacing with agitation, and chanted in a whisper, "Jesus, Jesus, Jesus."

"Lottie."

She had her back to him, but she lifted an arm his way, straight out, palm up, and ordered, "Give me a sec. I'll get it together."

She should come apart. Sometimes people needed to do that so they could put it back together stronger.

But fuck him, his hands actually *itched* to reach out and pull her to him so she could feel he was a big guy, strong, solid, and he had her.

He couldn't do that, so he did the only thing he could.

"You know it's okay to be freaked by this guy," he educated her. "He's a freak."

"I don't get freaked easily," she returned.

He could sense that about her.

But this was new territory for her.

Not for him. For Hawk. Jorge. Probably even Smithie.

Fanatics were the worst. It didn't matter if they were that about the Broncos or their God who would not be down in any way with their behavior, they'd just convinced themselves they were doing righteous work.

If there wasn't more meaning to your life than football or acting out your twisted version of what you thought God wanted you to do, you had a serious problem.

She turned to him, hands now to the belt on her robe, tugging it tighter.

But Mo wasn't watching her hands.

He was staring at her face.

And he arrested.

Nope.

This was his worst fear.

For always.

Terror was stark in her expression, big hazel eyes filled with tears.

"My sister covered me with her body," she said.

That wasn't what he expected to hear.

"What?" he asked.

"Jet, when we were shot at, or in the room where people were shooting at each other, my sister was there too. And when the bullets were flying, she covered me with her body," she explained.

Mo needed a minute.

She was in a room *with people shooting at each other* and her sister had to *cover her with her body?*

"Jet and Mom...Jet and Mom..." A fat tear fell from her eye. "Jet and Mom would lose their minds if they knew this was happening. And Mom barely survived her first stroke."

"When were you shot at?"

It was him that asked the question, but he didn't recognize his own voice. It sounded low and gritty and like it crawled up his throat straight from the acid in his gut.

"My dad was a gambler. He's recovering. And my sister had made some dude unhappy by jumping him at an Einstein's. We went to confront Dad gambling and..."

She kept talking but it was then Mo remembered her sister was a Rock Chick.

He needed to hear no more.

"They don't need to know," he said over her story.

Her eyes got big. "Of course they don't need to know! They can *never* know! Jet'll tell Eddie. Eddie will tell Lee. Then that whole crew will lay waste to Denver."

In that moment, Mo was feeling the need to lay waste to something.

The woman was standing in front of him terrified and crying.

"I don't even want to think about what Tex'll do," she went on.

Well, hell.

He forgot Tex MacMillan was part of that posse.

Not only part of that posse but married to a woman named Nancy.

Lottie's mother.

Fuck.

"They won't know," he assured her. "Hawk's all over it. It'll be done before MacMillan can get his duffle bag of grenades out."

"I hope so," she muttered, turning her head away.

Mo noted she didn't deny her stepfather had a duffle bag of grenades.

Mistake number one.

He watched her dance.

Mistake number two.

He left her sightline when she was exposed and needed to know he had her.

Mistake number three.

He let it slip his mind she was tangled up with the Rock Chicks.

Mistake number four.

He also forgot her stepfather was a lunatic.

He usually didn't even make it to mistake number one.

It was time to get his shit together.

"I need to get ready for my next set," she mumbled, beginning to walk to the mirror she'd used both the other times he was in this room with her.

"Lottie," he called.

She turned back.

"Nothing's gonna hurt you," he promised.

She looked him head to toe.

Mo knew what she saw.

Nothing she wanted to see.

He knew he was one ugly motherfucker and she could get any guy she wanted. Didn't even have to crook a finger. Just give a man a look and he'd follow her like a hungry stray.

But she also saw what she needed to see.

It'd take something to get through him to get to her.

And they both knew the man behind that letter didn't have dick (maybe literally).

Then she surprised him again.

She showed him vulnerability.

Oh yeah.

This was going to be a challenge.

"Don't leave me again, Mo," she said softly. "Please."

And oh yeah.

That letter had freaked her.

Fuck yeah.

Mo wanted to lay waste to something.

"I won't..." he trailed off because it was on the tip of his tongue to call her *baby*. He finished with, "I promise."

She stared into his eyes a beat.

After she did that, she nodded and moved to her mirror.

* * * *

"So what do you do the other four hours?"

Mo was fully clothed on his back on her couch that was a decent-sized couch, but it wasn't long enough for him.

No surprise. Most couches weren't.

His eyes were on the dark ceiling.

It was nearing on two.

Lottie went on at nine thirty, eleven and one.

She danced for ten to twelve minutes each set. Customers weren't allowed to touch her to tip, but even if they could, they wouldn't be able to reach her with the way she worked the stage. The other girls ran out and gathered the bills that drifted onto the stage for her.

The rest of the time, she sipped watermelon Perrier out of little cans from a pink paper straw with white chevrons on it, got ready for her next set and gabbed with whatever dancer was in the room with her.

And if there weren't any, she gabbed with Mo.

She was a talker.

This was Mo's lot in life. Being surrounded by women who were talkers.

"What?" he asked.

"You said you sleep for four hours a night. What do you do for the other four?"

He wanted her to go to sleep.

He wanted her to go to sleep so maybe he could go to sleep (though he didn't hold a ton of hope for that) and therefore stop thinking about her in that tiny, green satin nightie with all the cream lace she'd come out of her bathroom wearing.

Or the fact she wasn't ten feet away from him, that hot little body alone in that big bed.

He did not want to talk about what he did with the extra four hours he had that others didn't.

In fact, Mo wasn't a big fan of talking at all.

"I work out," he said.

"For four hours?" she asked.

"Havin' a job with Hawk isn't nine to five. I also work missions."

"Missions?"

"Yeah."

"You call them 'missions,' not 'cases?'"

"Yeah."

"Why?"

Lord save him from chatty women.

"Because we're all former soldiers, not ex-cops," he shared.

"All of you?"

"Yeah."

"How many of you are there?"

Good Christ.

"Lottie, go to sleep."

He heard her loud sigh and then, "I can't. I'm always jazzed after a night on."

She should be exhausted.

She only worked at most thirty-six minutes in the four and a half hours she was at Smithie's (not counting the hour and a half she needed to be there before her first set to get ready), but when she was dancing she gave it her all.

Not to mention, she did new full makeup and changed her hair for each set, not just the outfit she took off. It was an all-new Lottie every time she appeared on stage.

No one could say she didn't work for her percentage of the cover, if she got one. But no one bought a house like this on Gaylord a block from City Park who didn't make some cake.

Mo wanted her to be exhausted. Needed her to be. Not only so she'd shut up, but because he didn't need to be thinking she was "jazzed" which would only make him consider the varied ways he'd help her work that off, how much he'd enjoy them and how much more he'd enjoy making *her* enjoy them.

"Count sheep," he advised.

"Does that work?"

Fuck if he knew.

"Put your body to sleep inch by inch," he said.

That always worked for Trine, Sister #4. She was always on the move. Constantly busy. Found it hard to shut down. Even as a kid.

When they were little, Mo would sit with her and whisper, "Start with your toes, Treenz. Point. Flex. Then put 'em to sleep."

Always, by the time he got to her belly, Trine was out.

"Say what?" Lottie asked.

"Start with your toes," Mo said. "Point 'em. Flex 'em. Then put 'em to sleep."

He gave it a sec.

"You doin' that?" he asked.

"Yeah," she told him.

"Now your feet," he ordered into the dark. "Point, flex, then feel 'em get heavy and let them go."

Another second and he let that go to two.

"Now your calves," he continued. "Tighten 'em. Let them go. Feel 'em relax. Then put 'em to sleep."

Mo gave it another sec.

And another.

And one more.

"They asleep?" he asked.

"Yeah," she answered. "I think so."

"Now your knees."

"Is this what you do?" she asked.

"It doesn't work if you talk through it," he told her.

"Right," she muttered.

"Knees, Lottie."

"'Kay," she mumbled.

It took to her shoulders, Mo making his voice quieter and quieter, giving it more time in between, before he started on the neck and she didn't answer.

Good.

She was asleep.

Mo stared at the ceiling but could see nothing but Lottie in that nightie.

The nightie morphed into her dancing.

Fuck.

Torture.

He rolled to his side and closed his eyes.

And saw her face, terrified, eyes filled with tears.

He opened his, moved his hand, found his gun under the toss pillow right where he put it.

Mo drew in a big breath and released it.

He tried that again.

After that, he started with his toes.

They were still in boots.

He gave up after getting all the way to his scalp and fell asleep two hours later with his hand curled around the butt of his gun.

Chapter Four

Whitening Strips

Mo

The next morning, Mo sat on the couch he'd slept on while Lottie was in the bathroom doing whatever she did first thing in the morning.

He was on his phone with Hawk.

It was eight thirty and he was surprised she was up that early.

He'd been up since six.

"No on the prints. Got a sample to the DNA lab to see if we can catch something on that, but if he's not in the system for his prints, even if they can pull some, he won't be in the system for DNA," Hawk briefed him. "FBI is still running the language. That might take some time."

"And?" Mo asked.

"And, customers Smithie, Jorge, Joaquim and me tagged as possibles got tails home last night. We're goin' into their places today to take a closer look."

"I'll take odds that he didn't send that letter and knows Smithie's gonna get it around about yesterday and he's gonna show at the club. He's gotta know Smithie is gonna call someone in."

"He's also probably expecting cops."

"You and Jorge don't look like titty bar regulars, Hawk."

"You want us to work this situation or sit on our hands for a coupla days?" Hawk asked.

Mo shut his mouth.

His boss was older than him, not by much, so it wasn't like he was a father figure.

Mo had given up on a father figure a long time ago.

It was that he was his commanding officer, as such, and Mo had been trained not to disappoint his commanding officer.

And right then, Hawk didn't exactly sound like he was thrilled with Mo.

"It hasn't been twenty-four hours, Mo," Hawk noted. "Is she already getting under your skin?"

She was definitely a challenge.

But she wasn't under his skin. That couldn't happen. And he knew it the minute she opened the door to him and took a step back like she was getting ready to flee.

This was not an unusual reaction people had to him.

It just kinda sucked Lottie had had it.

"I'm good," Mo muttered.

"Stay good, stay sharp and ask her out after we know she's safe," Hawk ordered. After that, he gave Mo an, "Out," and he hung up.

But Mo was staring at the couch across from him.

Ask her out after we know she's safe?

He knew Hawk had seen his mug frequently over years. He also knew the man had 20/20 vision.

So why was he saying shit like that?

"Yo."

He turned his head and got smacked in the face with the view of Lottie in nothing but that nightie, her hair up at the back of her crown, but it was slapdash, so some of it was tickling her jaw, cheeks and neck.

All of those last, and including the rest of her face, looked like it was covered in shaving cream.

"Jesus," he mumbled.

"Firming mousse," she explained the shit on her face. "You want breakfast?"

He was starved.

She was in a nightie.

Was she intending to cook in that nightie?

"No," he answered.

"I do and you're covering my ass so if you don't eat, you get to watch me cook…" she tipped her head and smiled at him through foamy goo that was slowly melting into just goo, "then eat."

He realized, with the smile, and the way he was noticing her words sounded funny, that she had something on her teeth.

"What's wrong with your mouth?" he asked.

"Whitening strips." She bobbed out a hip, a move that felt like a sharp tug on his balls, and sassed, "Honey, all this," she swept an arm down her length, "doesn't come for free by *any* definition of that word."

With that she turned and bounced out of the room, the satin hugging her ass, the cream edge waving like an invitation.

Fuck him, fuck him, *fuck him.*

He had to get up and follow her.

Fuck him, fuck him, fuck…*him.*

Mo got up and followed her.

His legs longer, he caught up with her on the stairs.

She headed direct to the kitchen.

"Nespresso?" she asked, but she had a sort of lisp so it came out, "Nethpretho?"

Christ.

He wanted to laugh.

Laugh while walking across the kitchen to her, dropping to his knees and shoving his face under that lace.

"I'll make mine after you have yours," he replied.

"Coffee after whitening strips," *Coffee after whitening thtripth.* "Least twenty more minutes. I'll make yours now. Cream?"

"Yeah," he grunted, leaning a hip against the counter opposite where she was and watching her move around her kitchen.

He hoped dressing came after whitening strips too.

"Sugar?"

"No."

"Good boy," she murmured, opening a cover and grabbing a big clear bowl filled with pods.

He didn't want to be her good boy.

He wanted to be her *good boy.*

She turned to him. "I do natural cream. I try not to fill my body with too many chemicals."

Just strap them on your teeth and slather them on your face.

He did not say that.

He dipped his chin.

She got the coffee brewing, turned and leaned her back against the counter.

"Egg white omelet with herbs, mushrooms and machego. Turkey sausages. Hash browns. You wanna change your mind about breakfast?"

Abso-fucking-lutely.

His stomach nearly growled.

He just nodded once.

She gave him a foggy-toothed smile and set about moving around the kitchen again, getting out skillets, bowls, a whisk.

Apparently, she was going to cook in that nightie.

Thank Christ for the goo on her face.

Before she really got down to business, she handed him his coffee and announced she was taking away the only defense he had by declaring, "I gotta wash this off my face. I'll get on it when I come back."

And then she was strutting out of the room.

The goo was going.

Terrific.

Mo pulled air into his nose and assessed the situation.

He'd locked up last night.

She had a security system.

It was on for doors and windows.

Before she got up, he'd done a walkthrough. Doors locked. Windows closed and locked. Blinds down. Security system functioning. Backyard empty. Cars parked at the front empty or folks getting in them, going about their normal business.

He could let her out of his sight for long enough for her to wash her face.

But after taking a sip of his coffee, he set it aside and walked to the foot of the stairs.

It took maybe five minutes, the last thirty seconds of those he considered jogging up to check on her, before she showed. Face clean and gleaming. Tits jiggling as she danced down the steps.

She stopped four from the bottom.

"If I can rinse my face without you in the next room, why can't you shower with me somewhere else in the house?"

"I'm vulnerable when I shower. And unarmed. I'm not when you rinse your face."

Another big, blurred smile and an, "Ah."

Then more jiggling and dancing down the steps.

He'd lived a good life.

Clean.

Taken care of his mom and sisters.

Put up with them even after the taking care of them part was no longer needed (and they were a lot, every one of them).

Enlisted and was honorably discharged.

He did right by Hawk, never wheedled out of a mission (something that would get his ass canned, but that wasn't why he didn't do it), always followed orders, never fucked up.

The two long-term girlfriends he'd had, he'd treated them like gold. Living with five women, you learned a lot of shit. And he'd given it all and then some to the women he'd claimed. It had been them who'd scraped him off for something better.

So no cheating. No excessive gambling or drinking. Absolutely no drugs. No nights out carousing with his boys and not checking in. No getting up in their shit about how expensive their handbags were or why they couldn't rinse a damned plate and put it in the dishwasher rather than leaving it in the sink.

How he'd earned this punishment with Lottie, he did not know.

Maybe it was beating the shit out of his sonuvabitch dad.

Yeah, that had to be it.

He followed her back into the kitchen and she did her thing, in her nightie, while he watched, and it was while she was sautéing the mushrooms, and he was taking a sip of coffee, when she asked, "What do you think about my tits?"

He nearly did a spit take.

To avoid that, he swallowed hard, not like he was swallowing coffee, like he was swallowing a boulder, and he stared at her.

She was at the stove, wooden spoon in her hand, but twisted to look at him. "I'm going natural. Next month."

He tried not to look at her tits.

Swear to God he did.

He couldn't not look at her tits.

He then forced his eyes to her face.

He knew her tits had to be fake.

Still, they were fucking *awesome*.

"Your body, your choice."

"Do you think I'll lose customers?" *Do you think I'll loth cuthtomerth?*

Christ, she was too much.

He really should not have beaten the shit out of his dad.

"No."

"That's what I think." She turned back to the stove and fussed with the mushrooms.

"You want me to make you coffee?" he offered to have something to do that was not looking at her ass, her legs, her hair, her neck, her tits or her *at all.*

"Yeah. By the time it's done, strips will be about ready to come off. Splash of cream."

He moved to where he'd seen she kept all the stuff for coffee.

It was done brewing and he was sliding her mug on the counter by the stove next to her when he made mistake number five in his job protecting Charlotte McAlister.

"You don't need the strips, the goo or the tits, Lottie," he told her.

There was more to that message, he just didn't verbalize it.

She was beautiful and would be beautiful without all that shit.

She got the rest of his message and he knew it when her head slowly turned, tipped back (and then back some more) and she stared into his eyes looking shocked AF.

"You gotta know that," he continued.

And she did. For shit's sake, her living was her looks and her body.

"Maybe," she said in a sweet voice that played all kinds of havoc with his crotch. "But it's nice to hear it."

"Just sayin'," he muttered, moving away from her again.

She turned to face him. "You want toast?"

If she was going to ask him to make it, and it meant getting close to her again, the answer to that was a big, fat *no.*

"No."

"Good. Bread is bad," she declared and shifted her attention back to the stove.

If she thought that, did she even have any?

He'd learned therefore he didn't open his mouth to ask.

Mushrooms done, she got rid of her whitening strips right there in the kitchen before she started on the omelets, all this while the fresh potato hash browns from a bag were sizzling in olive oil next to turkey sausage.

Mo was a doer so he couldn't stand still for long.

This meant he got out the plates and cutlery, opening and closing doors and drawers to find it, and brought them to her.

She served up and he took his plate and fork all the way (which wasn't a long way, and that sucked) across to the opposite counter from her.

Lottie put the sole of her foot against the ankle of her other leg and tucked in at the counter.

Mo did the same, without the foot action.

"So which branch of the military were you in?"

"Army," he muttered, shoving omelet in his mouth.

Well, hell.

It tasted good.

That took chops, making an egg white omelet taste good.

"How long?"

"Full term."

"Did you, uh…see some action?"

Mo turned his head to her, got a load of legs, nightie, tits, hair and a pretty face with a hesitant and earnest expression on it.

And he'd had enough.

More than enough.

He wasn't playing this game and it was seriously fucked up she was trying to make him do that.

He was done.

"We're not doin' this," he announced.

"Mo—"

"No," he clipped. "And rules. You put some goddamn clothes on while I'm with you. I know this is an inconvenience and you know I'm gettin' paid to do this job. But have some respect and cut a man some slack. You know precisely how fuckable you are. Every night, you dance, and you got a huge room full of men gagging for it. Do you honestly need that in your kitchen?"

The look on her face made him wish he could net the words that just came out of his mouth and set them on fire.

She blanked it right before she retorted, "I think I prefer Quiet Mo."

"Great. I prefer that too. So let's do that."

"Fine," she spat.

He dipped his chin.

She picked up her plate and took it to the apron-front sink which was two feet in front of him. She then dumped the whole thing in it, hardly eaten omelet and the rest sliding off onto the white enamel.

"I'm gonna take a shower," she declared. "I suppose, cutting you some slack, you don't need to be around for that?"

"No," he ground out.

"Awesome," she snapped.

And then she marched out of the room, every muscle in her body screaming she was pissed off.

Or hurt.

Fantastic.

Mo drew in another breath through his nose.

Then he finished his breakfast and cleaned the kitchen.

Chapter Five

Trading Up

Lottie

Things did not go well after Mo was a supreme asshole.

If I wanted to look on the Brightside (which I did *not*), him making it plain how fuckable he thought I was, was not a bad thing.

Him *completely* missing the pass I was throwing at him *was*.

I mean, did he *honestly* think I was wearing my nightie making breakfast with a man I hadn't slept with just so I could be a huge-ass *tease*?

No!

I wanted the big lug to ask me out.

Jerk.

Asshole.

Fuckface.

Obviously, considering I was an adult, I realized a route to rectifying this situation was to explain where I was at, and considering he thought I was fuckable, he'd probably get with the program.

Fat chance of *that*.

I couldn't be an adult at the best of times, even actually *being* an adult.

Sure. I got to work on time.

I paid my bills.

I kept my house.

I got oil changes when I was supposed to (though I thought that was a huge scam, every three months? *come on*).

What I did not do, for three days, was talk to Mo.

Yeah.

Not very adult.

Okay, that wasn't exactly true.

We talked because I was my mother's daughter. I couldn't start my day with someone in my house silently trailing me and not offer him coffee.

So I'd said, "Coffee?" to him the next two mornings after he'd been a consummate jackass.

Other than that…

No.

Why?

Two reasons.

One, I was the kind of woman who held a grudge. I just did. I knew that wasn't right. It had cost me friendships and boyfriends and maybe I should work on that.

But not with Mo.

Oh no.

Not with Mo.

Two, because he didn't like strippers.

That was clear.

He might have been diplomatic during our first talk, though he *had* indicated he had a problem with it.

And he was not mean to the girls at Smithie's.

He was also not friendly.

Then of course there was that part of his outburst, the part I liked *the best* (not), where he'd said, *Every night, you dance, and you got a huge room full of men gagging for it.*

He thought I got off on it.

And okay, if I took a second to calm down and reflect (which I did *not*), there might be something about that.

It still wasn't cool he threw it in my face and the way he did.

But I knew that about myself.

I liked attention.

When I was younger, I went to LA to become an actress.

I ended up Queen of the Corvette Calendar because, first, how kickass was that? And second, I sucked at acting. And last, there was an operative word in that title.

Queen.

My sister was quiet and sweet and responsible and hardworking, and everyone adored her.

But I was not any of that. Not even close.

This wasn't sibling rivalry.

At least (if I was honest), not anymore.

And Jet didn't get *all* the attention, but everyone around us made sure she (and thus I) knew how awesome she was for being sweet and responsible and hardworking.

"Oh, what a good girl she is, looking after that wild sister of hers while Nancy's at work," and, "Oh, it just breaks my heart Jet had to get a job so she could help her momma out with the bills."

That said, years ago (around about the time we were in a room when bullets were flying), I'd grown up enough to see that my sister didn't have it all that great, what with our not-so-stellar life with a deadbeat dad who kept us all on a string with fancy plans and big promises.

I also saw how responsible and hardworking she'd had to be and that she'd sacrificed a lot for me.

I appreciated it.

And I loved her for it.

I also moved on.

From that.

Not so much the fact our dad was a loser.

And I was honest enough with myself I knew that I was that girl who needed to be daddy's little girl. Daddy's princess. His sun and moon and stars. The girl he threatened all her boyfriends so they wouldn't hurt her, but mostly he was working out his issues because he didn't want to let her go. The girl he choked up about when he gave her away at her wedding.

Our dad had gotten his shit together.

But I would never fully trust it, and that was part of my plight, and his punishment.

Because all of what I'd needed when I was a little girl and growing up was lost to me.

I could never again be five and walking through the fair with my hand in my father's and have him cry, "Gotta get some cotton candy for my best girl!" making me feel loved, treasured, safe, protected…

Special.

Okay, he'd done that when I was five.

And when he'd stopped because the poker table was more important than his wife and daughters, that was when I'd learned what missing something felt like.

And how that missing it could turn to needing it.

And how that need became seeking attention.

Not to mention how to hold a grudge.

So on Day Three with The Supreme Asshole of All Time (Mo), Sunday, one of my two days off (I had Sundays and Mondays off), Mo was still sleeping on my couch in my room. He was also still standing backstage when I danced (except the second dance, that was when he handed off to one of Smithie's guys and took a shower and changed).

And I had absolutely no idea what was going on with the crackpot who wanted to "cleanse" me because I couldn't ask Smithie considering he probably thought I was getting briefs from Mo and I didn't want to tell him Mo was the Supreme Asshole of All Time.

This was due to my desire for Mo not to get fired (or reprimanded or something) after I explained why we weren't talking, which would make Smithie do something rash, like attempt to Tase him then kick him in the balls while he was down.

Or demand Hawk fire him.

Mo was an asshole, but he was vigilant, I was still alive and safe (ish). Not trapped in a well only to be drugged and dragged up and "cleansed" repeatedly (though, according to that letter, a "cleansing" sounded a lot like rape and torture, and I wasn't real sure how that would make a girl clean, then again, I wasn't a crackpot).

So I decided not to rock the boat.

Mo wasn't the only person I'd run into who had a problem with strippers.

I was used to it.

It hurt (coming from Mo).

It sucked (coming from Mo).

He was still hot as hell and I really wanted to pounce on him.

And occasionally (all right, frequently), I remembered him telling me I didn't need the strips or the face mousse or the implants, remembering this while also remembering how nice that felt.

But…whatever.

I'd been wrong about him.

He was one of *those guys*.

And one day he'd be gone.

Of course, this was what I told myself.

But at night, while trying to put my body to sleep bit by bit, knowing he was right there in the room with me, and remembering how sweet it was when Mo had helped me do that, my mind often wandered. When it did, I'd end up feeling my throat close, my nose sting, and my eyes feel hot wishing I hadn't been wrong about him.

(Another reason for the grudge.)

Now we were in his truck, Mo driving, because I'd deviated from my one-word-a-day plan and told him I had to go to the grocery store.

Therefore, we were heading to King Soopers.

He had a badass truck. Black on black Ram that had all the bells and whistles (even illuminated door sills that said Ram).

Normally I wouldn't hesitate to wax poetic about illuminated door sills.

I was pretty sure Mo could live without knowing I dug his sills.

Silently he drove and silently I rode.

Silently he parked and silently I sat next to him while he did.

Silently we got out and silently we walked to the store while I dug out the list from my purse.

Silently I grabbed a cart and silently he followed me as we wandered through the store.

I was silently perusing the selection of Asian noodles when I heard, "Mo?"

It was hearing a woman calling his name that caught my attention.

It was feeling the wall of…*something* coming from Mo that made me tense.

I looked up at him to see his jaw so set, I figured if I watched long enough, a crack would form under the pressure.

I then looked to where his eyes were aimed.

A very beautiful brunette was walking our way, pushing a cart, trailed by a tall, built (but nowhere near as built as Mo), very good-looking guy.

I assessed the guy and his expensive clothes that he wore even when going to King Soopers on a Sunday.

Peacock.

Possibly small dick.

Definitely sports car.

Or at the very least a high-performance vehicle (probably BMW).

Totally up his own ass.

I then assessed the woman.

I should have done her first.

She was staring at Mo like she didn't care sex in public was very illegal because if he gave her a nod, she'd tear her off clothes and ride him against the Asian food shelves.

My back shot straight.

Her gaze cut to me.

Her back shot straight.

Without a thought about what I was doing, I gave her my patented, He's Mine and I'm Ready to Rumble Look.

She shot back her, We'll See, Bitch Look.

I was *this close* to growling when her boyfriend spoke up.

"Who's this, Tammy?"

Since I was ready to rumble, I couldn't but cut a quick glance at the Peacock.

He was staring at my tits.

Okay, he was with his chick and staring at my chest.

Maybe *he* was the Supreme Asshole of All Time.

"My ex," she answered. "Hey, Mo."

"Hey," he grunted.

Mo Translation: I have zero interest in conversing with you.

Then again, he had zero interest in conversing with just about everybody as far as I could tell.

I was understanding why she was an ex when she ignored his vibe and asked, "How's things?"

Another grunt of, "Good."

She sliced a glance at me. "Is this your new—?"

"Yup," I said, cutting her off before Mo could say anything, then shifting and putting my arm around his waist.

Or trying. He had a wide waist. It was trim, but it was wide.

I finally grabbed hold of the other side, barely, my fingers sliding off the slick material of his skintight compression skirt.

So I grabbed onto a beltloop of his cargos.

Her gaze dropped to my finger hooked through his beltloop, her eyes narrowed, and she didn't seem to notice it took long moments for Mo to drop his arm around my shoulders.

I nearly crumbled to the floor.

His arm had to weigh more than my entire body.

I held steady and took the shot of acid she aimed at me from her eyes.

I shot her an acid neutralization glare and followed it up with a laser beam stare.

She blinked (yeah, my laser beam stare *rocked*) then tried to deflect by looking back to Mo.

"I haven't heard from you in a while," she remarked.

Her dude gave her a look.

Mo said nothing.

I said something.

"That happens when you break up, Tammy."

"I'm sorry, you are?" she asked me.

"Lottie." I grinned saccharine sweet. "Nice ta meet ya."

"Well, Lottie," she doused my sweet with some bitter, "we only broke up a month ago."

Bitch Translation: It hasn't been that long for you to be this tight with him, so I got you.

"Though you were fuckin' him a lot longer than that, yeah, Tammy?"

I went still under the weight of Mo's arm as these words came out of Mo's mouth.

The "him" I assumed was the boyfriend since all the color ran out of his face.

No longer distracted by my chest, Peacock was realizing who "Mo, the ex" was.

"Let's move on, Tam, yeah?" the boyfriend said, and I figured he did this because he had the gift of sight and this conversation had taken a turn he did not want within reaching distance of Mo.

Tammy's eyes were full of regret when she looked up at Mo. "Mo, I--"

"You honest to fuck wanna do this in a King Soopers?" Mo asked.

"No, she doesn't," the boyfriend answered hurriedly.

"Well, *I* wanna do it in King Soopers," I snapped.

All eyes came to me, even, I felt, Mo's.

"Are you *high*?" I demanded to know from *Tammy*.

"Lottie," Mo muttered, that arm around me tightening, or more like squeezing.

Even with the real danger of him dislocating my shoulder, I glared at *Tammy*.

"You walked right up to him and said, 'hey,' after you cheated on him. Who does that?" I asked.

She looked to her cart and muttered, "Maybe we should just—"

I stepped out from under Mo's arm and stood in front of her cart, cutting her off by ordering, "No, bitch, answer me. Who does that?"

I felt Mo's fingers curl into the back waistband of my jeans and he probably had to stoop real low because I also heard right in my ear, "Lottie—"

But I had Tammy's attention again.

And her squinty eyes.

"Did you just call me a bitch?" she asked.

"Yeah, bitch, I called you bitch," I answered. Then I shrieked, "*You cheated on Mo!*"

Yeah, I *shrieked*.

But what was the matter with her?

"Fucking hell," I heard Mo murmur just as I felt my jeans get tight at the waistband since he jerked me back by using just that.

I whipped my head around then cranked it to look up at him and yelled, "Let go of me, Mo!"

"Lottie, cool it," he commanded.

"Fuck cool!" I shouted. "She cheated on you then walked right up to you at a *King Soopers* and said, '*hey!*'"

"I don't care," Mo told me.

"I care!" I yelled.

"How can you care if I don't care?" he asked, his face sharing genuine curiosity.

"*She said 'hey!'*" I screeched.

"Is there a problem here?"

Mo turned, and since he still had his fingers in my jeans, I was pulled around to see a woman standing there wearing a King Soopers apron with a nametag on it that said Rhonda with the word Manager under it.

"Yes, Rhonda, there's a problem," I informed her. "*She*," I swung a pointed finger to Tammy, "cheated on *him*," I jerked a thumb over my shoulder to Mo, "with *him*." I finished this pointing in the direction of the boyfriend.

Rhonda looked between Mo and the boyfriend, cast her judgment openly through her expression (that's what I'm talkin' about!) and was looking disbelievingly at Tammy when I carried on.

"Then she just strolled up to him. No! To *us*! Right here in the aisle and said, 'hey.'"

Rhonda's brows shot up at me and she looked again at Tammy.

"You said, 'hey?'" Rhonda asked.

"We'd really just like to move along," the boyfriend shared with Rhonda.

Rhonda again looked between Mo and the boyfriend before she told the boyfriend, "I think that's a good idea."

"Yeah, move along," I called after them as the boyfriend grabbed the cart, did a tight turn, and hustled down the aisle. "And you get near Mo again, *Tammy*, I'll tear your hair out."

Tammy turned, mouthed *fuck you* to me…

And then it happened.

Mo was a big guy.

Normally, Mo did not move like Mikhail Baryshnikov and definitely not like Usain Bolt.

But I learned when the man wanted to move, he moved.

I knew this when one second, he was at my back, holding onto my jeans, and the next second, he was five feet down the aisle, in front of Tammy, cutting off her retreat. He was also bent at the waist, hands to his hips, right in her face.

"No," he growled.

That was it.

Though that word rumbled down the aisle like a rock slide.

Tammy stood with her back to me, completely immobile for a second, then she did a wide side step and practically ran down the aisle.

"Keep ahold a' that one, sistah," Rhonda murmured to me. Then called to Mo, "We good, big man?"

"Yup," he grunted, moseying back to me, again moving cumbersomely, each step powerfully swaying his hips in a masculine cadence that made my mouth water.

What those hips could do between my legs I could not contemplate or I'd have an orgasm in King Soopers.

Right.

It appeared it was high time to take a moment to reflect.

I'd just acted demented in a freaking King Soopers of all places.

I wasn't fond of cheaters but that wasn't about Tammy being a cheater.

I'd staked my claim before I even knew she was a cheater.

Hell, before I even knew she was an actual ex of Mo's.

So that was about wanting Mo, Mo not wanting me, being in his presence twenty-four seven, sleeping with him in my room, and me letting off some steam.

A *whole* lot of steam.

But it had been me that pushed it.

If I'd kept my mouth shut, that whole convo would have been shut down by Mo at the get-go and the whole cheating scenario might not have been outed.

Something not a lot of men took a great deal of pride in (women either).

Rhonda wandered off after telling us to have a good day and thanking us for shopping at King Soopers and Mo stopped in front of me.

"I'm sorry," I said, looking up at him.

"Why?" he asked.

"I lost it with Tammy," I reminded him.

"You did that," he agreed.

"I should have just kept my mouth shut."

"I don't know. Been askin' around about you. Heard your premiere in Denver was havin' a wet T-shirt catfight with your sister on the floor of Fortnum's. Was kinda hopin' for an encore, though minus the sister, which would suck, but my guess is, you'd have won against Tammy, which would have been awesome."

He'd asked around about me?

And was he…

Wait.

Was he *teasing me*?

"It didn't start as a wet T-shirt fight with Jet. It just ended as one after Mom threw a pitcher of water on us."

His silver eyes danced and his lips tipped slightly up.

Okay, that urge to orgasm was coming back.

"I was young then. I'm an adult now," I babbled.

"Totally can tell. You just adulted all over the ethnic food aisle at King Soopers."

I sure did that.

"It would take a lot to make me get in a catfight now that I'm all mature and, uh…everything," I told him.

"Lottie, you were two seconds from taking her down by her hair in a real-life GLOW move."

I totally was.

"Fortunately, Rhonda appeared," I remarked.

"Depends on how you look at it," he muttered.

He was.

He was teasing me.

He might actually be flirting with me.

Damn.

"When do you have time to ask around about me?" I asked.

"When you shower. You take really long showers."

Ah.

Why are you asking around about me?

That question was not audible.

I couldn't go there yet.

Perhaps Mo wanted a détente, but still, he'd said some rough things and that conversation was not for King Soopers.

However, now that we were speaking again there was one thing I wanted to know.

No.

Two.

"I'm assuming that you all aren't close to finding that guy."

Any remaining amusement went out of his face.

"No."

Great.

"Right then, before we carry on, why did that woman cheat on you when she practically begged you with her eyes to do her against the udon noodles?"

Mo commandeered the cart and set us in motion, doing this by bending way over, crossing his forearms on the handle and moving forward.

I quickly grabbed some buckwheat udon and followed him.

I suspected his movements meant he wasn't going to answer and I didn't blame him. It wasn't my business.

"She likes dick."

After I tossed the noodles in the cart, I walked beside him and had the unusual sensation of looking down on him.

He kept his eyes aimed forward.

"And I work a lot," he finished.

"Ah," I murmured.

I murmured that like I got it, but I didn't get it.

Then again, I wasn't a cheater.

My man wasn't taking care of business, there'd be a chat, never a cheat.

But that was just me.

"And she's the kind of woman who's always on the lookout for the next best thing."

I stutter stepped to a halt.

"What?"

He stopped and looked over his shoulder and down his bulk at me.

"What, what?"

"The next best thing?" I asked.

"Can we get the shopping done?" he asked back.

I started moving again, and when Mo moved with me, I kept at him. "What do you mean the next best thing?"

"You saw her new man."

"Yeah."

He said no more.

"And?" I pushed.

"Let's not do this," he said on a sigh.

"Do what?"

"Go there."

"Go where?"

He stopped again and looked up at me.

"I'm a guy, Lottie, and even I can see he's better lookin' than me," he stated firmly.

I stared at him.

"He also makes more money than me," Mo continued. "He's an attorney."

That explained a lot, but only about the boyfriend and his apparel choices for a shopping expedition at King Soopers on a Sunday.

The rest was still unexplainable.

"She moved on from *you* to an *attorney*?" I asked.

"Yeah," he answered.

I busted out laughing.

And I did this so hard, I slapped him on the shoulder blade to work some of it out.

"That's *hilarious*!" I cried.

"It's really not," he said.

I ignored him. "Ohmigod. What an idiot. You dump her and—"

"She dumped me."

I stopped laughing and started staring at him again.

"She traded up," he stated conversationally. "Now can we finish this and get back?"

"She didn't trade up, Mo," I told him quietly.

He sighed again but said no words through it this time.

"She totally didn't. And she knows it."

"Lottie—"

"She either dumped you so you wouldn't dump her, because, really, she's a bitch and probably knows it and definitely knows you aren't stupid so you'd figure it out. Or she instigated a faulty play, thinking you'd come to heel if she not only cheated on you, but acted like she was down with losing you and prepared to move on, all this so you'd fight to keep her."

"You were around her for maybe ten minutes. I lived with her for two years. I was there, Lottie. I know what happened."

But I wasn't seeing straight.

I wasn't seeing *anything*.

They'd been *living together*?

From far away (even though he was still right there), I heard him murmur, "Oh fuck."

I started walking.

Fast.

"Where is that bitch?" I demanded, still walking (fast).

I came to a halt when he caught me by the waistband of my jeans again.

He used it to turn me to facing him and kept his hand there.

My breasts *almost* brushed his chest, we were that close.

We'd never been that close.

I was also standing in the curve of his arm.

He was almost…

Holding me.

Whoa.

"She's history," he shared.

"She's a bitch," I returned.

"Yeah. And so she's history. Move on. I did."

"She didn't trade up, Mo."

"Okay."

He said that just to appease me.

I was not appeased.

I was a lot of things, including laser focused on his face.

He thought that.

He honest to God thought that.

And something had to be done about it.

So I decided instead of finding *Tammy* and taking her *down* I had bigger fish to fry.

Though I couldn't fry them shopping in King Soopers.

"Let's get this finished," I mumbled.

"Thank Christ," he said and let me go.

He went back to the cart.

I'd lost my list somewhere along the way.
Oh well.
Fuck it.
I'd wing it and if we forgot something, we'd come back.
We had to get this done.
I had fish to fry.

Chapter Six

Tell Them to Work Faster

Mo

He'd thought he'd wanted her back in the way he could have her, that was chattering at him and being comfortable in his presence.

Another mistake.

He had her back, but she wasn't back, as such.

Any man would read it the way Mo was reading it.

She was his.

He knew this partly because the floodgates had reopened on the gabbing, but apparently, it'd been a rainy season because she seemed incapable of shutting up.

He now knew about all the girls at Smithie's, who was putting themselves through school, who baked the best cookies, who knew the best zit-covering strategy, and who they were fucking, one doing a bouncer.

He further knew that Smithie would find out about the bouncer, because he always found out, and fraternization between employees was prohibited.

He also knew Smithie would go apeshit, but in the end not do anything but be loud and threatening while going apeshit, which was why the strippers routinely slept with the bouncers regardless that it was against employee policy.

And he knew Lottie's mom and Tex were always on her ass about adopting a coupla cats.

Further from that, he knew she was considering it, she just was building herself up to go to the shelters because when she did, if she hadn't established impulse control, she wouldn't adopt a couple of cats, she'd adopt fifty (this, by the way, he did not find a surprise).

And he knew her neighbors were being dickheads not because they had an outdoor TV, but because they played it loud and they did this a lot.

Mo had no idea what this all had to do with grocery shopping, the subject around which he'd like any conversation to remain, except they weren't grocery shopping, him as bodyguard with his boss's client.

They were grocery shopping as a man and a woman living together and he knew this because when they did talk about shopping, it was when she made him go all the way back through the aisles they'd already been through, forcing him to tell her what shit he wanted in the house.

Making matters worse, personal space was now just gone.

Vaporized.

She didn't hold his hand or press up against him and give his neck a kiss or anything like that.

But she stayed close, bumped him with a hip if she was being funny or feeling saucy (something that happened often), grabbed onto his biceps to get his attention or hooked a beltloop and tugged to change his direction.

All this meant Mo was in agony.

And that agony wasn't just about all of that.

Lottie had thrown right down with Tammy, no hesitation, and this was *before* she knew who Tammy was and what she'd done.

There was no way to deny it.

That felt good.

But it was even worse.

It was clear Lottie had claimed her man.

The end.

And he was that man.

Mo couldn't think on this, mostly how it made him feel.

All of it.

Fortunately, she was talking so much, his mind didn't have the opportunity to go there.

The FBI had come back with a negatory on the language, or any religious radicals in the area they were keeping an eye on that fit this guy's description.

This meant they had zero leads on whoever this man was who wanted to harm her, and they'd all made the decision that the second letter, received yesterday, Lottie would not know about because she was already alert and not doing anything stupid.

But mostly they agreed on that because the degree of disturbing in the latest letter had ratcheted up about fifteen notches.

Smithie had called the ball on that one, not telling Lottie about it and not taking it to the police, or the FBI. The last two would, after the second letter, want very badly to get involved.

This was because Smithie wanted the threat eradicated, no dicking around, and although Mo agreed with Smithie (to a point), Hawk did not.

The guy was gearing up to make a move, building his confidence, getting his shit tight, getting off on the increasing extreme of his letters and the fact he hadn't been caught yet to take him to the place where he could act out his twisted fantasies.

They all knew it.

Smithie wanted it handled.

Hawk wanted this guy on FBI radar.

Mo just wanted Lottie safe.

But Lottie didn't need to know all of this was going on.

And Mo did not need Lottie being even *more* of all that was good about Lottie when this guy was on the loose, fixed on her, and working himself up, her being more of all she was only serving the purpose of making Mo want her more.

But for the life of him, he could no longer handle the anger and hurt that had poured his way from her the last three days.

So when Tammy opened it up, and Lottie rushed right through, Mo seized on it and he did not have it in him to shut it down, being a dickhead about it, or otherwise.

It would probably bite him in the ass.

Hell, it already was biting him in the ass.

But she seemed happy, so he'd find some way to deal with it.

On her street, a few houses down from hers, he saw it before she saw it.

And when he saw it, he knew things were going to get even worse.

Terrific.

"Ohmigod!" she cried, cutting herself off from talking about some peacock outfit she was thinking about stripping in, somehow getting this idea from Tammy's new man.

He knew then that she saw it too.

"You get to meet my nephews!" she exclaimed.

Yeah.

All three.

They were running around on her sloped front lawn, looking like they were playing tag, while a blonde woman who had to be her sister lounged on the front steps.

Eddie Chavez's woman and boys, and as Mo brought them closer, he saw he could call that without even knowing Lottie's sister was married to Chavez.

His boys were stamped all over with him. Put one in a kid lineup, Mo would have called Eddie, or his brother Hector, no sweat.

Seeing as they wanted whoever was after Lottie to know she had protection, Mo didn't park in the garage at the back in case the guy was watching. He parked in the front.

Something he did right then.

And Lottie was practically clawing at the door before he even came to a complete halt.

He threw his truck in park just as she hit the locks.

Then she was flying out.

And his day got worse even though many men would describe it as exponentially better.

This was because she dashed up the slope and was immediately hit with one boy, the tallest, so probably oldest, then two, and finally the third, the youngest, toddled over and jumped on.

Lottie started going down with the first hit. It was a feint. The kid was maybe seven or eight and not small, but she could have stayed standing.

But not if she wanted him to think he could best her.

Something she obviously did.

Slowly, forcing himself to take in the surrounding area as he did it, Mo got out, rounded the hood, noted the sister, Jet, was up, had moved a bit forward, had hands on hips, but she wasn't watching her boys wrestle with their aunt on their aunt's front lawn.

She was focused on Mo.

He could see Eddie going there. She was pretty, not as pretty as her sister, but pretty. Curvy. Way more curvy than Lottie. Dressed in jeans, flip flops and a tight, long-sleeved T-shirt that showed no cleavage but still didn't leave much to the imagination.

Mo would lay money on the fact that Chavez both loved and hated that T-shirt.

Loved it when she wore it for him.

Hated it when she wore it in public.

This unlike Lottie, who was in another skintight tank, this one neon pink, and faded jeans (but Lottie also was wearing flip flops).

Well, not now. Both of them had come off in the free-for-all.

He'd ascended the slope just as the oldest one got her to her back, straddled her, shoving her down at her shoulders while the middle one (maybe five or six years old) threw himself on her legs and the littlest one (maybe three or four) was engaged in the concerted effort of trying to tickle her sides, something that was thwarted by his big brother's legs.

"I got you!" the oldest one shouted in triumph.

"Give! I give!" Lottie yelled through giggles.

Well, shit.

Just shit.

He knew it before.

He knew it right then for certain.

He was fucked.

Because he could totally fall in love with this woman.

Yeah.

Shit.

"Let up your aunt, boys."

Yup.

Eddie's kids.

Mom spoke and all the boys immediately moved. He had a feeling "Wait until your father hears this" was immediately followed with the urge to piss their pants.

It was then, when they were forming a loose row, oldest to youngest, the oldest caught sight of Mo.

So that was when he whispered, "Holy smokes."

Number two turned his head to check out what had his brother frozen in wonder and he caught sight of Mo.

His response was, "*Dios mio.*"

"Dante! Mouth!" Jet snapped.

"Holy smokes," Dante decided to repeat after his brother.

"*Hey! Are you Annie Lottie's boyfrien'?*" the youngest screeched at him.

Jet's eyes cut to Mo.

"Whoa," Dante said.

"Cool!" the oldest called out. "Auntie Lottie's dating a badass!"

"Alex!" Jet spat. "*Mouth!*"

Alex was too overwhelmed with Mo to mind his mother.

This was why he stated, "Dude, you're *yooooooouge.*"

"Do we speak that way to people?" Jet demanded to know.

Alex twisted toward his mother. "But, *Mamá*, he's *yoooooooouge*."

"I don't care. You don't tell a man he's large. He knows he's large," Jet educated. "And you definitely don't tell your aunt's boyfriend he's large. It's rude all around. It's ruder in the family."

In the family.

Oh yeah.

Shit.

Mo looked to Lottie who had not only taken her feet but regained her flip flops.

She was smiling, big and white at him.

He felt that smile in his gut, his balls and his chest.

Yeah, he'd been claimed.

How the fuck had he let that happen?

Thankfully, she turned her smile from him and declared to the boys, "We were just at the grocery store. Who wants to help us carry in and put away?"

"Me!" Dante yelled, then raced to the truck.

"Me!" the youngest shouted, then followed his brother a lot less agilely.

"Is it all healthy junk?" Alex asked his aunt.

"Who am I?" Lottie answered.

So that explained the Dove ice cream bars, caramel M&Ms, Tostitos and salsa and pork rinds, all purchases Lottie had not, in three days, demonstrated she'd ever let past her lips.

Alex grinned up at her. "You're Aunt Lottie."

He knew there were treats in those bags for her nephews.

Mo'd been wrong.

He could not fall in love with her.

That shit was already happening.

"Go help your brothers," she said gently, grinning back at her boy.

Alex raced to the truck.

Dante was already digging in the back cab where the groceries were.

"And this is?"

Mo had felt Jet approach, but he was engaged in doing another scan of the street.

He turned back at Jet's question.

"Jet, this is Mo, my new mound of hunkalicious boyfriend. Mo, this is Jet, my sister," Lottie introduced.

As previously noted, Eddie Chavez and his crew, all of them, including the ones he was linked not-so-loosely to at Nightingale Investigations, did not know about what was going down with Lottie.

Another reason, after the second letter, they didn't bring in the cops.

Or the Feds.

This meant Lottie's sister couldn't know. If she did, she'd be on the phone with her husband faster than Lottie went down when her nephew tackled her.

This meant they needed a cover.

And being unprepared for this visit, he had no other cover to give even if Lottie hadn't already decided, and communicated, what cover he was going to have. No man like him would be with a woman like her just as friends helping her grocery shop unless he was gay.

He put out a hand. "Nice to meet you."

She stared at it, looked at her sister, then took it and looked in his eyes before her lashes swept down, and pink hit her cheeks.

"Yeah, nice to meet you."

Sweet. Shy. Pretty. Filled out jeans great.

No wonder Chavez went for that.

But the sisters couldn't be more different.

Yin and yang.

The kind of perfect balance that made life worth living.

He gave her hand a light squeeze, let her go and turned to Lottie.

"Gonna help the boys."

Not missing a beat, or an opportunity, she moved into him, leaned into him, pressing her breasts against hands flattened on his chest, gazing up at him with sparkling hazel eyes, and breathing, "You do that, pookie-loo."

If she was his, all of that would earn her a spanking.

Mo filed that away as he controlled his body's reaction to her that close, the feel of her, how much he liked that look in her eyes, the smell of her perfume with hints of her shampoo, and he moved away to supervise the carrying in of groceries.

"Why didn't you just go in?" he heard Lottie ask her sister.

"I keep forgetting your security code," Jet answered.

"You're a dork."

"*You* keep track of three boys, their laundry, their mess, their mouths that demand food, football practice, a house, a husband who likes your body a whole lot more after you gave him three sons, and he liked it a lot before you did that, and a full-time job working with Tex *and* Duke, most of the time with those two together and bickering at each other, and remember your sister's security code," Jet retorted.

"You could text me…"

Mo lost track of the conversation as he hit the truck and they went inside.

His job became mostly controlling squabbling brothers who all (even the youngest) thought they could carry in six bags apiece, and they didn't even have that many, and making sure the youngest didn't fall flat on his face grunting and groaning with the two bags he demanded to carry while they got the shit into the house.

They put the bags on the kitchen floor, an odd choice, one Mo got when he realized this was a relatively practiced dance and the boys couldn't reach the counters, and they all went into unpacking mode. They unpacked, but it was only Jet and Lottie, under Lottie's strict placement plan, who put away.

"So, are you a professional wrestler?" Alex asked him.

"No," Mo answered.

"A soldier?" Dante asked, his eyes on the gun on Mo's belt that was in its holster looped through Mo's cargo pants.

"No," Mo repeated.

"He's a commando," Lottie announced.

Alex froze solid and stared with his mouth open at Mo.

"What's a commando?" Dante asked.

"The coolest of the *cool*," Alex whispered, then shouted, "Even cooler than Uncle Luke!"

Dante's face smushed up and he told his brother, "No one's cooler than Uncle Luke."

"*Muchacho*," Alex threw a hand Mo's way, "look at him."

Dante looked at Mo.

His face conceded the point, but his mouth didn't.

Mo nearly burst out laughing.

He was helped in controlling this when the youngest one slapped him on the thigh.

Mo looked down at the kid. "I wanna be a 'mando!"

"Give it time, bub," he said.

"Oh my God, someone kill me," Jet begged. "Last week, Carissa was over, Joker showed to take her home, and Cesar wanted to be a biker."

"Well…I mean, he *is* Joker," Lottie muttered while obsessively lining up cans of La Croix in her fridge.

"I'm gonna be just like Uncle Luke," Dante declared stubbornly.

"I'm gonna be like Uncle Lee, except the commando kind, 'cause Auntie Indy is *fine*, and I want me a hot babe just like her," Alex announced.

"*I love Annie Sadie!*" Cesar shrieked.

"Nobody is killing me," Jet pointed out.

"What are you doing here?" Lottie asked her sister.

Dante shoved a bunch of bananas in Mo's gut.

Mo took the cue and the bananas and put them in Lottie's fruit bowl.

"One, to ascertain I still have a living, breathing sister," Jet answered.

Mo had to hand it to her, Lottie didn't even cut a glance his direction on that.

"And two, to tell you Mom and Tex want us over for dinner next Sunday," Jet finished. "The whole family."

Jet's attention came to him.

"Cool. Mo and I'll be there," Lottie shared.

His eyes went to her and his hands itched with the urge to toss her over his shoulder, carry her upstairs and tan her tight ass.

"You're…uh, *there?*" Jet asked quietly.

"You can talk in front of Mo. We're tight," Lottie told her.

That bought her five more swats.

"Oooooh…kay," Jet whispered, giving her sister big eyes.

Lottie just smiled at her.

Jet's eyes narrowed, and she started to look pissed.

Ah, hell.

"Dude, how do you become a commando?" Alex asked him before Jet could get into it with her sister about how she suddenly had a boyfriend that Jet had never heard about who Lottie was tight enough with, he was coming to dinner with the family.

"This *dude* is Uncle Mo," Lottie corrected.

Now he was "Uncle Mo."

And now he wanted someone to kill *him*.

"Righteous," Alex said to his aunt, then back to Mo. "Uncle Mo, how do you become a commando?"

He opened his mouth to tell the kid he wasn't a commando.

Though, with some of the missions Hawk took, he absolutely was.

But Lottie got there before him.

"He was in the Army."

"Righteous!" Alex yelled. "Just like Uncle Lee!" His gaze dipped to

Mo's weapon. "Why do you carry a gun?"

"I'm on duty," Mo told him.

"*Coooooool*," he breathed. He recovered from that awesomeness and asked, "Do you know how to put on camo makeup?"

"Yeah," Mo said.

"Do you know how to use a rocket launcher?"

"Yeah."

"Have you flown in a helicopter?"

"Yeah."

"Have you jumped out of a plane?"

"Yeah."

"Have you been to Afghanistan?"

Mo's body grew tight and so did his repeat of, "Yeah."

He felt Lottie and Jet's attention.

Alex opened his mouth again but didn't get anything out before Lottie said softly, "Alex, honey, find the ice cream and get your brothers and yourself a bar. 'Kay?"

"Sure, Auntie Lottie," Alex said, then started digging through the remaining canvas bags.

Mo avoided her eyes as he bent and picked up the spent bags, folding them in half, like Lottie kept them, and stacking them on the counter.

He heard ripping ice cream bar plastic and felt Jet move his way. He turned his attention to her and saw she was carrying noodles, Tostitos and boxes of granola.

When she got close, she said low, "Thank you for your service, Mo."

She meant it.

They all meant it, but she thought he was involved with her sister so it hit closer to home, thus she *meant* it.

"Not a problem," he muttered as she passed him to get to the pantry.

He couldn't avoid Lottie anymore, not with strength of warmth coming from her direction, so he shifted his gaze to hers.

Yeah, that was why he did it right there. That look on her face.

He'd known he was going to be a man who was going to be a soldier for a long time before he became one. That was about a lot of things that were too numerous to boil down to just that look on Lottie's face. It included his mother and his sisters and the sense of duty and loyalty he had to them since they had no other man in their life. They were not wallflowers or doormats. Not one of them. It didn't matter. It was the man he was from early on that dictated the man he was going to be.

But that look on Lottie's face and her wrestling without hesitation with her nephews on her front lawn and her throwdown with a woman she identified as possible competition to claim him morphing into a throwdown to avenge him were why he got in.

And in a different world, one where she really was his, they would be how he could live with what he'd seen, what he'd done and what he'd lost in the dust, dirt and sand.

To be the kind of man who earned that look.

Who deserved it.

And who could claim the woman who wore it.

"It isn't a big deal," he lied.

"You're absolutely wrong and you know it so shut up, pookie-loo," she returned.

A good ten swats.

Bare ass.

Mo cut ties with her eyes and bent down to pick up the last bag, forgotten in the ice cream rush, not surprisingly carrying the fresh fruits and vegetables.

He put it on the counter and unpacked it.

* * * *

"So…Afghanistan?"

She'd barely shut the door on her sister and nephews.

He was standing in her living room where he'd retreated, really fucking quick, after he hovered close at her back when she was saying goodbye to her family.

She was standing in the arched entryway that led off her foyer into her living room.

"Lottie—"

"And," she cut him off, "to go back to our discussion at the grocery store, you may have lived with that woman for two years, but I *am* a woman, so I know the plays she was making, and they were not what you think they were."

Mo shook his head. "We're not doing this."

She started to move forward. "We are so totally doing this."

He took a step back and she stopped.

"We're not, because we can't," he declared.

"We can, we are, and I'll get us started. Backtracking in a belated effort at being an adult, you should know, anyone else, no way I'd be in a nightie making breakfast."

He clenched his teeth because he had an idea he knew what was coming next.

"I was in a nightie making breakfast with you because you're hot and I wanted you to jump me," she kept at him.

That was what he thought was coming.

He still knew better.

"The minute you opened the door to me, you took a step back," he bit out.

"That's because you're enormous, Mo. There's a lot of you."

On that, she advanced again.

Mo took another step back.

She stopped.

But she didn't stop talking.

"Now let me share my first reaction to seeing your face through the peephole, something you didn't witness, and the exact time I decided I was pretty sure I was gonna want you to jump me. Okay, I'll admit, the amount of you took me by surprise, but in no way was I withdrawing because I didn't like what I saw, or I feared it. It was just surprise followed closely with the desire to climb you all the way to the top."

Shit, fuck, he couldn't listen to her talking this way.

"Lottie—"

She took another step forward.

He took a step back, hit her coffee table and began to skirt it.

She stopped so he stopped.

"You were a dick to me, Mo."

Fuck.

He knew they'd get there.

He just didn't want to be there because she was right.

He'd been a dick.

"I thought you were playing games," he explained.

"You didn't keep that secret," she reminded him.

"I also needed you to back off."

"You didn't keep that secret either."

"So how about you remember I need you to back off?" he suggested.

"No way in hell," she returned.

"Lottie, listen—"

She advanced again, he retreated, and she didn't stop until his calves hit couch and there was nowhere to go.

Which meant she got in his space but didn't touch him.

But her in his space was bad enough.

Christ.

"Let me make myself perfectly clear. I like you, Mo." She leaned closer. "*A lot.*"

"We're not going there," he grunted.

"We so are."

"We're not."

She put a hand to his chest and her eyes warmed as her voice went soft and sweet. "We are, baby."

"We're not because there is no way I'm gonna be in the position of being inside you and my attention all about you something that would give some whackjob the opportunity to get the drop on us and put a bullet in the back of my head."

Her face went slack and her hand curled into a fist on his chest.

But he wasn't done with her.

"After that, he'll drag you out from under my dead body, and no one will get the warning you've been taken because I'm dead in your bed and he's got you somewhere, making you wish you were as dead as me."

She pressed her fist into his chest but said nothing.

"Lottie, you get this is serious, but what you gotta *really* get is that I need to be focused and not on how badly I wanna make love to you, but on how badly I wanna keep you safe and healthy, physically, but more, *mentally.*"

"Okay," she whispered, understanding the intelligence of that right away, and that was his girl. "We'll wait until it's over."

Goddammit.

"We won't do it then either."

She showed her shock then her hurt before she said, her voice rising, "Why not?"

"Because it doesn't cut me up too much, the likes of Tammy dumping me, but I start something with the likes of you and you get the urge to move on, then do it, where do you think that'll leave me?"

"Have you thought about the fact that I might not get that urge?" she asked.

"They move on, Lottie. They *all* move on."

"I'm not them."

"You can do better than me and both of us know it."

They did.

They both did.

And he knew she did when she dropped her head, took her hand from him and stepped away.

Now *that*…

That cut him up.

Until she tilted her head back and speared him with her gaze.

"What's better than you, Mo?" she snapped.

"More money. Better lookin'. Trips to Tiffany's."

"You think I give *one real shit* about all that?"

Mo fully clicked into a conversation he thought he'd already been fully clicked into and he did that by realizing somewhere along the line he'd made her angry.

Very angry.

"Lo—" he began.

"First," she bit off, "you're hot. Not a little hot, *a lot*. You might not be everybody's cup of tea, but neither am I or anyone else. But trust me, Mo, I wanted to climb you like a tree the first time I laid eyes on you and Tammy would have gotten down on her knees to beg you to have her back. And that has a lot to do with you just being you, but the kind of woman she is, it also has to do with you looking the way you do and also the fact it's pretty clear by her behavior you know how to use your cock."

He'd had no complaints on that, as far as he knew, but he was not going to share that with Lottie.

Even if he was, he wouldn't get the shot because she kept going.

"So you're hot, and that's my call to make, you can't make it, so I don't wanna hear another word about it," she clipped. "*Second*, my dad promised us everything from trips to the Riviera to castles in the sky. He didn't deliver on *one single promise* he made, but more, he wasn't even enough of a man to fight the urge to hit a table in order to see to his woman and his girls. You're man enough to fight the urge to fuck me in order to make me safe. What else would I get if you let me have the rest? I don't know, you do, and I want a shot at that."

"Lottie—"

"And I don't want Tiffany's, Mo. If I did, I'd earn the money to buy something there. I doubt you're on food stamps working for Hawk, but I also make a good living and if a woman's about the living a man can earn, she's not much of a woman. I need a man with ambition and drive and a belief in what he's doing. I don't need a man to drive me to Tiffany's. I got my own damned car."

"Baby—" he whispered, with all she said, unable to stop that word from leaking out of his mouth.

But that was all he got out.

"I don't know what those bitches did to you, since my guess is Tammy wasn't the only one. And I don't know what happened to you in Afghanistan. I don't even really know *you*. All I know, and I know it good, Mo, is that *I wanna find out*."

"This isn't smart," he said gently.

"Now? Or ever?" she demanded to know.

"Now."

And possibly ever.

But he wasn't going to get into that with her right then.

"Call Hawk and tell him to find this guy, Mo."

"They're workin' on it."

"Tell them to work faster."

He said nothing because all his attention was set on stopping himself from smiling.

Christ, she really was something.

"Do you have a problem with me stripping?" she asked.

Mo now had no trouble not smiling.

"I don't like men watching you take your clothes off," he told her honestly.

"This is an issue because that's what I do to pay the bills and I like doing it."

"Yeah," he agreed.

"Can you get over it?"

He didn't know how he'd feel if he wasn't there every night, watching the crowd watching her take her clothes off.

Maybe.

But doubtfully.

He gave her more honesty.

"It's an issue, Lottie."

"I'm not getting any younger," she announced.

Outside his time in the Army and on Hawk's crew, most his life he'd spent with women.

So on that, he kept his mouth shut.

"And I want kids," she went on.

He kept his mouth shut on that one too, even if he knew it already with how she was with her nephews, and he liked it a lot.

"Do you want kids?" she asked.

"Yeah," he answered.

"How many?"

"Two or three."

"I'm not getting any younger, Mo."

Well, hell.

Now he was fighting smiling again.

"You aren't either," she pointed out.

"Right," he murmured.

"We'll work it out," she declared.

He drew an audible breath into his nostrils.

"We're gonna work it out, Mo," she assured him.

"It'll break me, you get shot of me."

Her body turned to stone at his admission, her face did too, and she stared at him.

"You're a good woman. A class act. Smart. Funny. Love your nephews and show it. They love you back, so much, and you make it safe, so they feel free to show it. You got sass. You got talent. You believe in what you do and go all out to be the best at it there is. You're together. You're kind to your friends. And you can cook. I want a shot at that, Lottie. I wanna find out how much better you can get. But I already have a clue, and havin' that clue, I know, you give it, then take it away, it won't be like Tammy. It'll break me. Now, knowin' that, where you at?"

She didn't wait even a beat.

She ordered, "Call Hawk and tell him to work faster."

Mo no longer had the urge to spank her.

He had other urges and he had to lock himself down in order to fight them.

It was then he found out she'd take hold of any opportunity she was given.

Even going after what she wanted when he was weak.

"What happened in Afghanistan, baby?"

"Lost two brothers and killed people who were probably civilians."

And it was then he learned she went after what she wanted so she could give him what he needed.

"You holding on with all of that?" she asked gently.

"This is why I keep busy."

"And why you only sleep four hours a night."

"Yeah."

"Oh, Mo," she murmured, both words heavy with the weight of compassion he saw in her eyes. "I can't touch you, right?"

"Right."

"Okay, I can't touch you now. But I can promise I'm gonna take care of you, Mo."

"That's a tall order, Lottie."

And she just had a piece of Afghanistan.

She had no idea about all the rest.

"I'm goal-oriented, baby," she said quietly.

Mo stood still, eyes on her, and breathed.

"Do you need to hand me off to another one of Hawk's men?" she offered.

Oh, hell no.

"No one is on you but me," he growled.

She nodded immediately.

Then she smiled.

Not victoriously.

Gratefully.

"You wanna watch TV?" she asked.

"Sure," he answered.

"Game's on," she said.

"Whatever," he muttered.

"A movie?"

"Works for me."

"Mo?"

"What?"

"Thank you, honey."

"You need to stop it, baby," he said, going soft.

She nodded, a lot and fast. "Right. Right. All professional."

Like she could pull that off.

But at least she'd have a mind.

And after that…

He'd let himself think of what was after that when it was actually *after*.

"I'll make popcorn," she said.

"I'll do a perimeter check."

She smiled huge at him.

Huge and happy.

So…

Right.

When all was said and done, he might come out a winner for once, or he might be ground to dust.

But he knew right then it didn't matter which way that broke.

Just as long and as much as humanly possible in the meantime, Mo had a shot to make Lottie happy.

Chapter Seven

Incremental

Lottie

The lights went dark.

I rushed off the stage and Mo was there, throwing my robe over my shoulders.

He smelled good. Clean. Like soap and man.

He'd had his shower and was back to me before my set ended.

I wanted to pounce on him.

Instead, I shoved my hands through the arms and barely had my fingers to the sides to pull the robe closed before his big hand had a powerful grip on my upper arm and he was practically dragging me down the steps to the side hall.

It was Tuesday night.

Suffice it to say, Mo knowing where it was heading between us after the threat was over, and me knowing where this was going, we were impatient for it to get done.

But Mo being all that was Mo, his impatience, like everything else about him, manifested itself in much larger ways.

The man was a ticking time bomb.

This partly had to do with him wanting to get to know me better, and it was hard (*very hard*) to try to keep things casual, keep a distance, be professional, when we were together twenty-four hours a day.

We cooked together. We ate together. We watched TV together. And after putting a sheet up over the windows (something I did not like, but getting what I got after, that being hanging with Mo, I was okay with it) Mo lounged on the couch opposite mine in my bedroom with his eyes closed while I read. Even with eyes closed, I knew he was awake, looking Zen (and insanely fuckable), but he was also undoubtedly alert.

We talked.

We had no choice but to get to know each other better and I knew I liked what I got (even though he wasn't much of a talker, and as the days went by, he got quieter and quieter due to his patience waning more and more).

I also knew he liked what he got.

From when we first met, Mo didn't need words to communicate. And the increase in dancing silver eyes and the addition of soft looks he'd give me...

Man.

Yeah.

This had to end soon.

Mo's ticking time bomb thing also had to do with the big lug wanting to sleep with me.

And by the by, I *adored* that he'd referred to it during our Come to Jesus as making love.

But he was very much all guy, and men needed to get some, he was sleeping in my room, living in my home, watching me strip. The need for him to do me was so strong, it had a taste, it had a smell, it had a feel, it was constant and grew more powerful every day.

Not being able to take it there had to be torture.

I knew, because it was torture for me too.

And it was getting worse every day.

Last, but I had a feeling this was the biggest part, Mo's impatience had a sharp edge that I did not think had to do with him wanting to take me out to dinner and ask my favorite color then take me home and fuck me stupid.

It had to do with the fact that this guy hadn't been caught yet and there was something really not good about that.

I didn't ask. If Mo felt I needed to know, or wanted me to know, he would tell me.

More, I was thinking it was another way he was protecting me. And he was that guy. He needed to give that to me.

So even though none of this made me want to jump for joy, I didn't push it with him.

Like I didn't tell him his grip was too tight and that he needed to slow down or I'd break my neck on my platform stripper shoes while he dragged me to the dressing room. A place I knew, because he communicated (nonverbally) he thought was a safe zone, unlike the stage (definitely) and the hall, and anywhere else that was accessible or visible to people he might not know.

I just moved with him as fast as I could.

He used the hand he did not have on me to pound on the door twice, bellowed, "Man coming in!" and as he was hesitating the two seconds he always gave it so the girls could get situated before he went in, I spoke.

"I'm good, Mo. Safe. Sound. Healthy. Right here. With you. You've got me. Yeah?"

He looked down at me and allowed me to see some of the harshness bleed out of his face.

Not all of it, but some of it.

I'd take it.

Then he pushed us into the dressing room.

Strippers poured out as we went in, and once in, Mo let me go and shut the door behind the last girl.

I finally tied my belt on my robe.

"Shit," he said.

I looked up at him then turned my attention to where his was and saw Carla wearing her robe, platforms off, sitting at her makeup station, holding a bag of ice to her ankle.

I rushed her way. "Ohmigod, girl! What happened?"

"Tripped coming off the stage for your set," she muttered, eyes cast down to her ankle resting on her knee, her face pinched.

"Did you tell Smithie?" I asked.

She shook her head and finally looked up at me. "I'm just gonna ice it for a bit longer and then get back out there."

Yeah.

She had to get back out there.

She had two kids from two different baby daddies, both pieces of shit, the dads, not the kids (her boys were great).

So she had three mouths to feed, her mom, who was a bitch, her dad, who was a drunk, her brother, who thought they were all wastes of space, especially his stripper sister who had two baby daddies (in other words, she had a brother who was a dick).

She also had a killer bod she knew how to move.

This meant she was on a stage, dancing in a thong, when the last thing she wanted to do was go home after doing that to her two young boys and then look them in the eye over Cheerios the next morning.

It wasn't like I didn't get Mo's point about stripping. I did.

And Carla was Mo's point.

Smithie paid well, but tips were essential for all these girls (including me) to up our quality of life (for some of us, significantly), and if we had dependents, give them some modicum of a quality of life.

These thoughts on my mind, I started in shock when Mo hunkered down beside me and said quietly, "Lift the ice. Let me see."

I was shocked because he didn't often engage with the girls.

After our last two days together, I understood this was not about him disapproving of them. It was about him being not such a talkative dude. But also, he was there to look out for me, not make friends with them. And last, he was in our space and therefore he wanted to make it as safe for the girls as he could when he couldn't exit said space, so he didn't call attention to himself (an impossible task for a guy like Mo, but you had to hand it to him, he tried).

I stared at his bald head fighting the desire to run my hands over it as he took a look at her ankle.

Then I stared at his large, long-fingered, veined hand as he gently prodded it.

Okay, he could drag me around with little effort.

And clearly he could go gentle.

I did not need to learn that about him when he was off-limits.

Shit.

His head tipped back to look at her face when he asked, "Scale of one to ten, ten highest, what's the pain?"

He was still gently prodding her ankle.

She answered, "Three."

I turned my gaze to her face and saw the pinch tighten into a wince with each prod.

Mo straightened, muttering, "Ice back on."

Carla put the ice back on.

Mo then looked down at me and I knew by his expression he didn't miss the winces that did not say she was at a pain level of three.

He confirmed this by saying, "Most urgent cares closed, she needs to get to the emergency room."

"No!" Carla cried, and Mo and I turned back to her. "No. It's gonna be fine."

"It's probably not broken but it's a bad sprain," Mo told her.

"If it's sprained, I'll be off the stage for a week," she returned anxiously.

At that, I crouched down to her. "Carla, you can't dance with a sprained ankle."

"The ice will work," she told me. "I just need to give it more time."

"You need to see to it and give it time to heal if it needs that so it doesn't get worse," I pointed out.

"It'll be okay."

"Just check it out."

She shook her head with agitation. "I can't go to the emergency room. This isn't urgent. I'll be waiting forever. And I have to be home to let my neighbor go. I pay through the nose for her to come over and stay late to watch the boys. She gets pissy when I'm even later."

In a normal situation, I would offer to go relieve the sitter after my last set.

Mo would never agree to that, so I told her, "I'll call my mom."

Carla shook her head again. "You can't do that, Lottie. It's after eleven at night."

I grinned at her. "My mom loves kids, she loves you, and she's the kind of person who gets off on doing things for folks. And you know Tex. He's the king of wading in when a damsel is in distress. They'll be all over it."

"Tex might scare my boys," she muttered.

This was true.

"Maybe, but in the end he'll have them eating out of his hand," I told her the truth. "But right now, they're asleep and you'll be home before they wake up, so they won't even see him."

She looked at her ankle then at me. "I can't be off the stage for a week, Lottie."

I reached out and gave her wrist a squeeze. "Just go to the hospital. Find out how bad it is." I scooted closer on my platforms and reminded her, "And you know, if you have to take a break, we'll take care of you. You know that, babe."

More shaking of her head. "I can't ask the girls to help me out. You all have your own bills to pay."

"You won't have to, but we will, and we won't be pissed about it. We'll only be pissed if you don't take care of yourself. And anyway, Smithie would rather cut off his own arm than have you and your boys in a bind.

You know that too."

She glanced up at Mo before she whispered to me, "Smithie has a lot on his mind."

All the girls knew about my sitch. Everyone had been interviewed and they'd all been tasked to keep an eye out for a possible crackpot that tweaked them, as crackpots were wont to do.

It sucked they were in on this, and knew this was happening to me, thus they were worried about me, and it gave me more fodder for nursing the hugest grudge I'd ever held, this being against said crackpot.

Through these thoughts, I shot her another grin, and after I had them, I said, "It's unusual for a dude, but Smithie's a multi-tasker."

Carla gazed down at her ankle again.

"Can I call him?" I asked. "He'll want to take you to the hospital."

She gave me her eyes. "He wants to be around to look out for you."

I jerked my head to Mo. "He gave me someone who'll look out for me. If he knows you're hurting, he'll want to look out for *you*. And please, let me call him. If he finds out we didn't tell him this, he'll be ticked, *at me*. And I hate it when Smithie's ticked at me."

This was a lie. Smithie was all bark, no bite. I didn't tick him off on purpose, but I didn't avoid it should such an occasion arise.

Finally, I got a grin from her which meant I got out of my squat, smiling back, then moved to my station.

Mo, for the first time ever in that room, did not follow me.

He stayed close to Carla.

As I grabbed my purse to get out my phone, I watched out of the corners of my eyes and saw that he didn't murmur reassuring words or offer to help hold the bag of ice or do anything but give her his solid, assuring presence.

But he gave her his solid, assuring presence. She was worried. She was in pain. And he gave her what he had to give.

All right.

Seriously.

I hoped that man was good in bed because I was totally falling in love with him.

I called Smithie to come and see to Carla.

After that, I turned, leaned back against my station, and watched Mo openly while I called my mom.

His silver gaze came to me.

And there it was.

A soft look from Mo.

Jeez, I *so* wanted to jump him.

I gave him a smile.

His eyes dropped to it, but he didn't smile back.

And again, I wanted to pounce on him.

Mom answered the phone.

"Lottie? Is everything okay?"

She sounded awake and alert, but not alarmed. Just awake and alert even though I knew I had to have woken her.

This was because she was the mother of a Rock Chick and the Queen of the Corvette Calendar. She had a lot of practice with being woken up in the middle of the night, needing to do it and be alert.

"Hey, Mom. Sorry to call late, but Carla turned her ankle bad coming off stage tonight. Mo had a look at it and thinks she needs to have it checked at the hospital. She needs someone to go relieve her babysitter until she gets home."

"Mo?"

Shit.

Wrapped up in all that was going on, I not only forgot about dinner on Sunday, I forgot I'd told Jet about Mo coming, but not my mother.

And obviously my sister had left relaying that news to me.

"My, uh…" I gave Mo big eyes.

His dark eyebrows shot up.

Dark brows that went with the dark stubble he normally sported (except at times like now, right after his shower, when he'd shaved) and then there was dark hair on his arms.

This possibly meant dark hair on his chest, and other, better places, something I could not *wait* to discover.

My thoughts turned to the choice he'd given me at our first meeting of being in the room with him while he showered. Considering current events, that was a choice I no longer had.

And that was a crying shame.

But indisputably prudent.

"New boyfriend," I finished, my voice kinda husky.

His lips twitched before his attention turned because Smithie was bowling through the door.

The bossman didn't even look at me. He went direct to Carla, concern evident on his face.

God, I loved that guy.

"You have a new boyfriend?" Mom asked in my ear.

I focused on the task at hand.

"She has a *what?*" I heard boomed over the phone before I could answer.

Tex was awake.

Not a surprise.

Definitely a wildcard.

Tex had no kids. Tex's history was a long story, and not much of it, until he met Indy Nightingale, was good. And one could say, considering after he met Indy he'd been shot, clubbed in the head, kidnapped and blew up a warehouse, that wasn't good for him either.

But Tex would tell you all that had been a hoot.

And Tex was the finest man who ever breathed.

But he was a character.

A *booming* character, in all ways that could be, including audibly.

And the years that he'd been involved with the Rock Chicks (this being from the beginning, when he rescued Indy after she was kidnapped, this being when he got himself shot for that effort), plus the years he'd been married to my mom, he'd adopted all of us.

Especially me and Jet.

He was not a man who would hold my hand at a fair and shout how he needed to get cotton candy for his best girl.

He was a man who would run into the burning building me, my sister or especially my mother was in, even if there was little chance he would find us alive.

He'd risk his life, and give it, to try.

Obviously, I adored him.

"You'll meet him Sunday," I told Mom. "Listen, can you help Carla out?"

"We'll meet him Sunday," I heard Mom say, not to me, to Tex. "His name is Mo," she went on.

"Mo? Hawk Delgado's Mo?" Tex boomed.

Shit.

Of course Tex knew Mo.

Great.

My eyes went to Mo to see him standing guard over Carla while Smithie prodded her ankle.

From Mom to Tex, "I don't know, sweetheart." To me, "Does this boyfriend work for Hawk Delgado?"

"Um…yeah," I said.

"Yes," Mom told Tex.

"Well, all right!" Tex bellowed. "Boy's as big as a house, built tough as a tank and he ain't no chatterbox. He's over, I don't gotta listen to him blather on about a play-by-play of the last Broncos game while I'm watchin' me a Bruce Lee film. Tell Lottie I approve."

I nearly giggled, even though I had no idea who made him listen to a play-by-play of the last Broncos game. All of the Hot Bunch were Broncos fans. But none of them were men to hang at Tex and Mom's house with their one hundred and fifty cats.

Though, I had a feeling they'd dig on Bruce Lee films.

"Tex approves," Mom told me.

"Great," I replied, now with a smile in my voice.

"I still haven't met him yet, Lottie," she warned.

Mom was going to *love* Mo.

"You will Sunday," I reminded her. "Now about Carla."

"Text us her address, honey. We'll head over there as soon's we're dressed."

"Thanks, Mom," I murmured.

"Anytime, darlin' girl," she murmured back. "Love you."

"Love you too. And tell Tex I love him."

To Tex, "Lottie sends her love."

A low boom of "Sheeee-it."

I smiled.

That meant Tex loved me too.

"Later, Mom."

"See you Sunday, Lottie."

We disconnected as I watched Mo lift Carla like she was a sheet draped over his arms.

My nipples tingled and my thoughts went where they shouldn't.

That being my hope he was just as much of a powerhouse in bed.

He carried her behind the screen so she could dress.

"I'm takin' her to the hospital," Smithie informed me.

"Good," I replied.

Mo came out from behind the screen.

"Mo's gonna help me get her to my truck. You lock the door behind us," Smithie ordered. "And don't leave this room. Mo'll be back as soon as we get Carla in the truck."

I nodded.

Mo scowled at me.

"I'll lock the door, Mo," I assured.

He scowled some more before he dipped his chin.

I turned my attention to the screen, thus Carla, and called. "Mom and Tex are heading over to your place as soon as they get dressed. You might want to call your sitter." I paused, "And warn her about Tex."

"I'll do it in the car. Thanks, Lottie," Carla called back.

"Don't mention it. Do you need help back there?"

"Uh...kinda," she answered.

Yeah, she needed to hit the hospital.

I gave Mo then Smithie a look and headed behind the screen.

We got Carla dressed, I went, grabbed her purse and gave it to her before giving her a kiss on the cheek and a wish of good luck, and then Mo picked her up to take her out to the car.

I trailed them close at Mo's heels so he'd know I was doing as ordered.

I started to lock the door practically before it was fully closed.

When I turned back to the room, I realized it was weird to be alone. The only time I'd been alone for days was in the shower.

I barely got Carla's address texted to Mom and my false eyelashes off to do a full makeup cleanup in order to do a full makeup put on when there was a pounding at the door and a shout of, "Mo!"

Well, he didn't jack around.

I felt my mouth turn up as I hustled to the door to let him in.

He crowded my space to get back in, which meant back to guarding me, and I realized with him, falling in love would probably be incremental.

He'd do things like that, every day. Little ones, maybe some big ones, but things like that every day that would make me fall more in love with him.

Which, taken to its natural conclusion, meant, if we worked, I'd be falling in love with him, little by little, more and more every day until the day I died.

And that *soooooo* worked for me.

I hid my smile at this thought and quickly backed out of his space so I didn't have the urge to pounce on him (or didn't give in to the urge I already had) and didn't make things harder for him to fight his urge to pounce on me.

I moved back to my station.

"I'm surprised you didn't make Smithie call a bouncer to take Carla out."

"They have four persons of interest out there. They need eyes on the crowd."

My head whipped around to him. "Really?"

He dipped his chin.

"New guys?"

"All of them regulars who haven't been back in a while. All of them guys who creep the waitresses out. All of them guys who bouncers have red flagged since they started coming. None of them guys who've been here since the letter was sent."

I felt a tickle at the back of my neck.

"You think one of them—?"

"I think they'll have tails tonight and Hawk will have men in all of their houses the minute they leave for work tomorrow morning and we'll know."

Holy shit.

This might be over soon.

And holy *shit*.

They were searching houses.

"They're searching houses?" I asked.

"Yup."

"They can do that?"

"They can do whatever they want if they don't get caught."

Whoa.

"But, won't it be inadmissible if they search like that?" I queried. "I mean, they can't get it to law enforcement and have the cops be able to get a real search warrant if they find something illegally like that."

Mo had moved closer to my station while I spoke.

What he didn't do while doing that, arriving, and stopping to stand close to my table was reply.

"Right, Mo?" I pressed.

He was silent a moment, but before I could push again, he spoke.

"When this guy is caught, Lottie, the jury that matters right now is still out as to what to do with him."

"The jury that matters?"

"Hawk, Smithie…" he said no more.

"And you," I whispered.

"I'll make my case to Hawk that I get a say."

"And that case will be?"

"I got claimed in a King Soopers. I don't mind I did. As in I *way* don't mind it. And seein' as I belong to you, you belong to me, so I get a say."

Oh my God.

I totally needed to pounce on my mound of hunkalicious, soon-to-be (I hoped) boyfriend.

"You need to move away, baby," I whispered.

His head jerked. His eyes went dark. The muscles in his neck stood out in a sexy way that was *so* not helping matters.

Then he moved back to the door.

I tried deep breathing.

Then I turned to my mirror to deal with my makeup.

It didn't help because I could see Mo in the mirror.

His wide shoulders were to the wall and his gaze was cast to the floor, I knew, so he wouldn't be staring at me.

God.

They needed to catch this guy.

They *so* needed to catch this guy.

I moved a shaky hand toward my cleansing wipes.

And for right then, I got down to business.

* * * *

"Start with your toes, Lottie."

Mo's deep voice coming to me in the dark told me not only that he wasn't asleep, but that he was hearing me toss and turn.

I rolled to my back and stared at the ceiling. "I tried. It's not working."

"You want me to help?"

First, I loved that he asked.

Second, his voice coming to me from ten feet away when I couldn't cross that space, and he couldn't cross that space, would be no help.

"You can't help, Mo."

He didn't reply.

Suddenly, an idea hit me, I sat up and looked across the moonlit room to the big body covering my couch.

"You need to ask Hawk to put someone else on me so we can move this along."

He did not move, except his mouth.

"Not gonna happen."

"Mo—"

"Not. Gonna. *Happen*."

I shut up.

I'd never heard him sound like that. His tone brooked no argument, none whatsoever, in a way that even I knew I couldn't argue with him, and I could argue with anybody.

"I'm on you," he stated.

"I know," I said quietly.

"No one but me."

Another thought occurred to me, one I did not like.

"You know, this isn't woman-falling-for-her-bodyguard syndrome, honey," I told him. "It's Lottie-falling-for-Mo syndrome. I'm not gonna get attached to some other guy on your crew."

He was again silent but even if I couldn't see his face, I felt him communicating.

Strongly.

However, considering I couldn't see his face, I didn't know what he was saying.

So I called, "Mo?"

"You're fallin' for me?"

Now his voice was low and tight.

Uh-oh.

Too soon?

"Well…uh—"

"Stop talking, Lottie."

I shut my mouth.

"It isn't about that," he said.

"So what's it about?"

"No one's on you, but me."

"I know, you said that, but if we—"

In a surge, he sat up.

I again shut up.

"I'll give you something," he declared.

Oh God.

I hoped it was fingering me to an orgasm.

Then I could give him a handjob, something I was relatively certain I could do at the same time looking out for a bad guy so I could warn Mo so he could neutralize him before getting a bullet in his head.

That said, if his member was as big as the rest of him, that might not be possible, not because I'd have to concentrate, but because I'd *want* to.

"I make you mine, officially," he continued, "no one ever has you again, Lottie, but me."

Chills slid over my skin at the same time my eyes got hot.

I never would have thought it, but what he said was *way* better than any orgasm in the history of time.

And that answered my earlier question.

What I said was not too soon.

"Are you understanding me?" he asked.

"Yes, Mo," I whispered.

I'd be his.

I'd be his to love (hopefully), treasure (hopefully)…

And protect.

No one else's.

Ever again.

But he was starting now.

"Now go to sleep, sweetheart," he said, all soft.

I loved it when he let himself call me "baby." It didn't happen often, in fact, not since our Come to Jesus.

That was my first "sweetheart."

I'd never forget it.

Not ever.

I settled back into bed, pulling the covers over me.

I didn't watch but I did hear soft noises from the cushions as he settled back to the couch.

It took a while before I said into the dark, "I hope it's one of the guys from tonight."

"Me too, baby. Now please, go to sleep."

It was the please that got me.

I closed my eyes.

And with Mo watching over me, keeping me safe, I drifted off.

And slept like a baby.

Chapter Eight

Piece of Cake

Mo

The next night, standing backstage, eyes scanning the crowd during Lottie's last set, Mo tried to control his thoughts that were on the fact none of the guys they'd tagged last night was their guy.

And his thoughts were on that because they were also on the most recent letter they got.

The ugliest.

The most troubling.

The one that was delivered to Smithie Monday and included the news that the guy knew all about Mo, and that Mo was going to be cleansed himself, this being executed, as in made dead for "consorting with the soiled."

The letter that also shared the members of Hawk's crew who were supposed to be doing drive-bys and randomly keeping an eye on Lottie's house while he was inside keeping an eye on Lottie, as well as Mo when he was out with Lottie, had missed this guy somewhere along the line.

The letter that had Mo so tweaked, he was close to having to admit that to Hawk, this being right before he shared he was taking Lottie to Bali.

All these thoughts clashed with all his thoughts about Lottie, and all his responses—mentally, emotionally and physically—that were making it nearly impossible to do his job.

The way she stepped in with Carla being the most recent. Not only getting her to go to the emergency room, getting her mom to look after the woman's children, and also her chat with all the girls that night, after learning Carla was out for at least five days, probably more like ten.

They were taking a collection.

Carla was on paid leave.

But she wouldn't feel the loss of her tips.

And finally, Lottie saying to Dominique, who'd brought in Lottie's first take of tips from her first set, "Everything I get tonight goes into the envelope for Carla."

No, Carla wouldn't feel the loss of her tips.

It was clear Lottie ruled this roost, not as the headliner, but as the benevolent queen who looked after her subjects.

It wasn't just her nephews, her sister, her mother, her "And tell Tex I love him."

It was just her.

With everyone.

And when he had her, he'd have all that in more ways than she was giving it now, and make no mistake, she was giving it now.

But she was holding it back.

And it was tearing her up.

She was nearly bursting at the seams to give all she had to Mo.

And he wanted it.

Bad.

He was gonna have to tell Hawk.

Before he got her the fuck out of there.

This guy going uncaptured, they might never be able to come back.

Mo was down with that.

Unfortunately, his mother and sisters wouldn't be. Not to mention his nieces and nephews.

They had to get this guy.

And Mo had to stay sharp.

He had to…

His body went solid when he saw him.

Every Guy.

Very carefully *Every Guy*.

Slightly faded red polo shirt. But crisp jeans, like they were new.

Not a match.

You didn't wear new jeans with an old shirt. Most men forced to go to the store, they stocked up. If he had an occasion he wore new jeans, he'd put on a new shirt.

And it was slightly faded, not stained, misshapen, fucked up.

Casual. Like he grabbed whatever and threw it on when he did not. He made that selection carefully.

Trying to fit in.

Trying to be Every Guy.

And he probably usually wore trousers. Or chinos. A suit. Way too uptight to wear jeans. Way too obsessive to let go even for that.

Mo knew this because of his neat haircut.

Clipped perfect. Not overly styled. His hair laid that way because it was cut to lay that way. And Mo'd lay money down the man went to the barber no less than once every three weeks.

Clean, close shave. Baby skin. Perfectly trimmed sideburns.

Hand on the table next to a bottle of beer that was untouched. Mo could see the thin line of foam at the top in the neck. The guy didn't drink, not alcohol.

Fingers rat-a-tat-tatting a nervous strum on the table.

Careful placement of his position, not in the front row, not in a booth at the back, so as not to appear too eager, not pretending to be too aloof, or worse, hiding. Second row of tables, side stage, where he could see Lottie.

But his eyes were on Mo.

When he saw Mo had eyes on him, casually, too casually, he tipped his chin to acknowledge the eye contact, then turned his attention to Lottie.

Bland face, carefully bland. No reaction to the best one-woman show anyone in that room had ever seen. No visible reaction to a beautiful woman with a fantastic figure in a sequined bikini and high heels twirling upside down on a pole.

And no open display of hatred or disgust, for certain.

No one, not a soul except the waitresses, and even they stopped serving when Lottie performed, had eyes on anything but Lottie when she danced.

There was all this, and Mo could read a person, it was an important part of the job.

But the most important part of it all was that Mo would lay his life on the fact he saw that guy looking at cucumbers in the produce section of King Soopers on Sunday.

Mo felt a curl in his throat and heat hit his gut.

This was their guy.

Mo didn't move, even though, from the second night on, Hawk had fitted the team at Smithie's, including the bouncers, with earpieces and wristband radios.

This was where training was crucial.

This guy bolted, not a man on the mark knew it was him and he might be able to outrun Mo if Mo had to take off from his current position. Though the team would see Mo make a break for him, he could slip through a crowd like this and do it easy.

Then, if he got free of the building and didn't park in the parking lot, which he likely wouldn't considering Smithie had cameras all over and they were visible, when he got out of camera range and to his car, they'd have no clue who he was or where to find him. And obviously, no car on camera, no make and model or license plate.

He needed a tail that night.

No, he needed put out of commission that night.

Mo couldn't lift his arm and alert the team, the guy might see him and know he'd been made.

His body screamed to do it.

No.

It screamed at him to rush the man and incapacitate him in a way he'd never recover.

But it wasn't Mo's job to take down the guy. He couldn't rush him from his position backstage.

It was his job to stay on Lottie.

So he had to hold.

His only choice was to keep him in his peripheral vision so he didn't tweak him with a movement that would communicate he'd been made and set him to running.

Something he might already know since they'd locked eyes.

Mo needed the lights to dim even though he would be concerned the guy would make his move when they did.

It seemed to take years for them to go out.

His hand went right up, wrist to lips.

"Red polo. Jeans. Thinning hair. Second row. Left side. Stay on him," he ordered before tagging Lottie's robe.

He was two seconds late in throwing it over her bare shoulders.

She took off her top only in the final few seconds of her last song and never her panties.

He still *really* hated it that hundreds (probably thousands) of people had seen her mostly naked.

But tonight, he hated it oh so fucking much more.

He didn't have headspace for that.

The second she had her hands through the arms of the robe, he took hold of her and started to move her to safe ground.

"Eyes on him," Axl, one of his buddies on Hawk's team said in Mo's earpiece. "I'm on him. Following through."

This meant Axl would tail him home.

He got Lottie into the room, the girls streamed out, and he looked down at her.

"Gonna step into the hall. Be gone half a minute. Lock the door. Get dressed."

She stared up at him, her hands arrested in the act of tying her robe closed.

"Lottie," he growled.

"Okay. Locking the door," she whispered.

He went out. Heard the lock go.

He then stepped two steps to the side and pulled out his phone.

He called Hawk.

"Status," Hawk said as greeting, not sounding like Mo just woke him, even though Mo knew he just woke him, and waking Hawk, he probably woke Hawk's wife, Gwen.

Undoubtedly a common occurrence for Gwen.

Fortunately, she was a kickass chick and she loved her man so much, Hawk could grow a beer gut and take up fishing every weekend and she'd simply wait for him to come home and still jump his bones.

"He's here tonight."

"He made a move?" Hawk asked.

"No. But I know it's him. Axl's on him. I want him taken tonight."

Hawk said nothing.

Mo didn't either, letting his boss think.

Finally, Hawk spoke.

"Gut?"

"Yeah."

"How sure?"

"Very."

"We'll take him tonight. You're wrong, we'll figure it out."

"I'm right, I want in."

A moment then...

"She's under your skin," Hawk murmured.

"She's not under my skin. I sleep on her couch. I guard her. But when this is over, she'll be in my life. My choice? For the rest of it. So that's not under my skin. She's just going to be a part of me."

Hawk did not sound surprised when he asked, "And her?"

"That part of where we're at for her has been difficult to contain."

"You should have reported this," Hawk said impatiently.

"I would have, but it's been contained."

"It's been contained, *and* you wouldn't let me pull you off her detail, which, if I knew this, was what I'd fuckin' do."

Mo decided not to respond to that.

"So, knowing this, I'll ask again. Your gut. How sure?" Hawk asked.

"This is our guy."

"I wouldn't normally ask, you know it, but—"

"She was dancing, he was watching me, not her. Second row. Faded-out polo. But new jeans."

"New jeans?"

Hawk didn't make that query because he didn't get it.

He made that query because that nailed it.

"And I'd stake my life that I saw him Sunday in King Soopers," Mo added.

"We'll move," Hawk declared. "Now. And you're in."

Thank fuck.

Hawk disconnected.

Mo pulled oxygen through his nostrils.

Then he turned and knocked on the door to Lottie, shouting, "Mo!"

Every inch of his skin crawled. His muscles felt twitchy.

He wanted to be out there.

He needed to be in the dressing room.

She opened the door.

He crowded her in.

He then said a prayer of gratitude that she hadn't fucked around putting on her street clothes.

"What's going on?" she asked as the door clicked behind him.

He locked it without looking at it. If a girl needed in, she'd just have to knock.

Lottie's face was pale.

"He's here."

"Ohmigod," she breathed. "How do you know?"

"I know."

"Are they—?"

"Just do your thing, Lottie. Let's get you home."

"But, are they—?"

He lifted both hands and framed her face.

Her eyelids went hooded and her body swayed to him.

Fuck.

Fuck.

She was so fucking *his*.

Mo fought how badly he needed to claim that and repeated his order of, "Just do your thing, baby."

It took her a beat.

But then she whispered, "Okay, Mo."

That was his girl.

He pressed in lightly and let her go.

It was slow, he could tell she was concentrating on her movements, but she walked back to her mirror.

Mo stood by the door, put his back to the wall and aimed his eyes at the floor.

"You okay?" she called.

"Don't think about me."

"That's impossible."

Of course it was.

God, he needed to fuck her.

"Just focus," he ordered.

"Right."

"And not on me," he added.

"Mm-hmm," she mumbled loudly.

She was totally gonna focus on him, just be quiet about it.

He kept his gaze to the floor.

Her voice broke the silence.

"You can't tear him apart when you get to him, Mo. I'm not visiting my man in the pokey and I hear conjugal visits are hard to arrange."

His neck still bent, he turned his head her way.

"Lottie, shut up."

"You got it," she whispered.

He looked back to the floor.

Lottie went back to being Lottie.

She took off her makeup. Brushed out her hair.

Saw to business.

Including the business of giving him room to do what he had to do.

Soon.

Fuck.

Soon.

Thank Christ.

Now all he had to do was stop himself from committing murder between now and getting her on her back in her bed.

With what he'd been through since meeting Charlotte McAlister…

Piece of cake.

* * * *

He'd been wrong.

It was not a piece of cake.

What he had not been wrong about was that this was their guy.

Threat neutralized, Lottie was home, asleep, had no idea he was not there, and Axl was sitting in her living room just in case she woke up and found out he was not there, Axl could tell her what was going down and she'd continue to feel safe, not all of a sudden without a bodyguard.

Mo was in the guy's house with Hawk and Smithie.

The man had been identified by Smithie and his bouncers as an irregular regular. He didn't come often, but they'd all seen him, more than a few times. Too innocuous to be red flagged, they'd never have called it.

Until Mo had.

In his house, there was no sick-fuck shrine to Lottie.

What they found after Jaylen asked the man for a word, he tried to bolt, Axl locked him down, they detained him in Smithie's office and got his wallet off him, then sent a team to his house, a team that included Hawk, were a number of very disturbing journals.

And a basement that was being equipped to do all the things to Lottie he'd written that he intended to do.

Yes. He was building his confidence and preparing to follow through.

That was part of his visit to the club that night. Keep an eye on his mark, or now his marks, build his hate and assess the lay of the land.

The man was still in Smithie's office.

This huddle was about next moves.

"Any involvement of law enforcement at this juncture that has any hope of sticking would include perjuring ourselves repeatedly," Hawk noted.

"I'm down with that," Smithie said.

Mo said nothing.

He was still trying to get out of his head how much plastic sheeting had been put up in the basement.

And the neatly aligned instruments laid out on a table.

But Hawk knew Mo would never perjure himself to the cops.

Unless ordered to do so for the good of the mission.

Or to protect someone who meant something to him.

So he didn't have to answer.

"Second option is I contact a man I know who's adept at disappearing people," Hawk went on.

Mo focused more fully on his boss.

"I'm down with that too," Smithie declared heatedly.

He was still seeing plastic sheeting as well.

Not to mention that table of instruments.

"I'm not talking a hit, Smithie. I'm talking forced relocation where the chance of return is nil. This includes check-ins to make sure that nil stays nil. For an added cost, it includes permanent incapacitation," Hawk explained.

"I'm down for that too, even if I don't know what permanent incapacitation means if it doesn't include this sick fucking *fuck* being very fucking *dead*."

Right.

Smithie was holding on by a thread.

Mo knew the feeling.

"No fingers. No tongue. No eyes. A combination. Or in extreme circumstances, no legs or paralysis," Hawk told him.

"And again I'm feelin' like I hit the lottery because none of these choices sound bad to me," Smithie returned.

"Smithie, you would have to live with that," Hawk pointed out.

"And you think this'll be a problem?" Smithie demanded to know.

"I think right now you're pissed as fuck and freaked as hell and all that is on top of you being worried, with that increasing with every day this guy went uncaptured and every letter you got. So I'm not sure you're thinking straight," Hawk retorted.

"Tell me, Hawk, you perform some magic with Mitch or Slim and they find cause to search this house legally and find what we found, what happens to this guy?" Smithie asked, calling up Hawk's buds, Mitch Lawson and Brock "Slim" Lucas, two DPD cops, two good men and the first ones Hawk went to if he needed law.

"I don't have the power of clairvoyance, Smithie," Hawk told him.

"Me either. But I'll tell you this, a sick fucking fuck like this guy has to do something sick fucking *fucked up* to be fucking locked away forever, where he needs to be," Smithie shot back. "And seein' as that's not gonna fuckin' happen, not this time, he gets caught, he maybe does some time, and that's a big maybe, since, so far, he hasn't really committed a crime."

"Those letters are threats, he used the postal service to send them, and that's definitely a crime," Hawk pointed out.

"That's thin and we all know it," Smithie spat.

They did, so Hawk nor Mo said anything.

Smithie kept going.

"But say he does some time. He gets out, fixates back on Mac or some other girl, and manages to get his shit together before someone finds out. And then some girl, if she's found before she's made dead, has a lifetime of having to deal with something that she didn't get a say in, like I got a say in having a lifetime of living with what we decide for this guy tonight." Smithie shook his head. "I'll take my demons. I won't have some woman facing hers."

"Smithie—" Hawk tried.

Smithie cut him off. "Or he gets off on the insanity plea, because there's no arguing the guy is fucked right the fuck up, and he's sent to a looney bin. Gets medicated. Gets therapy. Gets 'cured.' And that same end scenario happens, just after he goes off his government-funded meds and remembers he's a whackjob."

"So your vote is he disappears," Hawk deduced.

"My vote is the only vote that counts, motherfucker, seein' as I'm payin' for this shit," Smithie retorted.

"And Mo and me will know and we'll have to keep our mouths shut and live with those demons for your choice too, Smithie," Hawk returned fire.

At this juncture, Smithie glanced at Mo before he looked back at Hawk. "Can you share why your man is in on this discussion?"

"He has a say," Hawk replied.

"I get that, seein' as he's here," Smithie said. "I'm askin' why."

"Because I called him in," Hawk answered.

Smithie looked back at Mo.

Mo just stared at him.

"Shit, you fell for her," Smithie muttered.

Mo said nothing.

Smithie looked him up and down and his brows drew together. "And she fell for you?"

Mo remained quiet.

"Of course she did," Smithie muttered. "You're you. Before I even saw you, coulda drawn a picture a' you, someone asked me to conjure up Mac's dream man."

Well…

Hell.

Something occurred to Smithie, his eyes went to the ceiling before coming back to Mo and his hands went to his hips.

"Do not get any thoughts in your head, motherfucker. She's got talent. She's a headliner. She was born for the stage." He took a hand from his hip, pointed it at Mo, and declared, "*You* are not tellin' her she can't dance."

Mo felt his lips thin.

"There!" Smithie jerked his finger at Mo, not missing Mo's slight movement. "You're one of those guys! Christ!" He threw up both hands. "I thought I was done with those guys. Jack didn't mind his woman stripping."

Mo had no clue who "Jack" was. He didn't remember Lottie telling him about one of the women who had a man named Jack.

He still said nothing.

"And what about you?" Smithie asked Hawk. "Not real professional, one of your boys tags the woman he's guarding."

"It's been platonic," Hawk ground out.

"Right," Smithie said.

Mo was done.

With a number of things.

What they were discussing right then the least of them.

"I've touched her, that way, once. Tonight. When I needed her to focus and I put my hands on her face. *Once*," Mo growled. "Lottie wanted a new bodyguard so we could start things up, but no one could be on her, but me. We held off. Now we need to make a decision about this guy because it's done and that means my job is done which means I can claim my woman, so I'm done with this chat." He turned to Hawk. "What do you want to do?"

"What do *you* want to do?" Hawk asked calmly.

"I want him dead."

Hawk didn't even blink.

"But I'm pissed as fuck and I'm tweaked as hell right now which means I can't fully get behind that," Mo continued. "So I want you to call Lawson and Lucas and get his ass in jail. We really got no choice but to let justice take its course, not that I can't live with the other option, or Smithie can't, or you can't, but because I'll probably have to explain it to Lottie and she won't be able to."

"Shit, fuck, you just had to bring Mac into it," Smithie muttered irritably.

"She's not being brought into it," Mo shot back. "It's all about her and has always been all about her. If I had my say, any victim would be able to choose what punishment their offender would get. That would be random and chaotic, but I don't give a fuck. It'd be fair, and it'd give closure and power to the people who were stripped of it. I don't get to decide the way our criminal justice system works. But from the second those journals were found, I was unofficially off the job, and the path was cleared I could officially claim Lottie as mine. So now I *do* get to decide how she's protected in *all ways*. And I'm not gonna ask her to live with the fact that she knows some guy had his tongue cut out, even if I, personally, would like the opportunity to pull it through a gaping hole in his throat."

"I think I like you," Smithie announced.

"I don't care," Mo replied and looked again at his boss. "Are we done?"

"You might have to give false testimony, Mo," Hawk reminded him.

"I don't care about that either," Mo replied. "Are we done?"

"You were on her, so no one has to know you were in the house," Hawk muttered. Then said, "We're done."

Mo turned on his boot and walked toward the door.

"You got two days leave, Mo," Hawk called to his back. "Starting today."

Mo said nothing as he walked out of that house.

Though he did that thinking, not for the first time, his boss was the shit.

The sun was coming up in the sky.

The dawn of a new day.

Mo was looking forward to it.

He just hoped like fuck he didn't run anybody over getting his ass back to Lottie.

* * * *

Hawk

Hawk stood looking out the window at Mo's truck taking off.

He felt Smithie come up beside him.

"You're gonna let me call Mitch and Slim?" Hawk asked.

"Yup," Smithie answered.

"And you're gonna let justice take its course?"

"Yup."

"Then, after it does, if it doesn't swing Lottie's way, you're gonna bring someone in to neutralize this whackjob," Hawk guessed.

"Yup."

Hawk stared at the empty street.

"My girls gotta be safe, Hawk," Smithie explained.

"I didn't say a word."

"*All* girls should be safe."

He turned to the man at his side. "I got a daughter, Smithie, and I got a wife. Even if I didn't, you're still preaching to the choir."

"You won't know," Smithie assured him.

"I'd give you some names, you asked. But if you want to compartmentalize, this is your thing, she's yours to protect, it isn't my call."

Smithie studied him before he noted, "Your man, he had no say, you just wanted him to think he did."

"He was here speaking for her. The only thing I feel bad about is that Mo was right, she should have a voice in this. And in the end, she didn't."

"That's what men like us are for, Delgado," Smithie pointed out. "Someone's gotta make the tough decisions. This guy," he tossed up a hand to indicate the house they were in, "he's touched. Somethin' wrong with him. But that's not my problem. What's in that basement is anyone's worst nightmare. *That's* my problem. And that cannot stand."

Hawk nodded.

He could maybe argue, but he wouldn't know why, since he agreed.

"I'll lock the door when you go," he said.

Smithie didn't hang around.

Hawk locked the door when he left.

He dealt with the situation first through Jorge, then he called Slim.

Mitch was a straight arrow.

Slim had been DEA. He got shades of gray. He'd take care of it.

Then Hawk went home and was met with the sounds of pandemonium coming from the kitchen. This pandemonium being his wife getting breakfast for their three kids.

It wasn't just the kids, though both his boys were a handful.

Gwen was an even bigger handful, thankfully, and she got off on the chaos of family.

His youngest, Vivi, hit him in the legs before he even made the kitchen.

Hawk looked down and put a hand to her head.

His black hair, Gwen's blue eyes.

Pure beauty.

A letter was ever written about her, a room prepared...

No, he had no argument for Smithie.

"Hey, Daddy," she greeted.

"Hey, beautiful," he replied.

"Mommy's making us chocolate chip cookie dough pancakes."

Of course she was, and he had no idea such a thing existed.

To Hawk, it sounded repulsive.

But cookie dough was considered by his wife as a food group, maybe the most important one, and she had no qualms sharing this thinking with their children in a variety of creative ways.

Hawk smiled at his girl, but his thoughts were on his wife.

"Vivi, honey, get in the kitchen and control your brothers before I shoot them. Book bags, you know the drill," Gwen ordered, striding in wearing little gray shorts with lace at the bottoms and a loose gray tank, more lace at the bottom.

"Okay, Mommy," Vivi agreed, gave Hawk's thighs a squeeze then skipped out of the utility room and into the open-plan kitchen.

He lost the arms of one of his girls only to be in the arms of the other as his wife pressed into him.

Hawk returned the favor, but considering his children were in the next room, he didn't put either of his hands to her ass like he wanted to do.

Her eyes moved over his face. "Okay?"

"Yeah, Sweet Pea," he murmured.

"Tough night?"

"Job done."

She pressed closer and smiled up at him.

The minute she did, he started the clock.

It ran down to zero when he pulled back into his garage after taking the kids to school.

Kids at school.

Job done.

It was time to fuck his wife.

Chapter Nine

A Little Bit More

Lottie

I woke up when dawn was kissing the sky.

I didn't know what woke me, though since this all started, I'd wake on occasion, make sure Mo was there, then go back to sleep when I saw he was.

But that time, I knew something was off.

I got up to an elbow and looked to the couch.

No Mo.

This was concerning, though some mornings when I woke up in a way I was awake, he wasn't there. He'd be using the bathroom or doing a walk-through of the house, and then he'd come back.

I rested on my elbow listening in case that was what was happening, but I heard no noises from the bathroom or the house.

After Mo informed me the guy was there last night, he was so edgy, he was quietly wired, that live wire charging everything anywhere near him.

Even me.

I suspected he wanted to be in on the interrogation, or the takedown, or the search of his house, or whatever they were doing, but he had to stay with me.

We did our normal thing coming home, but when no word came, I'd had to ask him to talk me to sleep with his toes-to-feet-to-knees gig.

Not to get him to help me sleep, but to help him relax so his vibe would leak out of the room and I could go to sleep so he'd at least stop worrying about me.

Listening to his deep voice lull me, I did just that.

Now was now.

If they'd caught him, would Mo leave me?

If they'd caught him, wouldn't he stay and pounce on me?

Considering I very much needed to have answers to these questions, I threw the covers back, twisted my hips and tossed my legs over the side of the bed.

Since the morning of the egg white omelets, I'd made a habit of wearing my most unsexy nightgowns to bed.

I didn't have a lot of such items of apparel, though when I was on my period and feeling bloaty and devouring popchips by the bag, I went with one of those.

So this situation was taxing the limits of my unsexy stuff, but it wasn't for that reason I hoped it was over.

And my sleep drawer included the one I was wearing, which had little straps but the rest of it hung from a high-ish neckline down to my upper thighs and looked like one, wide, white cotton smock with a deep ruffle at the hem.

It wasn't ugly, as such. But it didn't make me feel like a bombshell.

I went to the bathroom, the door of which was open.

No Mo.

Okay, I wasn't liking this.

I crept to the top of the stairs and listened.

The house wasn't exactly brightening up with the September dawn seeing as Mo still had all the blinds closed.

And they were now closed.

No noises.

Shit, shit, *damn*.

I hoped the threat was over, I hoped Mo was off somewhere, having a quiet conversation or tying up loose ends.

But I should be prepared.

And with him gone, I had to admit, I was a little freaked.

He'd never leave me, unless it was safe to do that.

Still, he'd been around every day. I was used to him. I *liked* being used to him. And the situation was fraught.

So yeah.

I was a little freaked.

I moved silently back to the bedroom and assessed my options for a weapon, just in case.

I could use a shoe, though if I did actually have to use it, that would include getting in close proximity of someone I thought was a bad guy.

I didn't want to do that.

So no shoe.

I had a can of Mace, but that was in my purse which was on the seat of the hall tree downstairs.

I decided to buy some Mace for my nightstand.

And I went with hairspray. A shot in the face might incapacitate somebody long enough I could run away.

I had three different kinds (light hold, medium hold, and super hold).

I decided on super hold.

I uncapped it, put the cap on the counter, stole out of the bathroom and skulked down the hall, then the stairs, thanking God I'd had a thick, buttery-cream carpet runner installed in both.

It was when I hit the wood floors at the bottom I was glad my feet were bare.

I turned, moved through the arch into the living room and stopped dead.

This was because the lights were on in the kitchen and there was a very tall, very muscled dude (not taller or more muscled than Mo, but then again, not many were) standing at my Nespresso machine. He was wearing olive drab cargos and a white T-shirt.

His head was turned to me.

Thick head of silvery-gray hair, even though I could tell by his face he hadn't lived the years to earn that color.

Too far away to note the color of his eyes.

Totally not too far away to see he was gorgeous.

Undoubtedly one of Hawk's dudes for no man who looked like this could be a crackpot, or at least I hoped the laws of the universe weren't that twisted.

"What's with the hairspray?" he asked.

"To incapacitate you so I can run away," I told him. "I had a selection and went with super hold."

"Good choice," he replied.

"Who are you?"

"Name's Axl. One of Hawk's men. Buddy of Mo's."

I lowered my weapon, now on the subject that interested me. "Where's Mo?"

He turned fully my way and leaned a slim hip against the counter. "Caught the guy. Mo's with Hawk. He told me to tell you if you woke up before he got back that he'd be back as soon as he could."

I bet he would.

But…

They got him.

Ohmigod, *they got him.*

Instead of doing a round-off followed by an arms-up-in-the-air, heels-kicked-back jump, I walked to my coffee table and put the hairspray down.

When I gave my attention back to Axl, I saw I hadn't lost his.

"Mind if I have some coffee?" he asked.

"Help yourself," I answered, wandering toward the kitchen and stopping. "Pods in the cupboard above the machine."

He reached to the cupboard above the machine.

"Who was he?" I asked.

"Semi-regular. Total whackjob," he muttered, putting the bowl of pods on the counter and hitting the button on top, making it blink green.

Then he turned again toward me.

Whoa.

Clear, ice-blue eyes.

Nice.

"He comes to the club on occasion," he went on. "And—"

He cut himself off as he tensed, straightened and then used those long legs of his to move toward me, by me then stop four feet beyond me just as I heard the front door slam, heavy footfalls…

I stepped to the side so I could see past Axl.

Then I stopped dead.

Because Mo caught sight of me and he stopped dead one foot into the living room.

My panties grew wet and my mind went into a trance as Mo again very successfully communicated non-verbally.

This time he was communicating the wait was over.

And what was to come next was going to be worth that wait.

"Go," he grunted.

"Gotcha," Axl replied, humor dripping off that word. "Nice to meet you, Lottie," he said as he strolled across the room.

I stared at Mo and didn't say a word.

I'd apologize for being rude later.

Vaguely, I heard the front door open.

Vaguely, I heard the front door close.

I forced myself to speak.

"They got him?"

"They got him."

We stared at each other.

We stared at each other longer.

Then in a sudden burst of movement, I raced toward him.

I also raced right by him so I could sprint up the stairs.

All those nights with Mo on my couch wishing he was somewhere else, this was happening in my bed.

I heard the thunderous falls of Mo's boots hitting the steps behind me and I knew by their tempo that he was skipping some.

And my panties got wetter.

I ran into my room, twirled to face the door, the voluminous folds of my smock nightie flying out, exposing panty I was sure, and I saw Mo enter the room.

He stopped advancing but not moving. However, he moved only to take his gun with holster off his belt and toss it to the foot of the bed.

I started panting.

We stared at each other again.

My body felt so hot, I was certain I was about to burst into flame.

He put his fingers to his light gray compression shirt, pulled it up and it was gone, exposing the enormous wall of his chest, his bulbous pecs, the wide sweep of his shoulders, his bulging biceps, his demarcated abs and the thick, dark trail of hair that circled his navel and disappeared into the waistband of his black cargos.

Oh God.

I was gonna pass out.

"Mo," I whispered.

At that, he moved.

In two great steps, he was on me.

He hooked me with one arm at my waist and I was up, literally flying through the air to land with a couple of bounces on my back in my bed.

Oh God.

I was gonna come.

I got up on both elbows and saw him standing at the foot of the bed, his upper body rising and falling in a huge, smooth, but fast and deep rhythm.

He was getting control.

I needed to get control.

The problem was, certain areas of my body were begging me to get up on my feet, use the mattress as a springboard and land on him.

He bent at the waist, all the way, so all I had was a view of his back which might have been good except he was clearly taking off his boots and that meant he was using his hands which meant the muscles in his back and shoulders were moving.

And I was gonna come again.

"Mo," I whimpered.

Fast as a lash, he was up, his hands on my ankles, pulling my legs apart.

Lord, he had to stop doing shit like that.

"Baby," I breathed.

Then he went in, one knee to the bed, the other. Fluidly ducking his head down and moving forward like he was diving deep in a body of water, his head disappeared under the ruffle and his mouth was on me over my panties.

My fingers curled into the bedclothes and my head fell back as I spread my legs wider, feeling his teeth scraping at the material, *at me*.

So good.

So good.

"Oh God, oh God," I chanted, moving one hand to the back of his head, feeling the warm smoothness and quivering from top to toe.

I pushed him to me.

His mouth closed over me and he drew, *hard*.

So good.

"*Mo*," I moaned.

His mouth disappeared, I felt his finger hook in the gusset of my panties and my legs were forced back together and straight up as he got on his knees and tore my panties off.

He tossed them away, caught my legs at the calves, separated them and let them fall to his sides.

I stared up at him as he dug into his back pocket for his wallet.

"Yes," I whispered.

Wallet out, eyes locked on mine, he dropped it to the bed and his hands went to his belt.

"*Yes*," I panted.

The metallic noise of the clip buckle releasing gave me another quiver. The sound of his zip going down made me start to shiver. The movement of his arms which meant he was putting his hands to his waistband and was about to do the reveal made my eyes drop.

His cargos went to his beefy thighs and his massive, rock-hard cock sprang out from a thick bed of dark hair.

Oh yes, oh yes, *yes, yes, yes.*

God loved me.

"Hurry," I begged.

I watched him roll the condom halfway on before my gaze cut up to his face.

"Hurry!" I snapped.

He fell forward and I almost shouted, *Hallelujah!*

But he caught himself in a hand beside me, straight arm, holding himself away from me.

"Mo!" I cried.

His hand went between my legs, two fingers gliding tight over my clit then driving right inside.

Oh yeah.

I fell fully to my back, closed my eyes, lifted my knees, and reached to him.

Hard muscle, sleek, hot skin.

Beautiful.

I opened my eyes as he started to stroke. "You need to get inside me."

"And you need to be ready, baby," he said low, his voice tight.

"I think you can feel I'm ready for you, honey," I pointed out.

I wasn't wet.

I felt it.

I was *slippery.*

He separated his fingers inside me and dragged them out.

My eyes rolled back into my head and my fingers dug into his sides.

He withdrew and gently rolled my clit.

I looked at him again, fingertips compulsively clutching his flesh. "Mo, *please.*"

"Slow," he said.

Had he lost his mind?

We'd been waiting a hundred years!

"Not slow," I replied.

His fingers left me, and I felt why when he guided the head of his cock to me.

"Oh yeah," I breathed.

He slid in, stretching me. I took the head and then he rocked, giving me just that.

I glided my hands to his pecs and held on. "More, Mo. Come inside."

He gave me another couple of inches, opening me, filling me, then no more and he again rocked, giving me only that.

The wide stretch affected my clit, the gentle rub pure, delicious *agony*.

"Mo, baby," I pleaded.

"I'm a lot."

Through the haze, I focused on him and saw the strain, the sweat breaking out, the harshness in his face, the dark hunger in his gaze.

I reached up, grasped onto his thick neck, pulled myself up and stared in his eyes.

"I don't care, Mo. I want it all."

He gave me more, not all of him, and again rocked.

"Baby," I whispered, swinging my feet in so I could dig my heels into his ass.

God, his ass felt good, his cock felt good, the rest of him was just hot. *I needed him inside.*

"Lottie, you aren't helping," he gritted.

"I'm trying to," I snapped.

"Baby—"

"Mo."

"Sweetheart."

I seized his jaw in both hands. "Mo!"

He stared in my eyes, then dropped to his elbow, and with a powerful surge, I took all of him.

He'd filled me.

I had him.

He was finally *all mine*.

I arched up into him, the long, low moan from my throat slinking around the room like a cat as I dug my heels in, wrapped my arms as far around him as they could get, and I clutched him tight with my pussy.

"Fuck," he groaned.

And we were off.

He drove into me and I held on.

He moved faster and harder and I held on tighter.

When I started coming, a magnificent occurrence that didn't take long, I dug my nails in and called his name.

I got his thumb on my clit.

And I went flying, clawing at his skin, wrapping my legs around him so

I was holding his ass with my calves, moaning his name over and over like an incantation.

I kept coming and I kept coming and only when the fingers of both my hands found the back of his neck and head and held on did his thumb go away.

But he dug his arm under me and clamped it around my waist to hold me stationary so I could take his thrusts and he didn't fuck me into the headboard as his deep, fast, hot rhythm went super-charged and my powerhouse lost all control.

Oh yeah.

I liked it like that.

Coming down from my orgasm, I caught his eyes drilling into mine and I felt the rumble in his belly before it grunted out his throat.

His head snapped back, the cords in his neck straining, he slammed his hips into mine, then ground them there, and his grunt became a groan that I would swear shook the lamps on my nightstands.

God, he was spectacular when he came.

Breathtaking.

He did not collapse on me when he came down.

Oh no.

Not Mo.

I knew his climax was big, I saw it, felt it, *heard it*.

But even if he couldn't possibly be over it, he rolled so he was on his back, I was on him, and we were still connected.

I rested my cheek on his pec.

He clamped one hand on the side of my neck, one hand on the cheek of my ass.

It was quite a trip, riding the powerful rises and falls of his chest as his breath evened out.

It felt like riding a mountain.

I loved every second.

Eventually, his thumb came out to stroke my jaw.

"We'll go slower next time," he murmured.

"Okay," I murmured back, stroking the smooth valley between pectorals with the backs of my fingers.

"Hawk gave me two days off."

"I'm calling in sick."

At first, I didn't know what was happening. I also didn't know what I was hearing.

It took a second to realize the quaking of his big body and the deep noises that were tumbling low around the room were indications Mo was chuckling.

It seemed like a very long time since I heard him laugh and I'd never heard his humor come like that.

But hearing it, I wanted to see it.

So I lifted my head and looked down at him.

Face relaxed, sated, eyes soft and warm and aimed down his nose at me.

"You haven't kissed me," I whispered.

"I've totally kissed you," he whispered back. "Just not your mouth."

Oh yeah.

Right.

I smiled at him. "Our first kiss a pussy kiss. I like it."

His mouth quirked, his eyes dropped to my lips then his arms went around me, and I was on my back with Mo covering me, his lips on mine, his tongue gliding inside.

I made a mew, rounded him with my arms, my legs, and sucked his tongue deeper.

He tasted precisely like I thought Mo would taste and he kissed like I thought Mo would kiss.

Overwhelmingly amazing.

Yeah.

I'd been right.

Every day, little by little, or big by big, I'd be falling deeper in love with this man.

He ended it by running the tip of his tongue along my lower lip then asking, "How's that?"

It was the best first kiss I ever had.

Except the pussy one.

"I liked that too."

He smiled at me and stroked my cheekbone with the flat of the nail on his forefinger.

And there was a little bit more.

* * * *

I had both arms forward, hands pressing into the headboard, noises forced out of my mouth through my ongoing orgasm with each thrust I took.

Mo was on his knees behind me.

His thighs were so long, he had to fuck me with his legs wide, holding me up and spreading me open so I could take him.

This meant I was suspended from mostly nothing but his driving dick as he fucked me from behind.

I was coming down, how I didn't know, because each stroke I took blasted against my clit.

But Mo felt it, didn't like it, and I knew that when he reached around and pinched that sensitive bundle of nerves.

I cried out, whimpered, and came hard again.

"Fuck yeah, Lottie," he growled, those strong hips of his pistoning into me.

Suddenly, he did a dip and roll, and my eyes went back in my head as my body went into spasm.

"Fuck yeah, baby," he grunted, put me down, coming down with me, covering me, and fucking me to his finish with my belly to the bed.

Man, I loved listening to him come.

Though I preferred watching it.

But considering there was a good possibility he'd fucked a Lottie-sized dent in the bed, I'd take this one as it came.

After he was done, he commenced a slow roll, stroking gently inside as I felt his lips move from the tip of my shoulder, up, then he buried his face in my neck.

"Sweet pussy," he murmured there, sliding his cock in and staying in. "Sweet little body. Sweet hair. Sweet sex noises. Sweet smell. Seriously sweet fuck. My sweet Lottie."

"Don't say things like that when I can't kiss you," I mumbled into the pillow.

I felt his smile then I felt his tongue exploring the area behind my ear.

"Don't do things like that when I need to pass out after coming fifteen times," I ordered, but did it still mumbling into the pillow.

He nipped the back of my ear, the big lug, and through the tremble that caused, asked in it, "Fifteen?"

"I don't know. You've got a mammoth cock. And you're a powerhouse. And you fuck like a tank. I lose track of time when you're fucking me. And place. I don't know if we're still in my bedroom. I'm not even sure what year it is."

I felt that feeling I knew I'd come to love, his gentle laughter, before he slid out, lifted up, rolled me under him, then carefully covered me again with his bulk, taking weight onto a forearm, using his free hand to caress my hip.

I had to tip my chin up to catch his contented, handsome face, but with what I got, I didn't mind the effort.

"We're still in your bedroom," he informed me.

"What year is it?"

"Sweetheart, watching that tight ass of yours while your even tighter pussy takes my cock, I've no fucking clue. But I hope I drilled you for a decade."

"I don't. We can't make babies if you drilled me for a decade with a condom on. A decade, my babymaking years might be behind me."

That didn't freak him.

Not at all.

Not my Mo.

He dipped closer, touched his mouth to mine, pulled an inch away and asked, "How many do *you* want?"

"Seven thousand, but I'll take two or three and seven thousand cats."

His body and mouth both laughed again, I loved it again, then he said, "I'm not a cat guy."

Uh-oh.

"You don't like cats?"

"Take or leave cats, mostly leave. I'm a dog guy."

Okay.

This was a problem.

I communicated the enormity of that problem by grabbing both sides of his face and demanding, "Don't tell Tex that."

"I know about Tex's cats." He turned his head and kissed my palm (and there it was, a little bit more). He came back to me. "Swear to Christ, won't mention the cats."

"Do you have a dog?"

"Work too much to have a dog."

That'd end since I could take care of it when we got one (or two, or four).

Though he'd also have to put up with a cat (or two, or four).

"Axl seemed nice," I noted.

"Axl's a good guy."

"He says you two are buds."

"We are. Like I said, Axl's a good guy."

"Do you have a lot of buds?"

"Hawk's crew. Some old high school friends I keep in touch with. My family."

I tilted my head on the pillow. "Your family?"

"Mom in Denver, and four sisters."

Four?

"You have four sisters?" I queried.

"Yup."

"You the oldest?"

"Youngest."

I stared up at him.

Then I asked, "You're the youngest with four older sisters?"

"Yup."

"Ohmigod."

This seemed impossible.

No man his size was the littlest or youngest of anything.

"All but one is married," he shared. "All but that one have kids. I've got five nieces and nephews."

I loved this.

I loved it like crazy.

And not just the fact that I could freely ask him questions about his life, his friends, his family, and not try to keep things distant and professional.

But that he had a big family.

I loved family.

"Are they named Norwegian names?" I asked.

"Signe, Marte, Lene, Trine, in order, oldest to youngest."

That was a yes.

"And you're gonna meet them, soon as that can be arranged," he announced.

I started to smile.

Then something occurred to me and I didn't smile.

"Are they gonna have a problem with me being a stripper?"

A shadow crossed his face, which meant a shadow shrouded my heart.

But I would learn I shouldn't underestimate Mo, or his feelings for me, and I'd learn it quick.

Like right then.

Because Mo rolled us both to our sides, gathered me close, but kept a lock on my eyes.

"You know, baby," he said gently, "think the problem with what you do is with you."

Hunh?

"I don't have a problem with it," I pointed out the obvious.

"First place you go, first question you ask, is if someone has issues."

It wasn't *the first*.

But I saw his point.

"That's so I can ascertain if they have issues so I won't waste time or emotion on someone who's an asshole."

He looked dubious. "You sure?"

"Mo, honey," I said quietly, "can you imagine the shit I've come up against because of my job?"

The dubiousness fled, understanding replaced it, and he nodded. "I can."

We were on rocky ground here and I didn't want to be on rocky ground.

Not now.

Not when the wait was finally over and we were getting to the good stuff.

But maybe it was good to at least start the discussion, so it didn't get buried under all the goodness. Both of us trying to ignore it was there. Then it became harder to bring it up, but it was between us and needed to be dealt with, and since we didn't deal with it, it grew out of control and became a problem.

This was a very adult thought.

I still didn't want to broach it and this demonstrated why I wasn't a big fan of being an adult.

But I *was* a big fan of Mo's, so I had to be an adult.

Damn it.

"And we need to—" I began.

"Babe, I don't like you stripping," he announced.

Shit.

Fortunately, Mo wasn't done.

"But I also wouldn't like you being a journalist based in Syria. My job isn't often dangerous, but it is far from always safe. If you had a problem with it, we'd talk about it, but it would definitely drive a wedge if you put your foot down about it. It isn't what it is. It's who I am and if you asked me to stop doing it, it'd be you asking me to stop being who I am. I'll eventually have to get out of the field because this kind of job has a shelf life and I won't be as strong and quick as I need to be. What you do isn't the same, but it is in some regards. I like you and I've had enough experience with women to know I won't like every single thing about you. But the same goes for knowing that what I like, I like a lot so I'm willing to work at it and find ways to compromise with the rest."

Okay, that right there wasn't a little bit.

It was a huge truckload.

"I see you've been thinking about this," I noted.

"On the ride back to you. I knew if I started things with us, I had to be all in." He pulled me closer. "I'm all in, Lottie."

Yeah.

That was a huge truckload.

He gave me that. He gave me a kiss.

And when he pulled away, I whispered, "Thanks, Mo."

That was when he gave me a smile and pulled fully away, exiting the bed.

I wanted to get into his "experience with women" (and how they'd fucked him up) but I was learning this was how Mo was.

He had to get rid of the condom and he didn't make that announcement or a production of it.

He slipped out of the bed, took care of it, and came back.

I was hoping he'd brought a bunch of them because I decided, before we got into his "experience with women," I'd give him more experience with *this* woman because I had a hankering to ride my mountain of man.

We could talk about the bitches in his life after I got myself in the mood not to be pissed as shit about whatever it was.

In other words, after I had another fifteen orgasms.

Mo was walking back into the room, and I was watching him walk back in, precisely his hips, not covered in cargos, and that huge dick, which was impressive even soft, and how I'd decided just then to suck it before I rode it, when he stopped dead and his head jerked to the side.

This was right before we heard a pounding on the door and a faraway, but still loud bellow of, "*Lottie! Open this goddamned door!*"

I felt my face pale as I watched Mo look back my way.

"Oh shit," I whispered.

Then I finished.

"Tex."

Chapter Ten

Little Sister

Lottie

"I'll take care of it," Mo announced.

Say what?

You didn't *take care of* Tex.

No one could *take care of* Tex.

Especially when he was bellowing louder than his normal bellow and pounding on a door.

I suspected even my mother couldn't *take care of* Tex when he was doing that and Tex was head over heels in love with my mother.

Sadly, while these thoughts tumbled through my head, Mo had found his cargos and tugged them on.

He exited the room doing the fly.

Shit!

"Mo! Wait!" I yelled, scrambling to get out of bed.

It took me too long to find my panties and nightie in the mess of bedclothes and too much longer to struggle them on at the same time racing out of the room.

My nightie was floating down as I hit the top of the stairs and I started to bolt down them as I heard, "*You! You've* got some *explaining to do.*"

Tex.

Tex getting in the face of Mo.

I kept going, just a lot faster, and when I made it to the bottom, my feet squeaked on the floor as I slid across the hall and slammed into the arch to the TV room from my momentum.

This was when I saw that this situation was not just Tex in A Snit bad.

It was worse.

Way worse.

Because, filing through the foyer, was not just my big, wild-haired stepdad Tex.

Behind him came Lee.

Hank.

Vance.

Luke.

Hector.

Ren.

And Eddie.

The entire Hot Bunch (save Mace, but I figured he only wasn't there because he now lived in LA and he hadn't been able to catch a convenient flight).

Shit!

They all glowered at me as they trooped into my living room, trailed by Mo.

Mo was not glowering.

When he turned his head to look at me, he appeared to be having trouble containing his mirth.

No.

No, no, no, no, *no*.

He didn't get it.

This was *not* funny.

I'd been onboard when Smithie had explained why he brought in Hawk, *way* on board, for a variety of reasons.

First, and arguably the priority, because the Hot Bunch run amuck in Denver in protection mode of one of their own was a very scary thing.

Second, and arguably the priority, because Eddie would tell his wife, my sister, who would tell my mother, and the other Rock Chicks, and they'd all be worried, just like everyone at Smithie's.

And I couldn't have that.

Now, it was very clear the men knew.

And now, they were ticked, not that they'd been kept out of the loop, that they hadn't been asked to do the job.

And the Hot Bunch ticked was another very scary thing.

I needed to handle this.

Immediately.

I rushed to Mo.

"Mo—"

"Babe, go upstairs and put on some clothes," he murmured.

Was he insane?

We didn't have time for that!

"But—"

Tex boomed, "Get your ass in here, girl."

There it was!

No time for that.

Mo looked toward my living room.

I looked toward my living room.

It was filled with the Hot Bunch.

Tex appeared in the archway.

"What did I say?" he demanded (in another boom).

"Tex—"

"Eddie got the word. Smithie had some lunatic who was fixated on you and sending detailed letters of how he was going to *cleanse* you," Tex stated (loudly, as well as irately). "And *you. You* didn't call in me *or the boys.*"

Eddie appeared at Tex's side.

"Lottie, get in here," he growled.

Oh man.

I felt Mo's hand come to the small of my back and he put pressure there.

Apparently, he'd realized it was time to handle this.

Immediately.

But at that juncture I wanted to dig in my heels. However, since I was an adult and not ten minutes ago had decided to act like one, I probably shouldn't go back on that now.

Tex and Eddie got out of our way so we could hit the living room.

My living room wasn't small, as such.

And it didn't seem tiny with all those big men in there.

It seemed miniscule with all those big men being seriously ticked off at me in there.

"Uh—" I started.

"Hawk had it covered. I had her covered. It's done," Mo said over me.

Was he *seeing* these men?

I mean…

Did he *really* think that was going to work?

"We'll get to *you* next," Tex boomed at him.

See?

It did not work.

I looked to my side and up to see Mo had his head bent, staring at his feet, his profile telling me he was even more amused than he'd been before.

Yes, he was insane.

This was *not* funny.

I had to take things in hand.

"Listen, guys, like Mo said, it's done," I shared with the room. "It's been rough, but it's over and we're on to the celebratory phase. So if we could do the debriefing when there's beer and tequila handy, in other words, *some other time*, it would be appreciated."

"The celebratory phase?"

This came from Hector.

And the way it came from Hector had my body locking.

It was then I noticed that the Hot Bunch had been so preoccupied with being pissed at me that they hadn't quite noticed Mo was there, he was wearing nothing but cargos, and I was in a nightie.

Oh man.

"You do not, *ever*," Luke growled at Mo, "enter into an intimate relationship with the person you're protecting."

Mo's head came up and he wasn't amused anymore.

Oh man!

"He didn't," I said hurriedly to Luke. "We didn't start that until a couple of hours ago."

"Intimacy doesn't only involve fucking," Vance declared.

He had me there.

"It was totally professional," I lied.

"Looks professional to me," Ren remarked.

I glared at him, wondering what he was even doing there. He wasn't a member of the Hot Bunch.

Though he was married to Ally Nightingale, now Ally Zano, and he was most definitely hot, and his own brand of badass, and obviously, when it came to certain things, it appeared it was all in the family.

"It's over now," I snapped. "Like I said, we didn't start the fucking part until a couple of hours ago, even though *I* would have started fucking a week ago, Mo wouldn't let me. So from that, you can see it was all professional."

"Can you stop talking about fucking Mo?" Lee asked angrily.

"I'm a big girl, Lee," I shot back at him.

"You're every man in this room's little sister, Lottie," he returned. "So as such, can we please stop talking about you fucking *anybody*?"

I didn't answer him.

I'd gone solid.

I was Jet's little sister.

I wasn't…

Woodenly, my head moved so I could take in the men in the room.

Every last one was scowling at me.

Because it wasn't that my sister and all her friends' men (and okay, also my friends) were badasses and assumed they could take care of all the women in their lives' problems, no matter what kind of satellite that woman was in their life.

It was that all my big brothers had been kept in the dark when something was threatening me.

I didn't…

I didn't know.

I was just Lottie, Jet's little sister.

I had no idea they felt this deeply for me.

But they did.

They did.

They felt really fucking *deep* for me.

It was then my throat closed and my eyes got hot.

"You didn't come to me."

My attention went to the man who spoke.

Eddie.

Oh boy.

"Eddie," I whispered.

"If they didn't have it…" He shook his head. "If something happened to you…" He couldn't finish that either.

And I knew that, now, he couldn't not only because his life would be hell if something happened to his beloved wife's beloved little sister, his beloved boys' beloved aunt.

Also because something would have happened to his sister-in-law, a woman he cared deeply about.

Oh God.

"It didn't. It was Hawk Delgado, Eddie," I said quietly. "He had it."

"I've been to this guy's house, Lottie," Eddie retorted. "If they didn't have it…"

He again didn't finish.

With not a small amount of difficulty, I swallowed.

"Lottie, honey, look at me," Hank called.

I looked at Hank.

"There was more than just finding this guy," he said. "You had to be out of your mind worried. You should never take that on alone. It doesn't help you or the situation and it doesn't save the people you're keeping in the dark from anything. They're just going to feel what you've endured over a week in a second," he lifted a hand to indicate the room, "as you can see."

To be honest, I hadn't even thought of that.

I just put my head down and got on with it.

But I did that because I didn't want to worry anyone. Worrying the girls at work was bad enough, and that wasn't my choice. If it was, I wouldn't have done it.

And I was Lottie Mac. I was a tough broad. I could handle anything. I'd been on my own and doing that for a long time.

Not to mention, I had Smithie. Hawk Delgado. His team.

And I had Mo.

"Yeah," I admitted. "But I had Mo."

Bad idea.

Hank looked to Mo and his gentle big brother expression vanished.

"How about you go put some clothes on while we have a word with Mo," Luke suggested.

Oh no.

"Luke—"

"Lottie," Mo's hand came again to the small of my back, "go get dressed."

I looked up at him. "I'm not leaving you."

"It'll be okay. We have to have a chat," he replied.

My spine snapped straight. "I'm not leaving you, Mo."

"You need to put some clothes on," he retorted.

"I'm practically wearing a smock," I fired back.

"It's sexy *AF* and not helping anything," he returned.

It was not.

Was it?

"It isn't."

"Lottie, I would know," he pointed out.

"I would too, my eyes are burning," Luke muttered.

"Babydoll nightie, Christ," Vance bit out.

I looked down at myself.

Okay.

Maybe it was cute.

And a little hot.

I turned to the men. "You've seen me strip. All of you."

Luke's gaze bored into mine. "Don't remind me."

"I might hurl," Hector mumbled to floor.

Holy smokes.

They were *totally* my *big brothers*.

"Lottie, *go put clothes on*," Mo rumbled.

And there was the Brook No Argument Voice.

I glared at him. "Fine." I turned my glare to the men in the room. "But no one hurt him while I'm gone."

"We're not gonna hurt him," Ren said.

"I might hurt him," Vance murmured.

"I'm in on that," Hector added.

"You're not gonna hurt him!" I yelled at Hector.

"All right, all right. *Cálmate, hermanita,*" Hector replied.

To make certain that happened, I turned my attention to Tex and announced, "When the time comes, I want you walking me down the aisle."

Tex had been uncharacteristically quiet through all this, likely thinking the men had it in hand since they weren't letting up on me.

He remained that way after my announcement seeing as he went visibly still.

The room went still.

Time stood still.

"And prepare," I continued. "Because it's gonna be a huge-ass wedding and I'm wearing a sexy dress. Like Roxie's, except sexier. Lots of flowers. A colossal cake. Server passed hors d'oeuvres. Open bar. The whole shebang." I whirled on Mo. "You down with that?"

"Whatever you want, baby," he murmured, looking amused again.

"Good," I snapped.

"You're already getting married?" Eddie asked, his voice low and unhappy. "You said you just started things up a couple hours ago."

I whirled on him. "When did you move Jet in with you?"

He shut his mouth.

Mm-hmm.

Not a one of them could use the "you're rushing into this" defense. They'd each claimed their women at the speed of light.

Thank God I didn't have to put up with *that*.

"And no, not yet," I carried on. "We haven't even had our first date. But signals are showing he's the one. We'd see if all systems are a go if I'd stop having religious freaks after me or my living room filled with meddling *men*. Though," I turned back to Mo, "we do kinda have that crackpot to thank for bringing us together."

Mo's eyes narrowed and a noise that sounded like a growl came up his throat.

Okay, so, not yet in the threat-over, post-sex-haze-of-goodness benevolent mood.

Important to know.

Eddie sighed, and I looked back at the Hot Bunch.

Lee was grinning.

Hank was looking at his feet...and smiling.

Vance and Hector were looking at each other, still not happy.

Luke was watching Mo.

Ren smiled at me.

I turned to Tex.

"Well?"

Tex stared at me.

Then he came at me.

First, his hand went to the top of my head.

Once there, he used it to shove my face in his chest.

That was when his arms went around me.

I closed my eyes and put my arms around him.

Yeah, I didn't need to be my dad's best girl.

I just needed Tex around.

"It'd be my honor, Lottie," he low-boomed into the top of my hair.

Yeah.

All I needed was Tex.

And Mo.

And the Hot Bunch.

Life taketh away.

But if you're open to it, it also giveth.

And I had a lot.

"Now put some clothes on, girl," Tex ordered, let me go, spun me around, and gave me a gentle push toward Mo.

A knock came at the door.

"Christ," Mo muttered, the soft look he was giving me after watching the Tex hug turning to an impatient one. "I'll get that. You get dressed," he said to me.

"All right. I'm going," I replied.

He went to the door.

I went to the stairs.

I was up three of them when I heard. "Good, Mo. Glad you're here. We need to ask you a few questions too."

This meant I pivoted and went right back down to watch Mo ushering in Mitch Lawson and Brock Lucas.

Fabulous.

I knew Mitch and Brock because they were cops, they got around. And I worked at a strip joint, and there were always lots of people around and by the law of averages, some of those people did things cops were interested in.

We weren't best buds, but they were good guys that on occasion had to talk to me because of, say, one of the girls dating someone who was a fuckface or Smithie calling in the police when he suspected someone was dealing from a car parked in the club parking lot.

Though I liked them, they were two more men I had to get out of my house before I could suck Mo's massive cock and then ride it, this prior to getting to know him better in other ways.

"Hey, Lottie," Mitch greeted.

"Mitch."

"Lottie," Brock said.

"Hey, Brock."

"Lottie."

That last was a growl.

I looked to my mound of hunkalicious boyfriend and got his message.

Definitely time to get dressed.

"I'm gonna get dressed. Don't start without me," I said to Mitch and Brock, and before they could reply, I twirled and ran up the stairs to get dressed.

* * * *

Mo joined me in order to put on a shirt.

This was a heavy burden to bear, after waiting so long wondering what was under that shirt, finally having it, liking it a whole lot, and then again having it hidden away from me.

But hopefully this would all be over soon, I could call in sick, we could both get naked again and recommence the celebratory festivities.

I put on cloud-gray joggers with a matching slouchy top that fell off my shoulder, only to have Mo inquire, "You just can't do it, can you?" with his eyes assessing my outfit.

For goodness sake.

"This outfit isn't sexy," I informed him.

"Babe, there was time for me to get on my knees right now, I'd do it to thank God you don't got a dick. But I do. So that's my call. And it is."

I couldn't argue that.

So I used, "All those men are very taken, Mo."

His gaze cut from my outfit to my face. "Yeah, so am I. *By you*. And now I gotta be interviewed by the cops fighting getting hard."

Oh.

Well then.

I struggled against smiling while I asked, "What do you want me to wear?"

"Until this house is empty but you and me, a shroud."

Okay.

I couldn't not smile.

"I don't have one of those," I shared through it.

"Let's just get this done," he said through a sigh.

I was down with that.

We walked out of the room together, me under an additional burden, this being the burden of Mo's heavy arm flung over my shoulders.

This burden I didn't mind bearing.

"You okay?" I asked.

"You're safe, we've fucked twice, I'm good…for now."

"No, I mean with Tex and the Hot Bunch being here."

He stopped us halfway down the stairs, stairs that weren't exactly narrow, but they were with me jammed up next to my mound of hunkalicious boyfriend.

"The Hot Bunch?" he asked.

"The Nightingale Men, plus Eddie and Ren. Haven't you read the books?"

"Those *Rock Chick* books?" he asked.

"Yeah," I answered.

"No, I haven't read those books," he muttered.

That was probably good.

However…

"Don't you read?" I asked.

"I *can* read," he answered.

"No, I mean, enjoy reading, for fun."

"I'm too busy. If there's time I can, I listen to them."

I smiled up at him. "Cool."

He stared down at me. "Are you in them?"

Hmm…

I decided to start by playing dumb. "In what?"

His arm squeezed my shoulder.

He meant was I in the *Rock Chick* books.

And he knew I was playing dumb.

To avoid my collarbone snapping, I said, "Kind of."

"How *kind of?*"

"The kind of *kind of* that's more like a yes."

He stared down at me.

Then he blew out another sigh and resumed our descent of the stairs.

We joined the men who had decided to hang around (this being all of them) and I saw Eddie had made himself at home and was handing out coffees.

I made a mental note to buy more pods as Mitch and Brock suggested I sit at the dining room table while we chatted.

I took the head and there was a slight kerfuffle when Mo firmly positioned himself standing at my right side, which meant Eddie had abandoned his coffee post and was trying to position himself at my left, where Tex was also positioning himself.

"Who's givin' her away, motherfucker?" Tex asked to end the hubbub. He didn't allow Eddie to answer. "Me. So stand down."

"She's gonna make you wear a tux," Eddie warned, giving in badly.

"So what?" Tex asked.

Everyone in the room looked at Tex in shock.

He wore flannel shirts and jeans.

The end.

Unless he was under duress, this being when he got married, when a Rock Chick got married, and when he went on a cruise with my mother. On that he wore swim trunks for the sole purpose of wearing them, and since he was only slightly smaller than Mo, though older and a lot hairier, he cleared the deck by the pool on the ship because people were terrified of him.

"I didn't give Roxie away 'cause Herb horned in on that action," Tex went on, referring to his niece and Hank's wife.

"Herb's her father," Hank pointed out.

"Yeah, well, she's got *two* arms, am I wrong?" Tex noted.

He was not.

"And if I get Lottie to the altar and change my mind," Tex continued, "when I'm asked who gives her away, I can punch this guy in the face and take off with her."

On that he jerked his head Mo's way.

But on that, I was having second thoughts about asking Tex to give me away because Tex was unpredictable, and this sounded shocking, but with him, nothing was out of the realm of possibility.

"I'd really rather you not do that, Tex," I told him.

"Then you better be really fuckin' good to her," he told Mo.

"We haven't even been out on a date!" I snapped.

Tex finally looked down at me. "Don't try that shit with me, girl. I've been in on it since the beginning. I'm not sure Lee and Indy have even been on a date yet, and they've been married for years and got two kids."

"You really kinda haven't, have you?" Hank asked Lee.

"Can we talk about the lunatic with a basement covered in plastic sheets?" Mitch asked.

And my body went ice-cold.

"A word. *Now,*" Mo grunted, and didn't wait for Mitch to agree to said word.

He turned on his bare foot and stalked to the back door.

Mitch looked to me, the men, and followed.

Brock went after him.

"You didn't know?" Eddie murmured to me.

I stared at the dining room table.

"Lottie, *querida,* you didn't know?" Eddie repeated.

I tipped my eyes up to him. "Plastic sheets?"

Eddie's face got hard and he looked to Lee.

Tex's big mitt fell on my shoulder and squeezed.

"He was…he was getting ready to follow through, wasn't he?" I asked.

Eddie looked back to me.

"Yeah, Lottie," he said gently.

"Oh my God," I breathed.

Tex pulled out the chair beside me and settled his bulk into it.

His hand covered mine on the table.

"Safe now, girl. All good," he low boomed.

I stared at his hand covering mine.

"Lottie, look at me," Tex urged.

But something was wrong with me.

"Lottie, my girl, *look at me*," Tex repeated.

"I love you, Tex, you know that, don't you?" I said to our hands.

"I do, darlin', and I love you too," Tex replied.

The astonishing and magnificent event of Tex actually saying the words and not getting tongue tied and feeling awkward at open emotion didn't even register with me.

"I love you, Eddie, you know that," I told Tex and my hands. "I love you for my sister and my nephews and I love you for me too."

"Love you too, sweetheart," I heard Eddie murmur as I felt my hair gently pulled off my shoulder and a hand land reassuringly on my neck.

I wasn't reassured.

"I love all you guys," I said.

No one replied but I felt the goodness all around me.

It just didn't work.

"I need Mo," I whispered in a voice even I barely heard.

"Sorry, darlin'?" Tex asked.

Abruptly, I turned my gaze to his, totally lost the hold I'd been keeping now for a week, and shrieked, "*I need Mo!*"

The back door opened even before Vance and Ren took off toward it.

I heard heavy, fast steps then I was in strong arms and after that I was sitting in a wide lap, burrowing into a big body, trembling from head to toe.

"Victim's Assistance?" I heard Hank ask quietly.

"Give her a minute," Mo replied in the same tone, holding me close but pulling me closer. Then in my ear, "What do you feel?"

Terrified.

Plastic sheets.

His arms tightened further. "What do you feel, sweetheart?"

"Y-you."

"Me," he agreed. "Where am I?"

"R-right here."

"Right here. With you. Are you safe?"

I forced myself to nod, but the movement felt foreign, like I'd never done it before.

And I couldn't stop shaking.

Man, it was so cold.

"Get her sister here," Mo ordered.

"On it," Eddie said.

"And her mom," Mo went on.

"Got that," Tex replied.

"I'm okay. I'll b-be okay. Don't worry them," I said to Mo's chest.

"Lottie?"

"Y-yeah?"

"Shut up."

"'Kay."

Still trembling (okay, more like shaking), I pushed closer to Mo. And he held on.

Chapter Eleven

I Hit the Mother Lode

Mo

"Fuck, Mo. I'm so sorry. I didn't know."

Lawson hit him with that the second his foot hit the ground floor after he left Lottie in bed with her mother and sister.

Mo looked to the man.

He looked wrecked.

Mitch Lawson was about doing what he could to make things right, not the other way around.

Freaking Lottie like that wasn't in his DNA and knowing he did gutted him.

But that was on Mo.

She'd shown her level of fear that first night.

He should have known something like this would happen and the second Mitch and Slim showed, he should have been on that.

"I know you didn't," Mo replied. "She knows you didn't. She's a together woman. Puts on a tough front. Even I didn't know she wasn't hangin' in there, Mitch. And you couldn't know, Lottie bein' how she is, that we hadn't kept her up to date. That's on me. I should have warned you. But like I told you outside, she doesn't know anything. The first letter, that's it."

Lawson nodded.

"Right. Let's just get this done," Mo said, moving into the living room.

He was shocked as shit when they settled in, the Nightingale brothers

(Lee and Hank), the Chavez brothers (Eddie and Hector), Tex, Vance, Luke and Ren all stood at his back.

Guess his approval rating went up.

In that moment, he couldn't care less. He needed to focus on getting this done so he could get back to his girl.

He leveled his eyes to Lawson and Lucas who sat next to each other at the dining room table after Mo sat in the chair at the head, where Lottie had been.

Lawson had dealt with it (for now) and had his game face on.

And Lawson started it, taking point as bad cop, though Mo suspected Lucas might not take the role of good.

"Axl reports he locked this guy down because you called him in the crowd."

Axl would not report that.

Fuck, this wasn't going to go easy.

But it couldn't.

If they appeared to be sweeping shit under the rug, this whackjob could walk.

"I didn't get a good vibe from him, but he wasn't notable, which is why I didn't clock him at King Soopers where I saw him first," Mo somewhat confirmed. "But I made the call and Axl said he was on him. I don't know anything about locking him down and that wasn't our remit, so I can't confirm if he locked him down. But I'd be surprised Axl would do that unless the man gave Axl a reason to lock him down."

"The suspect reports, when he was approached, he tried to leave and wasn't allowed. Were you a witness to that?" Lucas asked.

"I was on Lottie in the dressing room. So no."

"You just tagged him as a person of interest and then you took care of Lottie," Lawson said.

Mo nodded.

"You need to make a statement on the record of that and the King Soopers sighting," Lucas remarked. "You sure it was him at the store?"

"A hundred percent, honestly, no. But gut, the second I saw him in the club, I'd bet all I had on the fact it was him checkin' out cucumbers."

Lawson and Lucas looked at each other.

"Receipt," Lawson muttered.

"Noted," Lucas muttered back.

That meant they'd search through the guy's stuff and try to find a receipt to place him at the store, verifying Mo's statement so Mo didn't have to be a hundred percent on placing him there.

And Mo hoped that guy bought something and kept the receipt.

"I'll go on the record about it," Mo added. "When I clocked him at the club, he wasn't watching Lottie. He had eyes on me."

"He threatened your life in the last letter," Lucas noted.

Mo felt the men behind him shift and wondered if they knew that part. "Yup."

"And you didn't want the police called in?"

"Smithie's call. Letters addressed to him."

Neither Lucas nor Lawson looked happy about that.

"But you were directly threatened," Lawson reminded him.

"I look like a guy who can't take care of myself?" Mo asked.

"No," Lawson replied. "The man states his wallet was forcibly taken from him in Smithie's office and he was detained against his will."

Well, hell.

No, this wasn't gonna go easy.

"I was on Lottie," he reiterated.

"You don't know about that?" Lucas asked, watching him closely.

He did.

"I was on Lottie."

"You don't know about that," Lucas repeated, not in question form this time, but it was still a question.

"Asked and answered," Lee declared. "Move on, Slim."

"Lee, let them do their jobs," Hank said quietly.

Hank, also a cop, knew the game and he knew it had to be played.

Lee just wanted them out of the house so it could quiet down for Lottie.

There was a knock on the door.

Seemed things weren't going to quiet down for Lottie.

Fuck.

"On it," Hector said, and he moved.

"I'm sorry, but it wasn't actually answered, Lee," Lawson pointed out.

"Tagged the guy. Waited until the lights went down seein' as I figured he knew me, and that I might know about him, I didn't want to tweak him by talking into my radio," Mo put in and Lawson and Lucas's attention came back to him. "The lights went down after Lottie's set. I informed the team. Axl stated he was on him. I got Lottie to the dressing room, she locked herself in. I called it into Hawk. I told him the level of my certainty this was our guy, which was high. Hawk made the call."

"And that call was?" Lawson asked.

"I told you that call, Mitch," Hawk said, striding toward them in front of Hector. "Now, Mo doesn't need an attorney, but I'm fuckin' gonna get him one just to fuck your day up if this shit goes on longer."

Hawk knew the game.

It just got under his skin when his men were forced to play it.

"Smithie, nor you, nor any member of your team, nor any employee of the club can detain a man, Hawk," Lawson retorted.

"Yes we can as hired security for that club," Hawk returned.

Lawson knew that to be true, so he let it go and switched subjects. "He reports his wallet was forcibly removed from his person."

"I'm not surprised he's offering false testimony, Mitch, considering what was found in his house," Hawk clipped. "But at the time, when we shared our concerns, he shared he had nothing to hide, was happy for us to enter his house and do a search, something we did. He thought we were bluffing, didn't understand the scope of our security remit with Smithie or thought this right here would get what was in his house made inadmissible after what he'll claim is an illegal search. Now he's falsifying his story, deciding this will be his defense when his shit got hot."

Mo remained silent.

The shifting behind him ceased.

"But we got witnesses to the effect of our story," Hawk carried on. "And he's got a basement fitted with soundproofing and other things I don't need to describe since you saw it. He got agitated during the time he chose not to leave Smithie's office, probably cottoning onto the fact we weren't bluffing. He was cocky at first, and if you read his letters, you'll get why. He thought he was on his way, his confidence growing."

They definitely knew that last.

"So we *did* detain him," Hawk went on. "Just not forcibly. But we were adamant about it once Jorge found what was in his house and I called you. I made that order. So that's on me. But Mo wasn't around for any of that. So how about Mo comes down to make a statement when his woman isn't upstairs, workin' off a week's worth of tension caused by the likes of this man having her in his sights and we move on from here."

Mo wondered who'd called Hawk in.

His guess was Lucas.

But it also could have been Lawson.

He'd never know because he'd never ask, and it didn't matter anyway.

It was just a game that needed to be played to put a sick man down.

"By the time we hit that club, Hawk, all the patrons were gone so we couldn't question them. And none of the employees are reporting the incident where your man Axl forcibly locked down the suspect and took him up to the office," Lawson noted.

"That was because Axl and Jaylen asked him up to the office and he came of his own free will," Hawk replied.

"And again, he says otherwise," Lucas pointed out.

"And again, with what Jorge told me was in his house, I'm not surprised," Hawk fired back. "Are you? You got him on intent. You got him on stalking. You got him on malice aforethought, times two." He jerked his head toward Mo, indicating the death threat. "And the Feds got him on using the United States postal service to deliver a threat. Three counts. You call in the Feds?"

"Yeah," Lucas said.

"Now you're tellin' me this guy who had that shit in his house is gonna roll into a court of law, whine about Smithie and my boys forcibly capturing and detaining him when the man doesn't have a mark on him, have pictures shown of that basement, his journals passed around to a jury, those letters read, and he's gonna get off?" Hawk asked.

Axl had a talent at that, a capture with no marks.

Downright skilled.

Mo did not smile.

But he wanted to.

"We're tellin' you, if we don't hand everything to the DA with all of it tied up tight, he's gonna find a crack to slip through so maybe you can back off and let us do our job," Lawson replied.

"And I'll repeat, I'm good to go down to the station, but I told you what I saw, where I saw it, what I did, what I reported to Hawk, which by the way, turned out to be correct, and that I was *on Lottie*," Mo butted in.

"And Lottie…?" Lucas pressed.

"Was in the dressing room, then in my truck, then in bed asleep and she doesn't know dick," Mo told him. "The only letter she saw was the first, everyone's call considering the escalation of menacing language."

"She might hear it if this goes to trial," Lawson said carefully.

"I don't know why, since she doesn't know dick, so there'd be no reason to call her as a witness. She doesn't even know what this guy looks like," Mo bit off.

"We're gonna have to talk to her," Lucas said even more carefully.

"You're gonna have to wait," Mo clipped.

Lucas nodded.

"So are we done?" Mo asked.

"We're done, but we'll need you to come in as soon as you can to make this official," Lawson told him.

"And with this whackjob makin' false statements, what's my girl up against?" Mo demanded to know.

"Hawk's right," Lucas answered Mo. "We got him on intent to do grievous bodily harm, stalking, malice aforethought and the Feds got a case. He typed out the letters, but handwrote the addresses, which might have been ballsy, but mostly it was stupid. Threats delivered, an employer took action to see his employees were safe. In these situations, bringing in security details is not unheard of. Even hired security using force when a threat has been identified isn't unheard of and that won't be a problem. The search of his home possibly against his will…"

Lucas let that trail, but he wasn't done.

"If the judge can get past that and what was in his house is admissible, though, he's fucked. Our search had a warrant. The judge just factors that, we'll be fine. As for bail, the letters alone will give any judge pause. The rest, the DA will drive hard to either have bail set out of his price range or hold him until trial since he's clearly not all there, so not only a likely flight risk, but just a risk. She's good. But we'll stay on this and if it comes to a point we're concerned, we'll be makin' a lot of calls, so she's covered."

That was what he wanted to hear.

Mo got up.

"Morrison, I'll tell her myself when I see her again, but if you can get it in, apologize to Lottie for me. Yeah?" Lawson asked.

Game over.

Mo lifted his chin.

Eddie started to make short work of getting Lawson and Lucas out of there, but Mo didn't hang around to watch.

He took the stairs three at a time and went to Lottie's bedroom.

Lottie was curled up in a ball, her head in her mom's lap, her mother stroking her hair.

Jet, on her other side with Lottie's feet in her lap, caught sight of him and gave him a small smile.

"Lawson and Lucas are taking off," he told Jet.

Lottie's head came up and her eyes found him.

"You okay?" she asked.

"I'm good, baby," he answered, moving into the room. "You okay?"

"She needs her sister's chocolate sheet cake," Nancy decided.

"I'll get on that," Jet said, scooting to exit the bed.

"How about you get on this and I'll get on getting those boys to move along?" Nancy asked him, tipping her head sideways and down to her girl.

He was one hundred percent down with that.

Lottie pushed up.

She was down with it too.

Jet touched his forearm as she moved around him.

Mo went to the bed.

He helped Nancy out of it. Seemed she had something wrong with her arm, not a lot of mobility with that. Though the rest worked fine.

Probably a lasting result of the stroke Lottie mentioned.

"Thanks, Mo," she murmured when she was steady on her feet.

He didn't wait a long time to ascertain that before he slid in and took her place.

Lottie didn't hesitate to put her head in his lap.

"Be back, baby girl," Nancy said.

"Okay, Momma," Lottie replied to his feet.

Mo gave Nancy a look, she gave him a small smile and moved out of the room.

Mo then gave it a beat, another, up to five.

Then he murmured, "Okay, now, how's my girl really doing?"

"I just had a blip. I'll be fine."

He curled his hand around the side of her neck, ordering, "Stop it."

She twisted that neck so his hand was light on her throat and she could look up at him.

"Really, Mo, I'll be fine."

"That for me, your mom, your sister, a combo, all of us, or are you just lying to yourself?"

She closed her eyes, rolled her body and shoved her face in his gut.

It was for all of them.

Including herself.

He slid his hand into her soft hair, cupped the back of her head and held her there.

It took some time before she said, muffled by his stomach, "I will, you know."

"What?"

She turned her head slightly to look up at him. "Be fine."

"It's just now, you're not."

A hesitation before she nodded. "I'm a little freaked."

"Natural," he told her.

Her gaze went vague and she muttered, "Feels weak."

"It's natural, Lottie."

She focused on him again. "Yeah, but it feels weak."

"It isn't."

"Okay."

"*It isn't*," he stressed.

"*Okay*," she snapped. "Jeez. Stop being all supportive and sweet. It's annoying."

He grinned down at her. "Right, I'll snap into being an asshole. How's that go again?"

"You know, in this moment it's troublesome you've no clue how to do that."

"I could share that the first time I had your face in my lap, this wouldn't be my call on how you'd be using it."

She rolled her eyes and mumbled, "That works." She stopped mumbling to tell him, "Though I will say my blowjob plans being indefinitely delayed pisses me off."

"We'll get there," he told her.

She narrowed her eyes at him. "Not a lot of dudes would be free and breezy with indefinitely delayed blowjobs."

"The guy who did this to you is fucked," he announced. "He's going to be charged on some serious felonies, three of them Federal indictments. It's doubtful bail will be set, and if it is, he can afford to post it. You're safe. You got a lot of people who love you and will look out for you. I got all that and I'm with you in your bed, somewhere I've wanted to be for what feels like years. I'm gonna sleep beside you here tonight, not on that fuckin' couch. And I'm gonna wake up next to you tomorrow. With all that, I can wait for a blowjob."

Her pretty hazel eyes warmed and she pulled herself up so she was curled in a ball in his lap, not beside him on the bed, her cheek tucked tight to his chest, his arms around her.

Her head in his lap didn't suck, no matter how he had it.

But still, having her in his arms was a whole lot better.

"I don't like that I didn't handle things too well," she told his pec.

"You handled them fine," he told the top of her head, pulling her closer.

"I buried it. Acting strong isn't the same as *being* strong."

"Whatever works, works."

She tipped her head back. "I fell apart, Mo. Lost it in front of everybody."

"Do you think any of those men care you lost it in front of them?"

"I—"

"Lawson's kicking himself in the ass a million different ways, he laid it out for you and the way he did," he shared. "Education, Lottie. Those men love you. As for Lawson and Lucas, they respect you. And the only thing they're feelin' now is honored you'd trust them enough to show weakness. I'll tell you what, if Tex, Eddie, Hank, Luke and the rest had a choice, only *one*, either to be there for you and catch that guy or be there for you to catch *you*, they'd pick the second. In a way, they got that. So move on. They have."

"But, they're action men."

"They're men like me," he declared, and her eyes widened. "When I saw him and knew it was him, my skin itched to be out there to take him down. But every other part of me needed to be *with you*. Trust me. You didn't fight Smithie's decision to keep them in the dark and I can tell you feel bad about that. But they got to be in on the important part, being here now *for you*, and they know it. So get over it. It's all cool."

"Right. You're hot. Have a huge cock. You're spectacular in bed. You approve of my OCD tendencies. *And* you're quick as a whip?"

He grinned at her. "That's me."

"Then I hit the mother lode."

Because he could.

He did.

That being, he pulled her up even as he dipped down, and he took her mouth.

He kept the kiss gentle and light.

He wanted more, and he'd get more.

But he'd take it later.

He broke the kiss and asked, "Chocolate sheet cake?"

"Yeah."

"You gonna eat that?"

"Probably. But Mom's just using this as an excuse to get Jet to make one because she loves it. Tex loves it. It's Eddie and the boys' favorite. But mostly it's just because Mom loves it."

He grinned at her.

It faded before he asked, "What's up with her arm? That happen from the stroke?"

"Yeah. Her stroke. She had it a long time ago. She fought to get her leg back, but we thought she'd never have her arm. A couple of years ago, some physical therapist was in Fortnum's, getting a coffee and chatting with Indy while she did. She'd had some success with stroke patients, even years after the event. Indy introduced her to Jet, Jet and Tex talked to Mom, they started working and she got some mobility back." She shrugged. "Not much. It isn't strong. She can't fully grip or lift anything. But she can use it to shove things around to position them and stuff like that. Anyway, something is better than nothing."

"Yeah," he agreed. "Though hate that happened to your mom, baby."

"Me too. But she survived and takes care of herself, Tex takes care of the rest, so it's all good."

"Yeah," he muttered.

"Mo?" she called, and his focus went back to her. "Chocolate sheet cake means the boys are gonna come over. Since Blanca's probably watching them, and will hear what happened to me, she'll wanna know I'm okay so she'll come over. If Blanca isn't watching them, one of the Rock Chicks is watching them, so they'll come over. I need to shower. Get ready, albeit belatedly, to face the day."

He bent in and kissed her forehead before he said, "I'll go down and make sure they're cleared out."

"I don't mind them here."

He studied her closely and saw what he needed to see.

"Then I'll make that clear."

She nodded and gave him a little smile.

"Mo?" she called again, even though he was looking right at her.

The smile he gave her wasn't small. "I haven't gone anywhere, baby."

"I know. And that was what I was gonna say. Thank you."

It might make him fucked in the head, but in that moment, he really didn't care.

Because Mo knew the most precious thing he'd ever heard in his life was Lottie shrieking, *I need Mo!*

"You really want a big wedding?" he whispered.

"Is that a problem?" she whispered back.

"Not even a little."

His girl smiled at him. It wasn't small that time.

And Mo smiled back.

* * * *

Much later, Mo stood on Lottie's back porch, feeling his jaw get tight.

Lottie was upstairs, horsing around with her sugared-up nephews.

The entirety of the "Hot Bunch" and "Rock Chicks," including Blanca, Eddie and Hector's mother, and two gay dudes named Tod and Stevie, had arrived, and they were having what could only be described as a party.

It wasn't a rip-roarin' one, loud and obnoxious.

But Lottie had given them the cue that they needed to be business as usual, so Mo was guessing this was that.

He was also guessing, since the more of them who came over, the more business as usual they acted, the more herself she seemed, this was exactly what she needed.

What was loud and obnoxious was the TV he could hear from the neighbors' place.

If Lottie was out there, trying to have a moment of quiet to find some peace, it couldn't happen because her neighbors seemed to want to hear their TV not only from any corner of their yard, but any corner of any of their neighbors' yards.

"Yo."

He turned his head and saw Eddie step out on the porch with him.

"Yo," he replied.

Eddie came to stand next to him and it took a millisecond for his brows to draw together and his head to turn toward the neighbors' yard.

"So this is gonna be you, not Tex?" Mo asked.

Eddie's attention came to Mo.

"Learn now, that man is a woman's man," Eddie shared. "After she lost it earlier, Tex is strugglin' with bein' five feet from her. Any other time, he'd be out here. This time, no fuckin' way."

Mo nodded.

He'd gotten that impression from Tex.

Though anyone who'd heard anything about Tex MacMillan knew that was the way already.

"She's deep for you," Eddie pointed out.

"Good to know, since I'm there too," he muttered.

"Noticed that," Eddie replied in a mutter.

Mo didn't mind he did since he wasn't hiding it.

Eddie continued.

"I probably don't need to tell you we'll put the hurt on you, you do that to her."

That message had already been made clear.

"Nope," Mo stated, hearing the channel change next door, now it was some baseball game, then he could swear he heard a door close.

"And—"

"Hang on," Mo said, turned, walked across the porch, into the house, through the people in the house, out the front door, across the lawn, to the neighbors' front door.

He knocked just as he felt Eddie come up behind him.

"Mo—" Eddie started.

The door opened and the woman who opened it took one look at him, her head tipped back, then she stepped back, and her face got white.

"Hey," he said.

"Uh, hey," she replied, her eyes darting to Eddie and back to Mo.

"Honey, who is it?" a man's voice came from in the house.

"Um, come here a sec, would you?" she called, not taking her eyes off Mo.

"You watchin' the game?" Mo asked.

"Sorry?" she asked back, and her gaze went beyond him again just as Mo felt more bodies at his back.

"You watchin' the game?" he repeated as a man appeared from behind her.

He got a load of what was at his front door, his eyes got big and it took him a second to decide whether to join his wife or yank her away and shut the door.

He joined his wife.

At least that said something about him.

"Can I help you?" he asked.

"Are you watching the game?" Mo repeated.

"Erm...what?"

Jesus Christ.

"The *game*," Mo bit off. "Are you watching the game?"

"I have it on out back," the man said.

"I know. I can hear it. But are you watching it?"

"Well, uh..."

"He's listening to it. I don't like sports on in the house," the wife said.

Like he suspected. This was why it was so loud. So it could be heard in the house.

"He got a radio?" Mo asked.

"I…I guess not really but he likes to pop out and look in on it when he can," she explained.

"While he's blasting it, but not even there to watch it, it's disturbing his neighbors," Mo pointed out.

"It's a weeknight. No one's outside," the man said.

"I was outside."

"You…do you live here?" the man asked, openly unhappy about the idea of Mo being a neighbor.

"No, but my woman does, right there." He tipped his head toward Lottie's house. "And today, she had a really tough day. Bad as you can imagine. She has her folks around her, but they'll leave and then she'll need peace and quiet. Not have to listen to the game. So can you shut it off or turn it down?"

"I wanna hear it," the man replied.

"I don't," Mo returned.

"Right, I'll go out and turn it down," the man allowed.

"Awesome. Thanks. But have a mind. My woman says it happens a lot. I don't wanna be comin' over here all the time asking you to have a mind."

The man glanced behind Mo, decided to save face and puffed up his chest. "I can do what I want in my own house."

Mo nodded. "Yeah, you absolutely can. You can even decide to be an asshole and not give a shit about your neighbors in your own house, all because you wanna hear a baseball game. And I'm free to come to the door and ask you not to be an asshole. Somethin' I don't mind doin' if it bothers my woman. I also don't mind callin' the cops and makin' a complaint. Now, you can deal with that hassle, or you can decide not to be an asshole. Your choice."

On that, Mo turned to leave.

And on that, the man called, "You know, it's not cool to come over and try to intimidate me like that!"

Mo turned back. "I made a request, did it as polite as I could in the face of you not bein' polite at all. And you decided to act your version of a man which is your call, but I'd argue it wasn't the right one. I didn't use intimidating language. I just asked you to turn your TV down and have a mind to that in the future."

"You're big as a house, you got ten big guys behind you and you told me you're gonna call the cops on me for listening to a stupid baseball game."

"I got ten big guys behind me because they're all my woman's family, and like I said, she had a bad day and needs her family around her and her neighbor not to act like a jerk. And I simply informed you what I would do if you continued not to behave in a neighborly fashion. Last, I can't agree baseball is stupid, but if you think that, why would you go to the mat for it?"

The man's face was getting red. "I—"

"Listen," Mo cut him off. "You're workin' yourself up for no reason. Just turn it down and have a mind."

The man's face twisted and at that point he decided to work out what were probably some life issues, considering the fact he wasn't all that tall, and not built at all.

"You know, guys like you think they can do whatever they want just because they look like you do," he clipped.

"What I know, even the way I look, I'd have a mind to the people around me and wouldn't turn my TV so loud, it'd disturb them," Mo returned. "But mostly that's because I don't think the world revolves around me and I couldn't give a shit about the fact that it actually doesn't. I use my turn signal too."

The man's face got even redder at that.

He didn't use his turn signal.

Mo sighed and through it said, "I think we're done. Thanks for your time."

The second he moved out, Eddie moved in and stated, "And just to confirm, I'm family. I'm your neighbor's brother-in-law. I'm also a cop. And any noise complaint reported on this address will be expedited. So in the end, you'd have been better off dealing with just Mo, considering he has courtesy, patience and restraint, like you'd have been better off just apologizing and turning down your TV. Every day, we can learn new things. This is today's lesson for you. Now you folks have a nice evening."

Mo didn't turn back to see the response to Eddie's message.

Because Lottie and the rest of the Rock Chicks were crowded on her front stoop.

Well, not all of them. There were too many. Some of them were poking their heads out of the front door.

She had her arms crossed on her chest, that top dropping down her shoulder, and it might be insensitive, but he hoped with all the love and support she'd gotten that day, his blowjob was a lot less indefinitely delayed.

"Your neighbor is kind of a dickhead," he told her when he got close.

"I knew that the first time he played his TV loud," she replied and tipped her head, the mass of her hair she'd arranged at the crown after her shower falling to her shoulder. "You just couldn't help yourself, could you?"

He stopped two steps down from her. "Nope."

She smiled down at him, white and huge.

Then she listed forward, like a tree falling.

Mo caught her.

And stepping through a sea of Rock Chicks, he carried his smiling girl into her house.

He felt bad he'd interrupted Eddie's "You hurt her, we'll fuck you up" speech.

But…

Priorities.

He had to look after his girl.

Chapter Twelve

The Only Good One Left

Mo

Mo's eyes opened, and he saw dark.

Not unusual. That happened every night.

What was unusual was he had a little bundle of heat tucked tight to him.

Lottie.

He was in Lottie's bed.

Not on the couch.

In the bed.

With her.

Mo stayed still and breathed in deep, taking in the scent of her shampoo, the feel of her in his arms, and just her.

He'd get up in a minute, hit his place, get some clothes, go to the gym, workout and be back to her before she got up.

But he'd give himself a minute, or a few, to feel having her like he'd wanted her for too long of a time.

Then he'd go so he wouldn't disturb her.

This plan was ruined when Lottie stirred then made a move in his arms.

He had to shift some of his bulk, since he was semi-cocooning her, as she turned from back to him to front his way and shoved her face in his chest.

"You awake?" she mumbled.

"Yeah, baby." He gathered her closer again. "Just go back to sleep."

She didn't go back to sleep.

She nuzzled his chest with her face and his cock took notice.

He was about to repeat she should go to sleep, but she tipped her head back and touched her tongue to the indent at the base of his collarbone.

His cock definitely took notice of that.

"Babe—"

"Shh," she hushed, lifting her hands to his shoulders and pushing him to his back as her mouth moved on him and her body followed his.

"Lottie, you don't have to—" he started, curling his fingers around her waist.

"Quiet," she whispered, her lips trailing down to his nipple.

Before he could protest again, her mouth covered it and she drew in, light and sweet.

Mo shut up.

Lottie didn't talk. Her mouth was busy. And she used it to take her time exploring his chest, his stomach, so by the time she got down between his legs, he was hard as a rock and aching.

She pulled the waistband of his shorts down so it cupped his balls, and he couldn't bite back the groan.

He also couldn't stop himself from coming up on his elbows to watch her through the shadows.

Mo felt the tip of her tongue trace the underside of his cock from root all the way to the rim of the head, where she stopped and tickled him there, back and forth.

Fucking fuck.

He opened his legs, this drawing the waistband tighter against his balls, and that was magnificent.

She fell through and positioned.

Her hand gripped him at the base, lifting him off his stomach as her tongue traced up to the head and then she took him deep, gliding a tight fist up the length she couldn't swallow.

And that was spectacular.

Mo's head fell back and another groan rolled up his throat and out his lips.

Sweet Lottie, he should have known she'd have a sweet mouth.

She blew him. She took her time. She did it right. And when she'd worked him up so much, he beaded for her, she dragged her tongue across the head to take in that pearl and then lifted up.

Christ.

She dropped to the side, her hip landing on his inner thigh, and she dragged her panties down her legs, doing this quick.

She repositioned straddling him, and honest to fuck, it took all Mo had to put his hands to her thighs instead of one to his cock and one to her ass to drive her down on him.

She then reached long to the nightstand, where he'd stashed his wallet when her sister and mother were there.

"Let me do it," he said, his voice alien to him, coarse and thick.

"I got it, honey," she whispered, tossing the wallet back to the nightstand.

And she did.

She took her time. She did it right. And by the time she got a goddamned condom on him, she had him so wound up, he nearly blew right into it.

But he held.

And he held through her positioning him so she could take him.

And he held when he caught on her sleek warmth.

And he held when she slowly settled in, taking him deep.

But he had no idea how he did that since she whipped off her nightie while she did it.

The silhouette of her sweet little body and perfect tits nearly undid him.

But it was Lottie who was in control of the unravelling.

She rode him, slow and tortuous, so much of both, he needed to beg her to go faster.

But he didn't say a word.

She drew his hand from her thigh to between her legs and he thumbed her clit.

After that, she rode him faster.

Fuck yeah.

When she fell forward to plant her hands on his pecs to ride him tough, Mo shifted his other hand around to her ass, clamped hard, the tips of his fingers pressing into the sensitive skin at the crease, and she made a sexy noise he felt sear through his balls and started bouncing.

That's what he needed.

Mo encouraged her by squeezing her ass, rolling her clit and bucking up inside her.

He heard her breaths come short but fast, blending with his coming rough and deep.

Suddenly, one of her hands went up to grip the side of his neck, the thumb on her other hand dragged hard across his nipple, his balls drew tight, and he clenched his teeth in an effort not to come.

"Mo," she breathed, and shot back, arching deep and riding untamed, bouncing with abandon on his dick.

Thank…

Fuck.

He clamped both hands on her ass, forcing her rhythm faster and harder, and thrust up into her as his cock exploded, his balls emptied, so did his mind. Everything that was him about his dick and his Lottie, and he was still coming when she collapsed on top of him, her body lax, her hips moving as he kept driving her down on his still shooting cock.

Eventually Mo settled.

Lottie was already spent.

They lay there, connected and silent, and caught their breath.

Finally, she turned her head and kissed the valley of his pecs.

Mo moved so he could wrap his arms around her. And there was so little of her, his arms so long, his fingers could grip his own flesh.

His sweet little Lottie.

"How you doin'?" he murmured, his voice still thick.

"Exceptional," she replied, shifting to rest her cheek on him again.

"Sweet mouth," he complimented.

"Thanks, babe," she murmured, but he felt that cheek on him move with her smile.

"You didn't kiss me either," he noted.

He felt her body move with a quiet laugh before she said, "Yes, I did. Lots of tongue."

There absolutely was lots of tongue.

Mo joined in her laughter before he pulled her off his softening dick and rolled her to her side.

He kissed the hair on top of her head and got out of the bed.

He adjusted his shorts and went to the bathroom, got rid of the rubber, grabbed one of Lottie's thick, cream washcloths to wipe down his cock, rinsed the cloth out, washed his hands and went back to her.

Face to face, he pulled her close then yanked the covers back over them.

"Now go back to sleep," he ordered.

She pressed closer and asked, "Is it nightmares?"

Fuck.

He didn't want to get into this with her.

This was one of the things that drove them away.

"No."

She didn't utter a follow-up question.

But for some reason, his mouth moved.

"Conditioned myself to wake up before they happen."

"Okay," she said softly.

"I don't go back to sleep 'cause…"

He didn't finish.

She still said, "Yeah."

She knew why.

If he went back to sleep, the nightmares would come.

She left it there.

Or she left *that* there.

"The other women—?"

It didn't take her long to deduce that.

"Not big fans of the nightmares or me getting up at two or three in the morning."

Her frame got tight.

"Lottie, it's okay," he assured her.

"It really isn't," she replied.

"It is because I'm not with them, I'm with you."

He heard her head move on the sheet and he looked down at the shadow of her face in the dark.

"This is true. It's still not okay. Didn't they talk to you about it?"

"Yeah. The rigmarole. Find a way to sort it out. VA. Pills. Groups."

"And?"

"The VA is a clusterfuck. Pills slow me up and I cannot be slow and do my job. And I got a group."

The pitch of her voice was higher with her surprise when she asked, "You're in a group?"

"It consists of Axl, Mag, Auggie and Boone. Sometimes, shit goes down with one of us, or one of us sees the other's got somethin' up, we hit someone's crib, have a few beers, talk it out."

"Axl, I know. Mag, Auggie and Boone?"

"More of Hawk's men, my boys."

"Oh."

"Mag's my roommate."

More surprise. "You have a roommate?"

"Tammy took off, he was looking for a place. Moved in."

"Right."

"Good guy," he muttered.

"I'd hope you wouldn't move an asshole in with you."

Mo grinned at her.

"What kind of name is 'Mag?'" she asked.

"Short for Magnusson, his last name."

"Is his first name Kourtney?"

He started laughing again, and through it, said, "No. It's Daniel."

"Speaking of Daniel. Boone, last or first?"

Mo kept laughing. "First. Last name Sadler. And before you ask, Auggie is Augustus Hero. And I'll confirm, his last name is actually Hero. He gets the most shit. He says it's Greek and since most women treat him like he's a god, I don't figure he's lying. Axl is Axl Pantera."

"I was pretty sure Axl was a god," she told him. "So if Auggie is a god, then I can't wait to meet him."

"Axl's a cat."

"As in tom?"

"Exactly."

That made Lottie laugh.

He pulled her closer so he could feel it better.

Lottie cuddled in and fell silent.

When she said no more for a while, he again urged, "Now go back to sleep."

"What are you gonna do?"

"Hold you for a while. Then I might get up and hit the gym. But I'll come back, probably before you get up again."

"Okay."

He waited for more, but that was all she said.

He felt her body relax and he knew when she fell asleep.

It was then he decided he'd make sure it was deep, less chance to disturb her when she woke up.

And anyway, he was getting off on being right there, with her, after fucking, chatting and laughing.

So he was good where he was.

* * * *

Mo woke again after a hand cracked his ass.

"Get up, sleepyhead. I'm making breakfast."

He tracked Lottie with his eyes as she rounded the bed and stopped on the other side, staring down at him.

"You could be lazy, but Smithie's given me the rest of the week off and you have to go back to work tomorrow so I have a weeks' worth of getting to know my mound of hunkalicious boyfriend to cram into a day so there are things to do," she declared. "Up and at 'em."

He pushed up to an elbow and stared back at her.

"Stop looking hot and pounceable," she ordered. "I'm hungry and you're out of condoms. So we also have errands to run."

After that, she shot him a smile and wandered out, wearing what she wore to bed the night before. A red satin nightie that barely covered her ass.

When he lost sight of her, he kept his gaze aimed where he'd last seen her, then he looked down at the empty expanse of bed beside him.

He'd fallen back to sleep.

Not only did it but did it and then didn't have the dreams.

"Jesus," he whispered.

How…?

He didn't ask.

He didn't care.

He kicked the covers off his legs and got out of bed.

* * * *

"*Mo*," Lottie moaned, coming in his mouth.

Mo took it and then licked her clean.

When he could leave her as he wanted her, he ducked out from under her nightie and grabbed hold of her panties which were hooked on one ankle, most of the material lying on the kitchen floor.

He opened them, muttered, "Foot, baby," and she moved to step in.

He guided the panties up her legs, coming off his knees as he did it, and pulled them over her ass, smoothing them around the waistband while he pressed a kiss to the side of her neck.

He then moved his hands to her waist, rubbing circles there over her nightie with his thumbs and looking in her hazy eyes.

Christ, he liked her like that.

He liked her all the time.

But he definitely liked giving her that.

"Now we can have coffee," he murmured, grinning at her.

Ascertaining she was steady, he moved to the Nespresso machine, mentally ticking that off the to-do list he'd been forming practically since he met her.

Now all he had to do was fuck her on the couch in front of her TV, in her shower, and in his bed.

Then he could make another to-do list.

* * * *

"Holy smokes, this place is *rad*," Lottie breathed as he led her into his LoHi condo.

Mo dropped her hand and moved to the kitchen, but did it looking around.

He had to admit, his crib was pretty awesome.

He'd just liked the space and it was a good investment, a hot 'hood in Denver, great scores for walking, restaurants, shops, transit. Central location. Excellent views. Fireplace. Easy access to I-25.

It wasn't spacious, something Tammy bitched about a lot.

But Mag and him didn't feel on top of each other.

Then again, one of them was always working, at the gym, Mag off scoring, or they both were sleeping, so it wasn't often they co-existed in the space.

Though seeing his neatly-stacked pile of mail, he was feeling good about his friend and roommate. Mag was not as obsessive as Lottie, but he was as obsessive as Mo. And that worked.

"Seriously, pookie, Hawk really doesn't have you on food stamps, does he?" she asked.

Hawk did not.

He stopped at the marble-topped island where his mail was and grinned at her.

"Wander around," he invited. "I gotta go through my mail."

"Which bedroom is yours?" she asked.

He was rethinking his invitation, wondering if he could concentrate on mail when Lottie was in his bedroom for the first time, but he saw the excitement on her face.

She liked his place.

Mo liked that she liked his place.

So he said, "To the left."

She looked that way before she walked that way.

He watched her go then cast his glance across the entirety of the space.

When he bought it four years ago, he'd moved his shitty-ass stuff in there.

He then listened to his sisters bitch at him for a year about his shitty-ass stuff being in a LoHi condo with a view of the city where you could hit Little Man Ice Cream with no hassle.

So he'd gone to a swank furniture store where the pictures online showed stuff he didn't mind. He'd found a chick who worked there and told her he needed a comfortable couch and chair, a rug, decent dining table, some stools, a bed and a dresser and asked her where he could buy a bathroom mat and some towels that didn't suck.

The woman had visibly lost her mind.

She'd then shared she was getting married in a couple of months, had just registered, therefore knew where the best stuff was, and told him she'd set him up. She even met him at other stores to sort his shit.

He'd gone to her wedding. She'd been a pretty bride. Her husband was top-notch.

And even Mo had to admit, with the grays, beiges, blues, woods, glass and kickass lamps, she hadn't done too badly.

And it had been three years and his towels were still the shit.

Tammy hadn't even griped about his towels.

She wasn't a fan of all the rest. Though she was, until he told her some woman he met at a furniture store kitted out his place. After that, she hated it.

At that juncture, Mo was wondering why he'd put up with her.

Then again, he'd had his first full night's sleep in years (albeit interrupted by some great head and an even better fuck), so maybe he hadn't been on his game.

And he hadn't yet met Lottie and cottoned on to what he might be missing.

No, what he could earn.

No.

What he deserved.

"Dude," Lottie said as she wandered back into the open-plan space, "next time I revamp something at my house, you're decorating it."

"Woman named Bobbi did it," he told her, and watched her as he did.

"Another ex?" she asked, entirely unconcerned, and coming to stand at the corner of the island next to him.

"A woman in a furniture store who'd just registered for her wedding. Gave her a clean slate." He tipped his head to the space. "She filled it."

"First, I'm in fits of glee you know what registering is," she began. "Second, you probably made her year, and since she was getting married, that says something."

Through his smile he replied, "First, I have three married sisters. I know what seating charts and cake tastings are too."

She smiled back at him, huge.

"Second, Josh, Bobbi's husband, thanked me at the wedding, seein' as she took care of my place, she wouldn't feel the need to do theirs all in one go."

"The gift of your all-around awesomeness just keeps on giving," she returned.

At that, he bent and pressed a kiss to her mouth.

Then he went to his mail.

Flipping through it, he asked, "You down with me getting online for a few minutes so I can pay some bills?"

"I've got until next Tuesday," she murmured, drifting toward the living room area.

When Smithie heard about her meltdown (this he got from Jet), he'd called Lottie to tell her he didn't want to see her until her first set next Tuesday.

Mo had to go in the next day, but he figured Hawk wouldn't put him on an assignment that would jam up his weekend because Hawk didn't do that shit. He'd been on duty twenty-four seven for a week. Hawk would give him his weekend or if he didn't, he'd lay light duty on him.

Next week, though, Mo would be fair game.

Which, with Lottie in his life, would suck.

But they had that day, all of it. And they'd gotten the worst part out of the way, going to see Mitch and Slim at the station after they'd had breakfast and showered.

Now it was just Mo and his girl.

"Gonna grab my laptop," he said to Lottie, watching her stretch out on his couch, her eyes to his view. "Want a drink?"

"No, Mo. I'm good."

He got his laptop from his room, brought it to the island and booted it up as he ripped open envelopes.

"So, sisters, mom, registries, cake tastings, nieces and nephews," she started, and Mo again looked at her to see her gaze still aimed at his view. "What about your dad?"

Shit, fuck.

He didn't want to get into that now.

Or ever.

"Can we talk about him later?"

She turned from the view to him. "We can talk about him whenever you want, honey. Though I have a feeling it won't be any easier then."

She was probably right about that.

"Think I mentioned he was a dick," he noted.

"You did," she confirmed.

"Those weddings my sisters had?"

She nodded.

"They part paid for them. Their future husbands pitched in. Mom pitched in and she did it a lot. Dad, not so much. That was his thing. Being around and being useless."

Also being a dick.

"Was he invited?" she asked quietly.

Mo nodded. "To one. Signe's a good girl. Oldest. Responsible. Played a big part of takin' care of us while Mom worked. She thought it was the right thing to do. Invited him. After that, no."

"Was he…did he behave—?"

"Like a dick?" he cut her off to ask.

"Yeah."

"That's what dicks do, Lottie."

"Does he drink?" she asked cautiously.

Mo shook his head and turned his attention back to dealing with his mail. "Teetotaler. Doesn't touch the stuff. Thinks anyone who does is weak. Same about drugs, for certain. Detests smokers. Even has a few things to say about people who drink caffeine." He looked back at her. "But didn't have any problem telling his daughters they needed to lose weight. Sharing with his son he thinks he's a piece of shit. Slapping his wife around until she got shot of him."

She pushed up to sitting on his couch, eyes locked on him, whispering, "Mo."

"Made Signe's day when he joined her at the back of the church to walk her down the aisle. Caught his first sight of his beautiful daughter in her wedding gown, told her she looked plump and she should have gone on a diet before the big day. Added that her dress made her look like she was trying too hard. Standing up front as an usher, took one look at her walking down the aisle and knew he got his teeth into her."

"Oh my God, Mo," she breathed.

"Thought Paul, Signe's man, was gonna march down that fucking aisle and rip his throat out. It ruined it. She was near tears the whole time they stood up there taking their vows, and not the good kind of tears. That's what you see in the pictures. That and Paul looking like he wanted to murder somebody."

"Honey," she whispered.

Christ, he hadn't talked about this in years.

But now that he was, it seemed like he couldn't stop.

Which was why he didn't.

"For him, he has no clue. Says he thinks he's bein' helpful. What he's being is controlling. He had no say in the wedding, even though he tried to horn in, about everything. And that flipped his switch. His choice, he would have planned the whole thing and it would have been an eighties throwback nightmare. But he didn't pay for shit. Didn't even offer. Even if he did, it wasn't *his* ass getting married. That was his payback."

"I can't believe what I'm hearing," Lottie said.

"I disinvited him before he walked into the reception."

"How did you do that?" she asked.

"I beat the shit out of him in the parking lot."

Lottie sat on his couch, staring at him.

Mo stood at his island, staring at her.

Seconds ticked by and through them, he watched her face get hard.

There it was.

He was an asshole, just like his dad, except an out-of-control one, not a control-freak one.

And now she knew it.

"Good," she bit.

He felt his entire body jerk.

"What?"

"Good," she snapped. Then she yelled, "What a dick!" She jumped to her feet just as Mo heard the door to the condo open. "Seriously! Total *dick*!"

"Everything cool?"

Mo twisted to see Mag standing there, looking alert while he glanced between Lottie and him.

"No," she clipped. "Mo's dad's a dick!"

Mag turned his attention to Mo.

"I mean, he ruined his sister's wedding day!" Lottie shouted, so in her snit, it was like she hadn't really registered Mag had entered, even if she was responding to him, which was something since not many women missed Mag doing anything. "Who *does* that?"

"I see your relationship has moved to Tales from the Darkside," Mag remarked.

"It happens," Mo replied.

"Warp speed, brother," Mag returned. "Heard you two didn't make it 'official,'" he did the air quotation marks just to be an asshole, "until yesterday morning."

"We didn't," Lottie butted in.

Mag looked back to her, fighting a grin and murmuring, "Mm-hmm."

"We didn't," Lottie repeated.

"All right, darlin'. I totally believe you," Mag said.

Lottie gave up on that (wisely) and turned to Mo, throwing an arm out at Mag. "So, he's not the one who's a god?"

Mag also turned back to Mo, brows raised, no longer fighting anything. Smiling flat-out.

"I told her about Auggie," he shared.

"Right," Mag murmured. He went back to Lottie. "Mo's the only real god among us. He put up with Tammy for two years before she did him the colossal favor of breaking up with him."

Mo looked to the ceiling.

Terrific.

He had no clue she'd already met Tammy.

Mag was in Test the New Woman mode.

Fuck.

"I hear that," Lottie returned. "Met her at King Soopers. Real peach."

"You ran into Tammy with her?" he asked Mo, jerking his head Lottie's way.

"Her name is Lottie," Mo replied.

"You ran into Tammy with Lottie Mac, Queen of the Corvette calendar and every other man on the planet's wet dream?" Mag amended.

Mo wasn't finding this even remotely acceptable anymore.

And damn sure not funny.

"Though I'm the *other* man," Mag stated, again grinning because he read Mo's face. "Seeing as she's dating my roommate."

"We did," Lottie affirmed, and regained Mag's eyes. "*And* her new man, Peacock Pete who wears a two-hundred-dollar shirt to go grocery shopping."

"Her new meat was there too?" Mag asked Lottie.

Lottie nodded her head, the bunch of her hair swept up at her back crown bouncing around. "Unh-hunh. When he stopped checking out my tits and figured out who Mo was, I'm pretty sure he pissed his two-twenty-five rag and bone chinos."

Mag burst out laughing.

Lottie smiled at him.

"Holy fuck," Mag pushed out through his hilarity. "That I would have paid to see."

"Tammy was the star of the show," Lottie shared. "I thought I'd have to scratch her eyes out before she begged Mo, right in front of Peacock Pete, to let her go down on him in the alley."

Mag busted out laughing again but he did it turning his attention back to Mo.

"Told you she was gagging for it. You totally should have tagged her convenient and left the scraps to Peacock Pete." He went back to Lottie. "Sorry, darlin'. No offense to women on the whole. Just referring to women like Tammy."

"She's not a woman," Lottie returned. "She just has the equipment."

Looking at Mo, Mag indicated Lottie with a thumb. "I like her."

"Take a number," Mo muttered.

"You want a beer?" Mag asked Lottie.

"It's barely eleven o'clock, Mag," Mo informed his bud.

"I'm feelin' like a play by play of the Tammy Incident and anything involving Tammy is better consumed with alcohol," Mag replied, then he returned to Lottie. "What'd she do when she got a load of you?"

"Nonverbal throwdown. Immediate," Lottie told him.

"I'll bet. Pea green. Fuck, wish I'd been there to see that," Mag replied.

Lottie then looked at Mo and declared, "I think I like him."

"He's an asshole, baby," Mo shared.

"The fun-loving kind who's only inappropriate when discussing women who are bitches and on occasion waxing poetic about a spectacular blowjob," Mag put in.

Lottie watched him say this and again looked at Mo. "I've decided I totally like him."

Mag chuckled and moved to the fridge.

"What are you doin' here anyway?" Mo asked his roommate. "Aren't you on mission?"

"Nope, it's done. Finished the debrief and now I'm gonna shotgun a beer then haul my ass to Coors Field for a day game. Meeting Boone there," Mag stated, tagging a beer from the fridge and turning to them. "You guys wanna come?"

Hell no.

"Mo has to pay his bills online and then I have to do a deep dive into his psyche as to why he put up with women like Tammy before he met me and after that we're gonna have a fuck-a-thon. I don't think we can fit it in our schedule. But thanks," Lottie answered for them.

Mag held his beer in hand and stared at her through all this.

Then he shot a shit-eating grin at Mo and announced, "I fucking hate you. You got the only good one left."

He might be right about that.

And Mo was down for the fuck-a-thon.

The rest?

"You want Lottie doing a deep dive in your psyche?" Mo asked.

"If I didn't think you'd pull my balls out through my throat, I'd share I would give it up about Nikki if I got all the rest."

"Nikki?" Lottie asked.

"You shouldn't have gone there, brother," Mo muttered.

Mag looked to Lottie. "How's this? You don't treat him like a piece of shit," he tilted his head to Mo, "I'll bust out my good Scotch and drown my sorrows while crying on your shoulder and laying my broken heart at your feet. You do end up treating him like shit, Axl, Aug, Boone and me will build an effigy of you and burn it, like we did Tammy, because apparently that works."

"I'll take that deal," Lottie immediately replied.

"Well, all right," Mag said quietly, eyeing Mo's woman up now with open approval.

They shared a moment of solidarity and Mo let them do that before he reminded his friend, "Weren't you gonna shotgun that beer and then get the fuck outta here?"

"Right, I have plans."

He then took out his army knife, set the beer on its side on the counter, slipped out the blade, shoved it in the bottom side of the can and put the hole to his mouth before pulling the cap, downing the brew like he was eighteen years old and standing in the living room of a frat house.

Mag gave out a big, "Ah," when he was done, crunched the can and tossed it in the recycling before he strolled to his bedroom, saying, "If you're behind closed doors, I'll lock up when I go out and catch you two on the flipside."

And then he shut his door behind him.

Mo looked from Mag's door to Lottie.

"Nikki?" she asked.

He knew she wouldn't let that go.

"I'll explain later."

"Scale of one to ten with Tammy being a five, what's my challenge?" she asked.

"Eighty-two. He was gone for her. Lost. Couldn't find his own ass if she was in the same room. And she was for him too, if he'd give up his job and go work at a bank or something."

"Oh boy," she muttered.

"Yeah," Mo agreed.

She wandered to him, saying, "I'll get on that later."

He bet she would.

Mo went back to his laptop to log in to his bank.

Lottie stopped at his side.

"Mo?" she called.

He lifted his eyes to her.

"I will never, not ever, treat you like shit," she whispered.

"I know, sweetheart," he whispered back.

They shared their own moment of solidarity.

"Pay your bills, honey," she urged. "We need to go get some lunch and carb up for our fuck-a-thon."

Mo decided right then they were having Italian for lunch.

He did this grinning at her.

Then he paid his bills.

* * * *

They were necking, Lottie sitting on his dick in his lap.

Mo was sitting up, his arms curled around her, his legs straight, her legs curled around his hips, her fingers trailing over the skin on his skull.

When his cock lost it, and her, they kept necking.

It was a while after that when he lifted her up and set her on her side on the bed, bent in and kissed her chest, then threw the covers over her and left her there to go deal with the condom.

They'd carbed up on pasta with the addition of a salad (Lottie eating a lot of the last, a little of the first) at a restaurant down the street from his house.

And since Lottie didn't want to waste time commencing their fuck-a-thon (and Mo didn't either), they'd walked back to his place and spent the rest of the afternoon doing that.

She hadn't done a deep dive into his psyche about why he put up with the likes of Tammy.

Then again, he suspected she knew she'd already handled that.

He rejoined her in his bed, pulled the covers over them, curled her in his arms and started making out with her again.

His bed had definitely been broken in.

And there'd been some action, if not the full go, in her shower that morning.

So that left her couch in front of her TV and finishing up what they started in the shower and he could dream up new places to have her.

His couch was going to be one.

The island too.

And her kitchen counter.

And the couch he'd slept on without her for a week.

These thoughts on his mind, Lottie's taste in his mouth, Mo broke the kiss, trailed his lips to her ear and asked, "You good?"

"Tremendous," she replied, pressing into him. "Though, hungry."

Yeah, he was too.

"And Mag got home a while ago," she went on. "We should probably come up for air and go see if the Rockies won."

This meant, go out and start laying the groundwork to find out what kind of guy Mag was so she could set him up with the right woman.

Mo grinned at her.

Lottie knew he knew what was on her mind and she grinned back.

He touched his mouth to that grin, pulled away and muttered, "Gotta do one thing first."

"Okay, baby," she replied.

He kept her close and reached an arm beyond her to his nightstand, tagging his phone.

He brought it back, engaging the screen, letting it see his face then he rolled to his back, taking Lottie with him so she was draped down his side.

She rested her cheek on his shoulder and commenced drawing random patterns on his chest.

Mo suddenly wasn't all that hungry.

He hit the phone button on his screen and made his call.

"Well, hello, Mo, so glad you called. This means I can talk Trine down from sending out a search party."

Mo smiled at the ceiling.

"Hey, Ma."

He felt Lottie tip her head to look up at him.

He kept his eyes on his ceiling.

"How are things?" his mother asked.

"Things are great," he replied.

"Great?"

Her tone was a mix of surprised, dubious and concerned.

To say his mother was not in the dark about some, if not all, of his issues was an understatement.

"Yeah, Ma, just got off a job."

"Hawk giving you some downtime?"

"Yeah. But back tomorrow," he told her. "Though after check in and debrief, hopin' he'll give me the weekend." He paused before he shared, "Listen, I met somebody."

Lottie tensed in his hold.

Complete silence from his mother.

To say Tammy and the others weren't beloved by the other women in his life was another understatement.

"And I want you and the girls to meet her," he finished.

"You...I...uh," his mother stammered.

Mo pulled Lottie further up on his chest and tipped his eyes down to her stunned face.

"You're gonna love her, Ma."

Lottie's face lost the stunned as it got soft and she slid her hand from his chest to the side of his neck.

"She's terrific," he continued.

At that, his girl's face got even softer.

He'd give her the hazy-eyed look of eating her out and making her come, and he'd love doing that as often as he could manage.

But that look right there he'd kill and die for.

"Well I'm not sure you've ever quite described one of your women as terrific, Mo."

Even his mother called him Mo, something he'd demanded around the age of six.

She'd saddled him with the name of Kim, Seamus was of his father, and even at six, he wanted nothing to do with that, so she'd relented without a fight.

Even his credit cards said Mo Morrison on them. Only his license shared that his mother had every faith upon his birth that he could handle bullies and douchebags without coming out scarred.

"That's because I'm seein' that they weren't," Mo replied.

"Well...*my*," his mom whispered.

"Can't do it this Sunday. Next Sunday?" he asked.

"I'd love to, but I think Marte's schedule has her on shift at the hospital."

"Sunday after that," Mo suggested.

"That'd work. I'll have dinner here," his mother answered.

"We can hit a restaurant."

"I'm not going to meet a woman you describe as 'terrific' in some stuffy place like a restaurant, Mo. I'll make my crab cakes."

He was not going to argue against his mother's crab cakes.

"Perfect," he muttered. Then louder, "Gotta go, Ma. Lottie's here and Mag's home from the ballgame so we're gonna get some food and hang with Mag."

Her voice went up in pitch when she asked, "She's there?"

He gave Lottie a squeeze. "Right here."

"Wow," she whispered. Then she got louder. "Mag's met her?"

"Yup."

"What does he think?"

"I got the last good one left."

Lottie pushed up and shoved her face in the other side of his neck.

There was a beat of hesitation before, sounding like she was smiling, his mom said, "Well then, Mo, I can't wait to meet her. Tell her it won't be formal. Just a family dinner."

His mother knew Mag would be a tough nut to crack.

And he was when it came to one of his buds.

Lottie had done it in about five minutes.

But Mo would not tell his girl anything like what his mother told him to say.

She was probably already walking to the hutch to pull out the china.

"I will," he lied.

"Glad you called, honey."

"Yeah, Ma. Love you and talk to you later."

"Love you too, baby boy."

He grinned, disconnected and tossed his phone to the nightstand so he could wrap both arms around his girl.

"Well, you didn't fuck around with that," she said into his neck.

"Nope."

"How nervous should I be?"

"She's gonna love you."

"How nervous should I be, Mo?"

He gave her a squeeze which got him what he wanted. She lifted her head and looked down at him.

"She's gonna love you, baby," he said gently.

She studied his face. She did it hard.

When she saw what she needed, she dipped in and kissed him.

Mo rolled her and kissed her back.

They necked for a while.

When they were done, they got up, got dressed and left the room they'd been in for five hours.

There was good soundproofing in his place. They'd heard Mag come in, but that was it. What they didn't hear was that Mag came back with Boone.

So over Chinese delivery, Lottie got Boone's version of Test the New Woman.

Mo figured, with Boone, she passed after she successfully shotgunned a beer.

It wasn't that Boone had lower standards than Mag when it came to Mo.

It was that Lottie was Lottie.

Chapter Thirteen

No Shit

Lottie

The massive spasm of his big body woke me and nearly sent me flying off his bed.

And then I wasn't teetering off the edge.

I was in Mo's arms, those arms so tight around me, I worried he'd snap my ribs.

And I couldn't breathe.

Just awake after coming out of a deep sleep, which came after a great fuck, unable to breathe, feeling the strength of him for the first time in a way that frightened me, it took me a second to figure out what the fuck was going on.

But I heard Mo's breathing, felt his skin was hot and clammy, and I figured it out.

"Okay," I pushed out. "It's okay. It's okay, baby. I'm right here. Right here. You're home. In bed. With me."

His arms got tighter.

Was he even awake?

I couldn't tell in the dark in his bedroom.

I forced my hands under his arms, shoved them up his chest and grasped either side of his neck.

"Mo, honey," I called.

He rolled into me, giving me all his weight.

All of it.

And his arms hadn't loosened.

God, he was going to suffocate me.

"Mo, baby." I squeezed out the words as I squeezed his neck. "Wake up."

"Awake," he grunted, putting his weight into his arms at my back, taking some of it from me, at the same time relaxing his hold.

I sucked in a big breath.

"Shit," he whispered. "Fuck," he said.

Then he let me go and rolled to his back.

Instantly, I rolled into him, climbing him, my chest to his, the rest of my body falling off his side.

"Dream?" I asked quietly.

"Christ," he replied.

I gave it time, carefully moving my hand to hold his neck and stroking his throat with my thumb.

When his breath came easier and some of the tension went out of his body, I tried again.

"Was it a dream, honey?"

"Yeah," he said to the ceiling.

It was the Sunday, the morning of the night I was going to meet his family.

In the ensuing two weeks, I'd met all his buds (and all of them were as awesome as Mag was). I'd hung with all of his buds (and hanging with all of them was as awesome as hanging with Mag was). He'd had dinner with my family. I'd gone back to the club. He'd been put on some surveillance job where, fortunately, he worked nights so he was working when I was working which meant we had most of our time together.

Though the first night I was onstage, Axl, Auggie and Mag were sitting front row to the side.

Not to watch me strip.

To make sure I was good my first night without Mo at my back.

Boone was working some other job.

Vance, Hector and Ren with their women, Jules, Sadie and Ally, as well as my sister, by the way, were sitting at the table next to them.

Eddie was at home with the boys (doing this avoiding having to watch me dance).

Jet, Jules, Sadie and Ally watched me dance.

Vance, Hector and Ren engaged in an apparently deep conversation while I danced.

I was loved.

And it was good to be loved.

But now, I wasn't feeling that goodness.

For nearly a month, being officially together for a two and a half weeks of that, Mo and I spent all our time together when we weren't working. We slept at his house, or mine, depending on a variety of factors.

He had a razor, shave cream and bodywash in my bathroom and a drawer and a rail full of clothes in my closet.

I doubled up on *all* my stuff, including a ton of makeup, a hairdryer and curling irons (that was fun, more fun, Mo was a man who didn't mind shopping—I had his sisters to thank for a lot, something I was going to get a chance to do that night). And since his big master closet was far from full, I'd filled my own rail and two drawers.

Neither of us was fucking around.

This was it.

He was the one.

I was his one.

And both of us knew it.

It hadn't been years, but we now had some time in and in that time, not once since Mo started sleeping at my side did he get up before seven in the morning.

No nightmares.

All good.

Until now.

And I had no clue what to do.

"You wanna talk about it?" I asked.

"No," he answered.

"Do you need to go work out or something?"

"Maybe."

"Wanna fuck?" I offered.

"Lottie, you don't have to fuck me every time I have a bad dream."

He sounded short and impatient, something I'd never heard from Mo.

"You've never had a bad dream," I pointed out. "And besides, in case you missed it, I wouldn't mind."

He lifted a long arm so he could rub his face with his hand.

I bent my neck and put my mouth to his skin.

"Really, babe, love you, but I don't want to associate your mouth on me after dreams like that," he announced.

But I arrested.

Really, babe, love you.

Love you.

He loved me.

Loved me.

His other hand came to the small of my back and drifted up until his fingers were in my hair.

"Go back to sleep. I'm gonna go to the gym," he muttered.

"Okay," I whispered, though no way in hell I was going to be able to go back to sleep.

He pulled me further up his chest, gave me a closed-mouth kiss and rolled me to the bed.

He threw back the covers and got out but tossed them over me and pulled them high up my shoulder before he walked to the bathroom.

He didn't turn on the light until the door was mostly closed.

Mo was a man who didn't turn the light on until the door was mostly closed when the room he left was dark and his woman was in bed in that room.

He was a man who pulled the covers up high to my shoulder.

Mo was a man who loved me.

Loved me.

I didn't feign sleep and Mo knew I didn't after he left the bathroom, went to the closet, put on workout clothes and came right to the bed to smooth my hair back before touching his lips to my temple.

"We'll go out and get breakfast when I come back," he murmured and gave my hair a soft tug. "Try to get some more sleep."

And then he was gone.

I lay in bed, unable to do what he asked (get more sleep), making plans of reading websites and finding books and bucking up so next time this happened, I'd have some tools to deal with it that could help Mo.

I was feeling this was a decent plan, but not feeling much better (except about the part that he loved me, *loved me*, and said it), when I heard noises coming from the kitchen.

You couldn't hear much in Mo's place, even if Mo and Mag's rooms were both right off the open-plan living space, just on opposite ends of the condo.

Though if it was early, silent, you were jazzed and not entirely in a good way and had already made your plan about how you were going to help your boyfriend with his PTSD so your mind wasn't jammed up, you could hear.

I got up, dashed to the walk-in, tore off my nightie, threw on some sleep shorts, a bralette and a cami, darted to the bathroom to take care of business, wash my hands, slap water on my face and brush my teeth.

Then I walked out.

Two Sundays ago, in the morning, Mo and I had been confronted with something Mo warned me later I'd see a lot of at his place: one of Mag's girls. A pretty brunette who spent the time Mag allowed her before getting her ass out of the condo to take her home looking at him like she was wondering if she should tranquilize him so she could successfully put a ball and chain on his ankle.

She hadn't been seen again.

That said, last Sunday morning, we'd met a redhead. She also had the ball-and-chain look.

And she, too, had been hustled out the door by Mag so he could take her home.

The good news was, he was not a man who made them Uber it.

The bad news was, he was a Slam Bam Thank You Ma'am Man.

Mo explained, unnecessarily, this was about Nikki. He'd been rabidly faithful to Nikki, and with any woman he was seeing, staunchly monogamous.

But now, his bud was attempting to fuck Nikki's memory away.

This was doomed to fail. I knew it. Mo knew it. Mag probably knew it. Though it was clear he needed this pointed out so he not only knew it subconsciously, but also consciously, and then he could stop breaking hearts all over Denver doing it.

I wasn't prepared to get into that just then.

I wanted to take care of the Denver sisterhood at the same time help Mag over his heartbreak, but…

Priorities.

Luckily, right then, I didn't have Mag's latest random piece of ass.

I had Mag, Auggie and Boone filling camelbacks with water (Mag) and downing a protein-load breakfast (Auggie and Boone) which, along with them all wearing various forms of running gear, shared with me they were going to take to the streets.

"Is there a marathon I don't know about?" I asked in greeting, and got three big, white smiles.

Just to share, Mag was nearly as tall as Mo, built tough, but lean, and he had a mess of black hair that was longish, prone to wave, curl, flip and often fell in his eyes in a way that he knew worked so good, or he'd tame that mane. This was paired with rugged, rough-hewn features and electric-blue eyes.

Boone, on the other hand, was pure, classic male beauty. The angles of his face could have been drawn by Michelangelo. The cut of his cheekbones probably had numerous poems written about them. They definitely had countless orgasms attributed to them (amongst other things about him). He had dark blond hair that was a thick swath on top, short on the sides and brilliant green eyes.

Oh yeah, and he was tall and built, but instead of being Mo's six five, or Mag's six four, he was probably around six two.

Auggie had not turned out to be a disappointment. It was no wonder women treated him like a god. Thick black hair that curled quite a bit around his neck, black eyes, olive skin, dense brows with a perfect arch, long stubble, sublime nose with slightly flared nostrils and a generous mouth, even I would be down with worshiping at the altar of him. And I had all that was Mo.

He was slim, not slight. Sinewy. Not an ounce of body fat on him (not that the others had any). And he was the shortest of the bunch, including Axl. Auggie probably measured in at six one, whereas Axl slotted in at number three, behind Mo and Mag, who, at my guess, was six three.

In normal circumstances, this was a lot to take in of a morning.

At that time, I didn't even think about it.

"Mornin', Mac," Boone said.

"Yo, Lots," Auggie said.

"Hey, girl," Mag said. "Want some breakfast?"

"Mo and I are going out later," I told Mag. "But thanks."

Mag looked to Mo's door.

"Trail run," Auggie declared, and my gaze went to him.

"Sorry?"

"Going up into the mountains to do a trail run, babe," he said, shoving a sausage link into his mouth, biting off a chunk, chewing a bit and saying through it, "Not a marathon."

"Oh. Right," I muttered, standing at the side of the island.

"Mo still asleep?" Mag asked, not hiding, if Mo was, Mag would be surprised.

I looked right into his eyes. "No. He's working out."

Mag stared right into mine.

He knew why Mo was off working out when I was in his bed.

They all knew.

They had a trail to conquer.

And I had a mission.

An important one.

So no fucking around.

"He had a dream," I told Mag.

The relaxed feel of the room took a hike as I watched Mag's handsome face grow troubled.

Okay, so they were also in the know about Mo's dreams.

"I knew about them, he told me. But it's his first with me," I shared to Mag.

"Right," he muttered.

"I didn't know what to do," I admitted.

Mag turned his attention to the men sitting on stools at his island.

I did too.

"Do you guys dream?" I asked straight out.

Auggie was studying Mag.

Boone shook his head at me.

"It's just Mo who gets the dreams," Mag told me.

Shit.

They might not be able to help.

"Mac, just be there for him, yeah?" Boone suggested.

"How do I do that?" I asked him.

"Don't tell him to get on some pill so he won't wake you up when he gets outta bed would be a good start," Auggie muttered.

God, I seriously *really* hated Tammy.

"She's not like the others, Aug," Mag clipped at his friend, then looked to me. "But Auggie's right, Lottie. So is Boone. Just be there for him. Listen if he's willing to talk. Be cool if he isn't. Press it if you can but back off if he's not down with it. And let him do what he needs to do to deal, like getting up and working out."

"And if it gets bad," Boone cut in. "Talk to one of us. We'll wade in."

"That's it?" I asked.

"You don't get it," Mag said.

I looked to him.

"And you can't get it, Lottie," he continued. "And that's good, darlin'. Seriously good. That said, it doesn't help seein' as you don't get it. What he's going through but more, why he's going through it. You have to be able to get it to help."

"Misery loves company," I replied depressingly.

"Just that, babe," Boone put in.

I stared at the marble countertop of the island, wanting to think happy thoughts, seeing as my mound of hunkalicious boyfriend loved me.

But I was not thinking happy thoughts.

Auggie caught my attention by speaking.

"You know, it helps that you give a shit, Lots. It might not feel like it. It might get frustrating. But it does help, even if you don't feel like it is. And it should get better. Mo's dreams might never fully go away. But he's been out a long time, they have gotten better since I've known him, and he's developed tools to deal with them. If he tries something new, being with you, hopefully they'll come less frequent. Just give a shit and don't give up. If it was you, he wouldn't."

No, he wouldn't.

I believed that totally.

"I like to be more hands on," I shared, and Auggie smiled.

Yep, could see a woman worshiping at the altar of that.

"That probably works too," he replied, and his smile dimmed, but didn't fade before he said, "But as awesome as you are, babe, it's not the miracle cure. And that's gonna suck for you because when you care about somebody, you think that emotion, if you give enough of it, will cure anything. It'd be fantastic if it did. But it doesn't. It won't go away because what he saw and did will never go away. He'll learn to cope with it his way, part with your help, but this is something that isn't about you."

Oh yeah.

Love and care and support not being the cure?

That was going to suck.

"Where it goes wrong is when you make him feel, whether on purpose or not, that you think you should be enough," Auggie carried on. "When you make him feel what you can give should be the only therapy he needs. That backfires because he'll know you'll be thinking that, he'll feel shit that you're thinking that, and he can't give it to you. It will add guilt to other crap he's got piled on him. All that gets twisted, for both of you, and if you're not careful, it gets twisted sometimes in a way you can't get straight."

I wondered if he knew this from experience.

I didn't ask then, and not only because I didn't get the chance.

"Sounds simple," Boone entered the discussion. "'Just be there for him.' But as you can see, it isn't. It's a challenge. But you got a leg up, Mac. Most women look at a man like Mo and it's a turn off, what they perceive as a weakness. They don't wanna know. They want him to sort himself out so he can be strong to take care of their shit. So you're already doing what you need to be doing. It just doesn't feel like it."

I glared at Boone while he spoke, and when he was done talking, declared, "I totally should have torn Tammy's hair out when I had the chance. Stupid Mo. He made me stand down. If I see that bitch again, it's gonna make my fights with my sister seem like a cakewalk. And both Jet and I have *grips of steel*."

"We'll arrange a takedown," Mag offered, now not looking troubled, only looking amused. "One condition. We all get to be there to watch."

"Grip of steel," Boone muttered. "Mo is one serious lucky fuck."

That made me feel better.

Slightly.

But it made me feel better.

I shot Boone a smile and said to them all, "Don't clean the kitchen before you go. I'll need something to do waiting for Mo to get back."

"I went to the store yesterday. Does this mean, while you're waiting, you're gonna adjust all the smartwater and Nakeds in the fridge so they're facing forward like you did on Tuesday?" Mag inquired.

"Of course," I answered.

"Can I clone you?" Mag asked.

"No," I answered through a smile.

"Bummer," he muttered through his own smile.

I headed to the stove to grab the greasy skillet, ordering, "Eat. Go take on the mountain. But leave some of it for other nature lovers."

They did the first part.

But before they took off to do the last, I got warm hugs and a few kisses on the top of my head (this relaying precisely how much it meant to them I gave a shit about Mo, which in turn relayed to me precisely how much they loved Mo), and Auggie, the last one out the door, called to me, "Everything's gonna go good tonight, Lots. But we'll see you later for the pep talk."

Later for the pep talk?

"Be cool," he bid and then the door closed on him.

Again, *pep talk*?

They were gone, so I couldn't ask, and they thought I was awesome, and they might not think that if I ran to the door, opened it and shrieked, "*What do you mean, pep talk? Do I need a pep talk?*"

So I didn't do that.

I cleaned the kitchen.

And I tidied the fridge.

All while I waited for Mo.

* * * *

"Be better if you were in here with me," Mo groused.

He might be right.

But from where I was sitting on the bathroom counter watching him in the shower, he was *so very wrong.*

"I already took a shower," I reminded him.

"Another reason we're gonna have words," he muttered irritably.

"Dude, you totally cheated me by falling for me and then catching the bad guy before I had the chance to sit in the bathroom while you showered. Throw a girl a bone," I replied.

His silver eyes turned to me while water sluiced his big body, making it all wet and slippery.

"I would, if you got your ass in the fuckin' shower with me."

I grinned at him.

He scowled at me and turned back to face the water.

I settled in to enjoy the show.

He'd squirted bodywash in his hands and was rubbing it on himself when I said, "You know, I have no clue if I would have fallen for you before you went into the Army."

Slowly, his arms crossed on his wide chest, his hands soaping his pits, he stopped moving except he turned his head to look at me.

I kept talking.

"Though my guess, no. Because back then, you wouldn't be Mo. Not *my* Mo. The Mo I need you to be. I'm sure you were still awesome. But not as awesome as you are now. And it's not I'll take the bad with the good when it comes to dealing with shit, like your dreams. It's that it's all good. It's all *you.* It's who you are and what you did and how you come to me. And I'll take it all, Mo. Because I want it all. Who you are and what you did and how you come to me is precisely what I need you to be."

Mo said nothing and remained unmoving.

"Just so you know, the boys were here having breakfast after you took off. I talked to them. About your dreams."

This did not make him appear to be pissed or even annoyed.

He just kept staring at me.

"I don't want to talk about you, have you find out and have you thinking it was done behind your back," I explained. "They told me some stuff, but not anything I wouldn't have done anyway. So we'll just get this out there right now, so it's there and over. If you want to talk about your dreams, I'll listen. If you don't want to talk about your dreams, I won't push. If you need to get up and go the gym, I don't care. If you need to do anything, save injecting heroin, to deal, I'm at your back, on your side or whatever you need. But if shit gets extreme and you aren't talking to me about it, I'm going to the boys. There it is. You cool with that?"

Mo didn't speak or move.

"You cool with that, honey?" I pushed.

He finally spoke.

"Get in the shower, Lottie."

"I already took one, baby," I whispered.

"Get. In the *shower*. *Lottie*," he said a lot lower, a lot slower and in a way one part of me didn't have to get in the shower to get wet.

I hopped off the counter and took off the shorts, panties, tank and bra I put on after I showered.

Then I got in the shower with him.

Waiting for Mo, I'd had time to shower.

I had not had time to do my hair.

I didn't think about that.

I didn't because Mo's hands were under my arms, I was lifted up and pulled around, my back slammed against the tile, and Mo was pressing into me.

"Legs around my back," he ordered.

We'd had the talk. Absolutely. Since Tammy had cheated on him, he'd gotten tested. He was clean and didn't go in ungloved with the two chicks he'd had since her.

Before him, I'd had a long dry spell and was on birth control.

So after I wrapped my legs around his back, Mo wrapping a fist around his big dick, guiding it to me and thrusting right in was just about him and me.

Him and me.

"Love me?" I whispered as I held on with all I had and did that *everywhere*.

His mouth took mine in a hot, wet, *long* kiss.

After he broke it, he grunted, "Yeah."

That was when I gave it to him.

"Love you too, baby."

"No shit?"

Uh.

Wait.

What?

No shit?

What did he mean, *no shit?*

"Is that what you say when I first tell you I love you?" I demanded to know, though it came out "Is THAT what you SAY when I FIRST tell you I LOVE YOU?" seeing as I took his powerful thrusts while demanding it so his cock forced every few words to be louder.

"Words don't mean dick, Lottie. You've been showin' me you love me since you threw down with Tammy. Now shut up, babe, and get fucked."

I glared at him.

His hips dipped and rolled.

I bit my lip and stopped glaring at him.

Mo grinned at me.

He was still doing it when he kissed me.

And he fucked me.

We both came.

After, I helped him finish washing up.

I'd watch him shower to fruition some other time.

Or I wouldn't.

It didn't matter.

I could have what I wanted with Mo anytime I wanted it.

I knew that to my soul.

So either way was good with me.

Chapter Fourteen

Dream Girl

Lottie

I raced down my steps as best I could wearing only one shoe, and turned into the living room.

My ears had not deceived me in what they heard while I got dressed upstairs.

The boys had arrived.

Hot guy action was everywhere.

Axl stretched on my couch.

Auggie lounged crossways across my armchair.

Boone sitting on my counter in the kitchen.

Mag with his head in my fridge.

And Mo standing in the kitchen, wearing a dove gray shirt with a sheen that made it almost silver, dark gray trousers, head tipped back, corded throat on display through his open collar, downing water from a black Hydro Flask.

I did not have it in me to react to all this goodness in my living room and kitchen, even Mo looking extra *double* hot wearing nice clothes and downing water in a way I got that view of his throat.

We were leaving in five minutes for his mom's and I was in a state.

"Babe, what the fuck? You don't have beer?" Mag stated after pulling his head out of the fridge.

"I only drink beer on special occasions or at your place," I replied.

He stared at me saying, "That's impossible."

"Crib is tight, Lots," Auggie told me as I rushed by him (or limped by him on one spike heel, one bare foot, clutching my other shoe to my chest as well as the bag I was switching out to).

"Thanks," I muttered to Auggie.

Mo had come out from behind the Hydro and was staring at me in a way that, if we weren't imminently going to dinner at his mom's, and his buds weren't hanging around being hot, I would be on my back on the kitchen floor getting fucked.

Good to know he liked the dress.

But I couldn't even let that penetrate.

"How can you not drink beer?" Mag demanded to know.

"She's fit, asshole," Axl called. "That's how. Not everyone has your metabolism and a cast-iron liver."

"Mac, babe, seriously, that calendar on your fridge," Boone said to me as I dumped all that was in my hands on the counter by his hip.

I looked up at him.

"What?" I asked.

"Three-month oil changes?" He shook his head. "Check your manual. Unless you drive a Chrysler Lebaron circa nineteen eighty-two, it's either five thousand or seven thousand. Sometimes even ten. That three-month or three-thousand-mile gig is totally overkill."

"I just *knew* that was a scam," I snapped.

He grinned at me. "Good you now got men in your life who'll look out for you."

I already had men in my life who looked out for me.

But none of them told me about the oil-change scam.

I would have words with Eddie.

Then Tex.

Later.

At that moment, I needed to freak out.

"Can I ask when my woman became all of your woman?" Mo requested to know from behind me, and he didn't sound happy.

"Until we get our own," Mag answered breezily. "You know sister wives? We're like brother husbands."

"No you aren't."

There was my man's Brook No Argument Tone.

"Without the benefits, of course," Mag added.

"Lottie, babe, step up the matchmaking shit," Mo ordered, leaning hips against the counter beside me as I reached to my purse so I could switch out what I needed to my clutch.

But I felt it, that "it" was strong, and I had to stop what I was doing to look around.

I turned my head side to side to see everyone's attention on me.

Even Axl had pushed up on my couch so he could look around the back of it my way.

"Matchmaking shit?" Boone asked.

"Lottie's gonna set you boys up," Mo told them.

I was?

"Let them be strippers. Please, God, if you love me even a little bit, let them be strippers," Mag prayed, head tipped back, eyes to my ceiling and everything.

"Actually, Mag, we have a girl working her way through college at the club. She wants to be an engineer. And she'd be *so* your thing," I told him.

His eyes came to me. "An engineer?"

"Software."

Mag started to look like he might be quietly choking.

He clearly was when his next words sounded strangled. "A computer nerd?"

"Yep," I said and turned back to my purse, trying not to smile.

Though I would never, in a million years, introduce Evan to him. He was a dawg. He was hot and he was funny and he loved Mo and he was sweet to me.

But he was a dawg.

And Evie was very pretty, in an understated way, when she didn't have teased-out hair and wasn't (somewhat awkwardly, she never got the hang of it, but she was so pretty, it didn't matter) slithering on a stage with bills poking out of her g-string.

I already felt bad enough—for Mag *and* the women he involved—that Mag was working out his heartbreak from Nikki by tapping as much ass as he could to block out the pain.

Mo had told me she was the reason he needed a place to live. Nikki and Mag broke up three weeks before Tammy and Mo broke up. He'd been sleeping on Axl's couch, until Mo's breakup saved him from chronic back pain.

I wasn't going to subject Evan to his This All Could Be Yours If Some Other Woman Hadn't Fucked Me Up Routine.

Until…

"No offense to your friend, but I'll pass," Mag told me.

That bought him my attention again.

My attention with squinty eyes.

"You got a problem with smart girls?" I asked sharply.

"Well…" he shrugged, "yeah."

I couldn't believe my ears.

"Why?" I rapped out.

"Babe, if they're smart, they can figure you out. Not everyone is level-headed, even keeled and adjusted like Mo," Mag returned. "I don't need some smart girl figuring out my shit. *I* can't even figure out my shit. What I know is, my shit is such shit, I don't *want* it figured out."

"Has it occurred to you that if you had a smart girl around, she might help you with that?" I asked.

"As he said, this would require him wanting his shit sorted, and Mag prefers to be a hot mess," Axl declared. "And not because he doesn't want to figure out his shit. Because him not doing that is a woman magnet."

"The broken one they think they can fix," Auggie added.

"Better that than the lost puppy," Mag fired at Auggie.

"That's me," he said through a grin. "All ready to go to a good home. Happy just to be fed and watered. But I'll perform for treats."

I looked to Mo. "How do you put up with this shit?"

"It's a lot easier to tune out when I got a beer in my hand and some game is on TV," he replied.

I'd bet.

"What are you all doing here anyway?" I asked the boys.

"Moral support," Axl said.

"Preparing you for the Morrison women onslaught," Boone said at the same time.

Onslaught?

There was going to be an onslaught?

Every fiber of my body grew tight.

"Jesus Christ, when are you motherfuckers gonna stop being scared of my sisters?" Mo demanded to know.

Scared?

These badass commandos were *scared* of Mo's sisters?

"When they stop bein' scary," Mag pointed out.

"You get, Mag, that they're only scary because they've figured out your shit," Mo returned.

"Yeah. There you go. Fuckin' *terrifying*," Mag replied.

"Ohmigod, ohmigod, ohmigod," I chanted.

Here I was again.

Nervous!

I'd met boyfriends' families. And okay, if I cared about them, I got nervous.

But not like this.

No other way to say it.

I was a wreck.

"I'm gonna kill every motherfucking one of you," Mo threatened, sounding like he'd do it.

After he did, I felt his fingers curl around my chin and he used them to pull my head around and tip it back.

I blinked up at him.

"Look at me, sweetheart," he urged gently.

"I am," I choked out nervously.

"Okay, *focus* on me," he amended.

I tried to do that.

When I somewhat succeeded, I felt the boys had surrounded me.

"It's gonna be fine," Mo declared.

"What if they don't like me?" I asked. "I can't have them not liking me, Mo. They're part of you. They're blood. They're *sisters*. I have a sister!" My voice was rising with the increased beating of my heart which was keeping pace with the increased level of my panic. "I know how important sisters are! If they don't like me, I'm gone. I can't have that. Ohmigod!" That last was nearly yelled. "You beat up your dad for one of them. If they don't like me, I'm not even a memory."

I lost his attention as his eyes slid up and did a half circle and his lips growled, "Yup. Gonna kill every motherfucking one of you."

"Babe," I heard Boone call.

I pulled my chin from Mo's hold only to have my body tucked into Mo's hold a different way (this being with his arm) as I turned my head to look up at Boone.

"You may or may not believe this. Regardless, it's true," Boone started. "To get Mo, the tougher wall you had to climb was us."

He jerked his chin to the others and I shifted in Mo's clinch so I had my back to his front and I could take them all in.

"You might not have noticed, you bein' you, together like you are, sure of yourself, but I threw down with you practically the minute I laid eyes on you," Mag reminded me.

He did that. It was semi-subtle, in the sense it was not like getting hit by a freight train, more like getting hit by a bus.

But he did it.

"I know," I told him.

"You won me over in about a minute," Mag told me something I knew at the time, and was happy about at the time, but being reminded of it in *this* time made me feel a whole lot better.

He wasn't done.

"It was you bein' pissed Mo's dad is a dick. It was hearing about you takin' on Tammy. It was you bein' hilarious. It was knowin' we were gonna have a beautiful woman among us who was also one of the guys. But most of all, it was the way you were with Mo. First time at our place, it was like you'd been there a hundred times before and you two were just chill." Mag shot me a grin. "Outside you shoutin' about his dad. Mo was goin' through his mail and you were shoutin' about his dad and you were all about him. I had to push it, 'cause he's my boy. But I didn't have to push hard."

"For me," Axl put in, "it was the fact I was worried I wouldn't get out of your house before you jumped on his dick."

I couldn't help but smile at him.

"I wasn't even there for you," Axl went on quietly. "He walked in, and suddenly, everything was gone, including me. You were all about him."

"Axl told us that," Auggie added. "Before Mag even met you."

All the rest I knew.

But that last was news.

"We don't trust people easy, Lottie," Mag said. "But the people who might become a part of the lives of one of our own, that's worse."

"I'm sure sisters can be tough to crack," Boone shared. "They might not show it, but brothers…"

Boone let that hang but I understood him.

They weren't brothers of the blood, and blood was thicker than water, but doing what they did for a living, all having served before, the trust that had to build, the men those experiences had made them, what they had was stronger than steel.

"We're here right now, for you, and we've known you two weeks," Auggie reminded me. "The Morrison women are gonna love you, Lots. You got nothing to worry about."

I felt Mo's arm tight around me, holding me to the strength of his big body.

And I saw all Mo's boys around me, giving me strength.

I'd fallen for Mo.

And along the way, I started falling for all of them too.

I looked at Mag.

"Evie for you. She's a nerd. But she's gonna sort your shit."

Mag blinked.

I looked to Auggie.

"Pepper for you. Just trust me on her. Perfect."

My attention went to Axl. "Hattie. You'll flip your shit for her. And she totally won't for you. You'll have to work for it. But she'll make it worth it."

Axl tipped his head to the side, openly intrigued.

Finally, I turned to Boone.

As suspected from nuanced vibes I was getting from him, there was something guarded in his expression, and I wasn't sure if it was me he didn't want to see it, or the others.

So I went out on a limb he didn't know was a limb.

"Ryn," I stated. "Kathryn. She'll be beyond your wildest dreams. Your *wildest* dreams, Boone."

There was a flash of understanding that told me I'd guessed correctly, and I moved quickly in order not to allow the others to catch it.

I'd have that conversation with Boone later.

Alone.

I turned in Mo's arm, looked up at him and said, "I just need to finish sorting my purse and get my shoe on, baby. Then I'm ready to roll."

Mo looked down at me a beat.

Then he smiled.

Pep talk delivered, I was good to go.

Still smiling, Mo dipped way down to touch his lips to mine and let me go.

I sorted my purse, but it was Mo who crouched down to put on my shoe.

And with hugs and kisses on the top of my head from the guys while standing by Mo's truck, and promises from Mag that the next time they came over, he'd bring beer, we were on our way.

* * * *

I was not surprised at Mo's mom's house.

He'd told me, in order to raise five children after his father ditched them without doing them the favor of actually ditching them, his mom worked hard to become a CPA. She'd semi-retired the year before, a partner in a big firm in town. She still worked VIP clients, two to three days a week, because if she didn't, she'd go crazy seeing as she didn't knit, paint, birdwatch (or the like).

She'd also downsized houses after Mo had entered the Army out of high school years ago.

So the brick Park Hill bungalow with the pergola over the front porch, brick path, thick, green lawn and tidy but not effusive landscaping that included black-eyed Susans in their final blooms was expected.

Sadly, by the time Mo parked behind a shiny Chevy Silverado, the pep talk had worn off.

This was the reason Mo turned to me and took my hand.

I gave him my gaze.

"The men hated Tammy," he announced. "They hated the ones before her that they knew. And they didn't hide it. Part of me was pissed at 'em. Those relationships weren't working and the way the guys treated the woman in my life, it didn't help."

I didn't like to think of how even one of them not liking me would feel.

Fortunately, I didn't have to.

"But I gotta admit, they were right," he went on. "I should have ended things. Lookin' back, havin' you, I see that now. But they already knew it. They knew I didn't have what I deserved. Now I know, and they know I do. With that, do you think, the minute they meet you, Ma and my sisters won't feel the same way?"

I loved what he was saying to me.

I loved that he found it in him to say it to me.

I still knew I needed to win over the women in that house, not for me. For Mo.

But I leaned into him and replied, "I'm glad you now know what you deserve, honey. And I hope I always give you that."

"I don't hope it, I know you will," he returned, came to me, kissed me hard but closed-mouthed, and pulled away. "You ready?"

I was not.

I nodded.

He let me go, shifted to open his door but turned back to me.

"I help you out."

"Right, okay," I whispered.

It was then Mo nodded.

It felt funny sitting there, waiting for Mo to help me from his truck, but it felt nice when he did.

Like I was what I was by Mo—loved and looked after.

We were halfway up the walk when the front door was opened by a blonde woman who was tall—not as tall as Mo, but really freaking tall, and built—not like Mo, of the feminine, curvy variety.

She took one look at me and shouted, "Holy crap! That dress!" She then turned her head back toward the house and kept shouting. "I'm going on a diet immediately! After crab cakes, of course. And meringue cake, of course again!"

With my dress, I'd gone black. I only had clingy because I only did clingy. It was sleeveless and halter neck with a racer back. It was also mid-thigh with a small slit on the left side.

It was me.

And I thought they should know who I was, no matter how nervous I was about it.

The woman at the door turned back to us as we walked up the three steps to the porch then immediately back to the house she yelled, "She's teeny! And she's *everything*."

Oh my *God*.

I wasn't exactly teeny.

But I was beyond thrilled she'd taken one look at me and described me as *everything*.

Before I could feel the fullness of this relief, Mo ordered, "Marte, quit shouting."

"Mo, get her in here," Marte ordered right back. "Mom wouldn't let us touch the hors d'oeuvres until Lottie arrived and she made mini-corn muffins and smoked salmon sandwiches. You know Taylor isn't into fancy food, but he's into eating, and since he hasn't since lunch, he's getting cranky. As for me, if I don't eat something soon, I'm gonna kill somebody."

"Right then," Mo returned, and now we were standing on the welcome mat in front of her. "You wanna get out of the door so we can actually come in?"

"'Course," she replied, but didn't do that. She pushed a hand my way and said, "Hey, I'm Marte. And I'm the least annoying one, no matter what Mo says to you."

"That's a lie," Mo muttered.

I took her hand, smiling because this night was starting a whole lot different than I expected.

"Hi, I'm Lottie."

"Jeez, Marz, what's with the bar-the-door routine?" another tall, blonde, built woman asked, doing this while physically shoving Marte out of the way only to take her place. "Hey, I'm Lene and I'm just gonna say right now, Rick brought his poster of you. And if you don't want to sign it, just don't. I told him it was rude. Not at the first dinner. Not when Mom's making us dress up and demanded we get babysitters. More like when Paul has his Columbus Day barbeque. And heads up, Paul uses every excuse to barbeque. So that's not weird, *for him*. Labor Day, Memorial Day, Veterans Day, totally Fourth of July. Even Halloween. He tried to barbeque a turkey for Thanksgiving once, and Signe lost her mind."

I couldn't help but stare at her, but when she stopped talking, I asked, "Your husband has a poster of me?"

"Don't be nervous," she advised quickly. "He's not a stalker or anything. He's just a huge fan of those *Rock Chick* books. I swear, I nearly had to take him to the hospital, he was laughing so hard at the part where your sister goes to the poker games with her girls." She leaned toward me. "He's gonna ask you to ask them to sign his books. Don't feel weird about telling him to shove off about that either. I got you, girl."

I kept staring at her.

They knew who I was.

They knew what I did.

And she was okay with her husband having a poster of me.

I had a variety of posters from back in my Queen of the Corvette calendar heyday.

And in *most* of them I was clothed.

Albeit scantily.

"Do you mind if I actually take my woman *in* the house?" Mo requested, sounding beleaguered. "Or does one of you wanna bring a plate of corn muffins out here?"

"Oh, right, sorry," Lene said, then grabbed my hand, and I could do anything in heels, but I nearly tripped at the strength of her dragging me inside, inviting, "Come in, come in." She barely got me a foot into the living room when she yelled, "Look everybody! Lottie's here!"

There were no children, and I would realize later this was about Mo's mom not wanting to bombard me with all that was her family.

What was in that living room was enough.

At first glance, it was innocuous. Women in lovely dresses. Men in trousers and shirts, like Mo. Classy platters of elegant-looking food. Candlelight. Sinatra on low in the background.

She'd gone all out.

The whole thing was the shit.

And every Morrison sister had the same look, so much so, they didn't appear to be just sisters, but quadruplets.

They also had the same type.

Their men were all tall and huge (if not bald), like their brother Mo.

I met Signe, Trine, Paul, Taylor, Rick, and finally, Ingrid, Mo's mom.

She folded my hand in both of hers and gently moved me further into the room, saying, "It's so lovely to have you here, Lottie. Thank you for coming."

"Really, my pleasure," I murmured. "Thank you for asking me here."

She nodded charmingly, giving me a graceful smile, and asked, "Now, what can Mo get you to drink?"

"I'm having a John Collins. Make her a John Collins, Mo," Marte ordered.

"Sidecar," Signe demanded. "Mo makes *the best* sidecars."

"Singapore sling," Lene declared. "But let Taylor make it. He's the master of the sling."

"Margarita," Trine said. "I already made a pitcher, Mo."

Mo let them all say this then looked down to me and lifted his brows.

"Margarita sounds good," I told him.

He nodded, gave me a small smile, bent to me and touched his lips to mine.

He then walked to the bar cart.

Ingrid had an actual bar cart.

Total class.

Totally the shit.

"Can we eat now?" Taylor demanded to know.

"Yes, Taylor," Ingrid said serenely.

Instantly Taylor, Rick and Paul fell on the hors d'oeuvres like they hadn't eaten in a year.

I almost burst out laughing.

"Would you like me to wade in and make you a plate, Lottie?" Ingrid offered. "Before the trough expires."

"Don't you eat all those corn muffins, Rick!" Lene snapped at her husband before I could answer her mother. "Those are Mo's favorites."

"They're mine too," Rick retorted to his wife, mouth full of corn muffin.

"Save him five," Lene returned sharply.

Rick gave a harassed look to Taylor.

Taylor didn't field it. He was busy shoving a muffin in his mouth.

"Mo, now that you're seeing someone famous, you need more shirts like that," Trine decided, eying her brother's awesome shirt.

She then turned to me.

"You'll probably be doing fancy stuff and he'll have to come along, which he won't want to do because it'll be stuff like book signings and movie premieres. But he'll do it because he's Mo and you'll be wearing hot dresses like that one. Though probably it'll be more because you'll be wearing hot dresses like that one. We'll go shopping. He looks *fabulous* in blue. He needs more blue. He's always wearing black. Or gray. I blame Hawk for that."

I didn't tell her I didn't attend book signings or that there hadn't been any movie premieres.

I didn't because I didn't get the chance.

"Hawk doesn't buy his clothes, Treenz," Marte rejoined.

"He promotes an environment that's manifestly *male*, Marz," Trine shot back. "If given the choice, men would only wear black, gray and army green."

At that, Paul looked down at his burgundy shirt before he muttered to Rick, "Could have sworn I hauled my own fuckin' ass out to buy this."

Rick grinned before shoving a mini-smoked salmon sandwich in his mouth.

"Speaking of that," Signe put in, ignoring this exchange, "when is Hawk going to hire a female commando, Mo?"

Walking back to me with my margarita that was in an actual salt-rimmed, stemmed margarita glass that was the only one of the pure-class variety I'd ever seen, Mo didn't have a chance to answer.

Lene did it before him.

"Never. He's *never* gonna hire a woman. Except Elvira."

"This is because Elvira's more woman than fifty women," Marte mumbled under her breath.

"That's for certain," Trine agreed.

"I would not wish those boys on any woman," Marte said. "Except Elvira. She's the only one who can handle them."

"It's still hardly equal opportunity," Signe pointed out.

"Seenz, you think Hawk has ever given the concept of 'equal opportunity' even a second's thought?" Lene asked.

The four sisters looked among each other, and then on a sister wavelength, in unison, they burst out laughing.

Though I didn't know Hawk very well, I did have firsthand knowledge he was a purveyor of quality badass and I wouldn't think he'd discriminate if he thought the job would get done.

I decided not to share this.

"Mag'd tap their ass before they even were assigned a flak jacket," Rick murmured.

"Rick!" Lene abruptly stopped laughing to snap.

"Am I wrong?" he asked.

"No!" she kept snapping. "But Danny is Mo's roommate. Don't give Lottie the impression he's a player."

That cat was out of the bag.

And…

Danny?

I was *so* going to give him shit by calling him that from this moment on.

And sharing it with Evie when the time came.

I had a margarita in my hand and Mo's heavy arm slung around my shoulder, so I coasted mine around his waist.

"Get out of my way, Paul, I'm making Mo a plate. And Lottie. I'm making Mo and Lottie a plate," Signe announced, nudging her husband out of the way and picking up a small, delicate, china plate with a graceful gold design on the edges.

"The man can feed himself," Paul muttered.

"No he can't, with all you boys guarding the food like rabid dogs," Signe fired back.

I heard Mo's quiet sigh.

I also again beat back laughter.

And last, I was understanding how Mo learned to communicate nonverbally.

He grew up with four older sisters who wouldn't let him get a word in edgewise.

I took a sip of my drink.

"Perhaps, if my girls can give Lottie the impression we've got a modicum of manners and aren't one step down from lunacy, I could sleep tonight. Rather than tossing and turning at the thought my son's new girlfriend is buying a one-way ticket somewhere very far from here to get away from *us*," Ingrid suggested smoothly before taking a sip of what appeared to be a martini with olives from a stylish glass.

Clearly, after my intro to the Morrison women, she'd retrieved her cocktail.

Actually, probably *because* I was receiving said intro, she'd *had* to retrieve her cocktail.

"And he *can* feed himself, Signe," Ingrid continued. "And as it appears Lottie has full use of all her limbs, I'm sure she can too."

Mother spoke, Signe gave big eyes to her sisters, all three of them, put a corn muffin and salmon sandwich on her plate and retreated from the coffee table where all the food was laid out.

When she did, Paul dropped a heavy arm on her shoulders.

Rick cleared his throat and started, "Lottie, if you could—"

"Don't," Lene interrupted him.

"I'm just—" Rick tried again.

"Nope," she cut him off.

"Laynz, she won't be—"

"Shut it," Lene bit.

"I'd be happy to sign your poster and ask the Rock Chicks to sign your books," I offered. "I even know the author and can ask her too. They all like doing that, so they'll be happy to and so will I."

Rick smiled big at me. "Thanks, Lottie."

"Not a problem," I told him.

He gave a look to his wife.

She rolled her eyes.

"Lottie, now that we have some calm in the storm my girls are so adept at blowing, why don't you tell us a little about you?" Ingrid invited, and then, class act that she was, guided my way, "I hear you have a mother and sister that live in town."

"Yes," I agreed.

"I'd enjoy meeting them," she replied.

"And they you. They already love Mo. I'm sure you'll be fast friends."

Her gaze darted to her son and came back to me. "They've met?"

Uh-oh.

Mo hadn't shared.

He also didn't share now.

He was nonchalantly drawing off a bottle of beer.

This meant I had to do it.

"He came to dinner at my mom's house."

"Of course they love Mo," Trine butted in. "Mo's lovable. Tammy's parents *adored* him. I think her mother is still wearing black in grief that Tammy messed that up."

"*Treenz*," Signe clipped. "Don't mention *Tammy*."

"He wasn't in a monastery before he met her, *Seenz*," Trine shot back.

"Lord save me," Ingrid whispered.

"Not that we're Catholic," Trine said over her, aiming this my way. "And not that we have a problem with Catholics. We don't. We're just not Catholic."

"I'm Catholic," Lene put in.

"Because Rick's Catholic," Trine returned.

"I'm Catholic because I'm Catholic," Lene retorted. "I just converted prior to marrying him."

"Because Rick was Catholic," Marte butted in.

"It doesn't matter," Signe snapped. "Talking about it is making Lottie think we think it matters when it doesn't." Signe looked to me. "We're cool with all races, religions and creeds. I promise."

"I wasn't worried," I assured her.

"Except white supremacists. We're not cool with that," Trine declared.

"No one's cool with that," Marte replied. "And that isn't a religion."

"It *is* a *creed*," Trine fired back.

"Right, would you four freakin' *shut it?*" Mo demanded.

All four turned to him.

Or five, since I did the same.

But he was looking down at me.

"Rewind to our talk in the truck. You got nothin' to be worried about. It seems *I* had somethin' to worry about. You findin' out my sisters are a bunch a' kooks and runnin' for the hills."

My mound of hunkalicious boyfriend looked hassled.

I smiled up at him.

"*Ohmigod*," Marte breathed, moving toward me. "You were worried, Lottie? That's *so* sweet." She threw a look over shoulder at her sisters before she drew me out from under Mo's arm and toward the coffee table. "Isn't that sweet?" she asked her sisters.

"That's *so* sweet," Lene said, crowding into me. "We don't bite, promise."

"We're just a little crazy," Marte told me, reaching to get a little plate and handing it to me.

Signe snatched up a square cloth cocktail napkin, also handing it to me, doing this saying, "We're not crazy. Crazy makes it sound bad. We're *zany*."

"Yeah, zany. Zany is good," Lene agreed. "Now let's get you some corn muffins. Mom's corn muffins are *to die for*. And she only pulls them out for the special occasions."

Special occasions.

I looked back at Mo, who had eyes on me.

He no longer looked hassled.

His sisters fussing over me, he looked happy.

I then turned my gaze to Ingrid who was moving toward Mo.

She had a small smile on her lips and this was pointed at her son.

In other words, she looked happy.

A corn muffin landed on my plate and females babbled around me while their males gravitated to Mo.

As for me?

I had Mo.

Mo had a great family.

He was giving it to me.

And that meant I was happy.

* * * *

Mo

They were on meringue cake, eating it in the living room, the women sipping Amaretto and Kahlua from his mother's snifters, sitting on his mother's couches, absorbed in woman talk.

Mo was standing with the guys, having already devoured his cake and setting the plate aside when his phone vibrated.

He pulled it out, looked at the screen and glanced to Lottie, who had her head bent way back, laughing at something Trine had said (or Lene, whatever).

"Gotta take this," he muttered to the men and moved to and out the front door.

He'd received a text.

Standing on his mother's front porch, he made a call.

"Mo," Brock Lucas answered.

"Hey, Slim," Mo greeted. "What's up?"

"We had a situation last night in lockup."

Mo drew in breath.

"This guy," Slim went on, "the one who sent those letters about Lottie, some of the other men set on him at chow and did a number on him before the guards could break it up."

Jesus shit.

"No idea why," Lucas kept going. "He's an easy mark, uptight like he is, no priors, slight, no experience lookin' out for himself, definitely not in a situation like that. They could have just scented weak blood and went after it. He'd already had some trouble bein' pushed around. Complained to the guards he'd been threatened. They put him in solitary a couple of days and the men who were causing the problem were moved out, either transferred or they made deals or bail. So they put him back in gen pop. Apparently, those men had friends and he was still a target."

"And?" Mo prompted when he didn't say more.

"They got him to the hospital and fixed him up. But in recovery, he developed a pulmonary embolism. Lost oxygen to his brain. They took him back into surgery, got that fixed too, but the damage was done."

Mo's entire body felt tight.

"What damage, Slim?"

"Man's alive, but braindead," Slim said. "He's on a respirator. Considering his inclinations, something my guess due to their reactions to the trouble he was in they suspected, his family is not tight with him. They've been called in. I don't know if they'll elect to take him off the machines. I just know, even if they don't, this man isn't gonna be in a position to hurt Lottie, or anyone. There's not a blip on him, Mo. He's breathing, but he's still gone."

Mo didn't know what he was feeling.

Because he was human, he didn't want it to be good.

But mostly it was good.

"So it's over," Mo noted.

"Not for the boys in lockup who are now also facing manslaughter charges, but for Lottie, yeah. It's over."

Yeah, what he was feeling was good.

He wondered if Smithie or Hawk had some hand in this guy being hassled in jail.

Or for that matter Lee or one of his men.

But he stopped wondering almost before he started because he really didn't care.

"Thanks for telling me, Slim," Mo said.

"Not a problem. You'll inform Lottie?"

"Absolutely," Mo told him.

"Great. Thanks. Later, Mo."

"Later."

He hung up.

He then heard the storm door open behind him.

Lottie stood in it, holding it open.

"Everything okay?" she asked, watching him closely.

"The man that sent those letters about you got jumped in lockup," he stated straight out. "They did some damage. He got an embolism which made him braindead. He's on a respirator but if they pull the plug or not, it doesn't matter. He's not coming back from that so he's no longer a threat."

She stared at him.

Mo let her and kept his eyes locked on her as she did.

Eventually, he asked, "You good?"

"I don't really feel anything," she replied, then asked, "Is that bad?"

"Could come up later, baby," he noted carefully.

"I'm probably the safest person on the planet," she returned. "You. The boys. My brothers. I had my freakout but then…" She shrugged. "It was already over for me before it was over *over* for him."

That was when Mo moved into her, entering the house pushing her back into it with him and letting the storm door hiss shut as he pulled her in his arms.

She slid hers around him too and gave him a squeeze.

"You good?" she asked, her head tipped back to catch his gaze.

"Totally."

Lottie took a moment to assess this.

Then she smiled.

"Everything okay?" his mother asked at their sides.

Mo looked her way and answered, "No. I need more cake."

His mom also took a moment to assess this, her silver eyes shifting back and forth between him and Lottie before she also smiled.

Tammy never got his mother taking her in with Mo and then smiling.

This was the fourth time that night he'd caught that from his ma.

He'd been right. So had his boys.

Lottie being Lottie and giving what she did to Mo, she had nothing to worry about.

"I'll go cut you one, darling," she said then she was off.

Mo moved Lottie out of the way and shut the front door.

He then walked his girl back to his family.

And got more cake.

* * * *

Lottie

As far as I could tell, Mo Morrison was great at everything he did.

But he had a particular talent with giving head.

Something right then, in my bed, he was demonstrating.

I had both hands on his smooth scalp, holding him to me, but I didn't need to do that.

He had me spread open with two fingers.

And my man was hungry.

When it happened, I hoped he got enough because he'd driven me to the edge and once there, I leaped off and went flying, coming hard in Mo's mouth.

He licked me clean like he had the rest of his night to do it and only rose up and settled over me when I gave him the sign by gliding my fingers over the top of his head.

Once in position, he pushed his face in my neck and worked me there.

I could feel his hot, hard cock pushing against my thigh.

So I encouraged, "Come inside."

Mo glided his lips up to my ear. "Gonna let you come down, play with you, work you back up, then you're gonna take it, in my lap, doggie style."

If he wanted me to come down, saying things like that didn't help.

His mouth eventually worked its way to mine and in the middle of the deep, sweet, wet kiss that tasted of him mixed liberally with me, I pressed up into him and Mo, being my Mo, got my message and took us to our sides.

He broke the kiss and murmured against my lips, "My weight too much?"

"Never," I whispered, ducking down to press my face into his throat running my hands over his warm, smooth skin, feeling the power underneath, liking the power underneath but loving that it was all mine.

I tipped my head back and kissed the underside of his jaw.

"Sweet Lottie," he said softly, cupping my ass in one hand, holding me tight with his other arm.

"Tonight was the best, Mo," I told him.

"Yeah," he agreed.

"Your family rocks," I shared.

"My mom rocks. The guys are the shit. My sisters are nutcases."

They were.

But the good kind.

"I liked them."

"Thank fuck," he mumbled.

I smiled against his skin.

And there, I informed him, "The day I met you, Smithie and I had a conversation."

I heard his head move on the pillow, so I tipped mine further back in order to catch his eyes in the moonlight.

"About what?" he asked.

"About the fact I was giving up since I hadn't found my dream man and never thought I would."

His big body grew still against mine.

"Then, hours later," I carried on, "he walks right up and knocks on my door."

It was guttural when he groaned, "Baby."

But I didn't need to hear the emotion.

I was feeling it since he was squeezing the breath out of me.

I let him, knowing he'd do what he did.

Relax his hold but keep me close.

I thought this was a good way to start the festivities back up.

But unusually in times like this (and other times besides), Mo was feeling chatty.

He shared this by saying, "You got that wrong."

"I do?"

"Not wholly, but importantly."

"How do I have that wrong?"

"I'd given up too. After Tammy, I was done. I thought it was me. I thought it was my shit that was driving them away. Then one day my boss hands me an assignment, and not an hour later, I walk right up and knock on the door to the house of my dream girl. And she made me see a lot of really fuckin' important shit differently."

"Mo," I whispered.

His big hand shifted to cup my face as his dipped closer to mine.

"I don't know what's gonna happen, baby. I know some of it probably isn't gonna be great. But who you are and what you give to me, most of it's gonna be awesome. You know I have bad dreams and they may never stop. I don't want that for me, or for you. But I can handle it a lot better now, knowin' I'll get those and wake up to my real dream, right there beside me."

It was my voice that was hoarse when I declared, "We need to fuck right now."

"Yeah, we do," he agreed.

But he didn't fuck me.

Not immediately.

He kissed me, hard, deep and for a long time.

Then he rolled me to my belly, positioned between my legs, shoved his knees deep underneath me so he was sitting back on his heels and pulled me back on his cock.

Taking him, my neck arched, I came up on my hands, and my powerhouse thrust into me.

Mo was feeling it at the same time feeling like making a seriously good memory of it, so he didn't let me control it.

To do that, he had to stop the action to switch positions so he could fuck me in a variety of different ways.

But we ended with me back in his lap, face to face, my legs up his chest, Mo on his ass, his arms around me, driving me down on his cock.

And we were kissing.

Later, I fell asleep in his arms and the last thought I had was that I'd been right.

That night was the best.

But add the end of it?

It was living the dream.

So I didn't get a Hot Bunch guy.

I got my Dream Man.

And the best of all of that…

My Dream Man got his Dream Girl.

Epilogue

"Not While I'm Around"

Lottie

I stood in my bathroom wearing some pink satin sleep pants with a cream, brown and pink striped waistband that made them look like girlie boxer shorts.

I wore nothing else.

I was staring at my breasts.

I'd had the surgery.

I'd also had the drama before the surgery.

It was same-day, even if I also got a lift to repair some of the stretch. And I was out of commission for only five days, though that was about not trying to do too much or lift anything too heavy.

The bummer was, I couldn't dance for six weeks.

That said, the whole thing wasn't that big of a deal.

However, I learned it was when I was going under the knife with Rock Chicks, Morrison Sisters, Hot Bunch and Commando Boys at my back.

But the worst was Mo.

You would think I'd had heart surgery.

There had been a standoff the day before I was scheduled to go to the hospital.

Although everyone agreed Mo would drive me and take me home, the around-the-clock care I *did not need* after all was said and done was hotly contested.

As they discussed the schedule of who would make me chicken soup, change my dressings, grocery shop and clean my house, somehow, the conversation took a turn for the worse with Morrison Sisters wanting to prove to Rock Chicks that I was one of them and Hot Bunch and Commando Boys jockeying for position as the favored brothers-not-of-the-blood in my life.

Though, for me, I would have paid to see any of those men bringing me chicken soup or running my vacuum.

That said, I would be perfectly capable of doing the first on my own, and my vacuum could hold off for long enough I could wield it myself.

By the by, through this, Mom and Ingrid sat at my dining room table, drinking coffees Tex had sent over from Fortnum's Used Books, where he was their premier barista, and chatting calmly like it wasn't happening.

It ended with Mo shouting (shouting! until that moment I'd never heard him shout), "*None* of you are gettin' anywhere *near* my woman's breasts! And *I* can and *will* feed and take care of Lottie. I got this. Back the fuck *off!*"

I learned then that when a big guy like Mo who was usually quiet and not easily ruffled bellowed, people listened.

I also learned then that there was family of a lot of different varieties.

But with that, Mo was claiming him and me (mostly me, obviously) as just *ours.*

I was sure he appreciated the love and support they were showing.

But in the end, it was just him and me.

They could bring flowers.

They could not bring me chicken soup.

In the ensuing days after the surgery, he took care of my incisions, changed my dressings, brought me food, ran the vacuum, got the mail, did the grocery shopping, wouldn't hear of me doing any of this for myself, even if I could, and didn't let me take that first peak at my breasts. Not until the volume had returned and the bruising had faded.

I'd had implants for a while, switching them out to freshen them up, because I looked great with big tits.

But now…

"Put a shirt on."

I turned at these words to see my man hulking into the bathroom.

"Mo—"

He walked to me, tagged the lacy pink bralette I'd laid out on the counter and held it my way.

"Put this on," he ordered.

My stomach plummeted, and I stared up at his gorgeous face.

"Do you like them?" I asked quietly.

He also stared down at my face.

"Of course I like 'em."

"You're not even looking at them," I pointed out.

His eyes dropped to them then came back to my face.

"You look beautiful, Lottie," he said. "You always look beautiful. It's impossible for you *not* to look beautiful."

I knew my strengths.

I knew my weaknesses.

I was pretty.

I was not beautiful.

Except to Mo.

That was sweet, incredibly sweet, and he could say that, but after my days of rest, it wasn't like we hadn't had sex in the five weeks since surgery. We did. A lot. Gentle at first. Then not so much.

From what I could see, I was fully healed.

I felt great.

And I was due to go back to work the Tuesday after next.

I was ready.

I was also not.

And the not part was mostly the fact that Mo and I made love, but he never touched my tits.

He barely even looked at them.

"Mo, when we have sex, you don't—" I began.

That was as far as I got because he cut off my words by tossing the bralette to the side, putting two big hands on my waist, lifting me up, planting my ass on the counter and then he put those two big hands to my breasts.

He lifted one up.

He bent to it.

Then he sucked my nipple deep into his mouth.

Oh…

Nice.

My head fell back and my hands went to his scalp, gliding over, fingers linking at the back.

His head and my hands moved to the other nipple while he rolled the one he'd left gently with his thumb.

I was breathing heavy when his mouth went away, his hands covered my breasts, and his lips came to mine.

"You were healing," he whispered, looking into my eyes.

"I'm fine now," I whispered back.

"Okay," he said.

That was it.

Mo said it was okay.

And it was okay.

He ran his thumbs hard over my nipples before he slid his hands to my back, slanted his head and took my mouth.

It was getting serious. I was enjoying the feel of that serious. Mo had moved one hand back to a breast and was kneading it, his other hand shoving in at my back so I was arched into him, when a pounding came at the door.

Mo lifted his head up.

"*Mac, open this goddamned door!*"

Oh man.

Smithie.

What now?

"I love my job. You love your job. I got a great family. You got a great family. We both got kickass friends," Mo growled. "And we're still moving to Hawaii."

On that, he turned on his bare foot and stalked out.

I moved to snatch up my bralette and pull it on. I then grabbed the cream cotton camisole that matched the cream in the waistband of my shorts and was skintight, even if in the chest area there was less to be tight against, and tugged that on.

Then I went flying from the bathroom just as I heard, "*You are not horning in on my action!*"

That wasn't Smithie.

That was Tex.

Oh shit.

I kicked up my pace and rounded the corner at the bottom of the stairs only to slam into Mo's immovable back.

He twisted to catch me with an arm and pull me to the side just as Tex caught sight of me, jabbed a finger Smithie's way, and boomed, "*Tell him! He's not hornin' in on my action!*"

"Tex, honey, what are you talking about?" I asked in what I hoped was a calming voice.

"You asked Tex to give you away?" Smithie demanded to know…from me.

Yeah.

Oh shit.

"Tex?" he bit out. "Not me?"

Shit.

"Smithie—" I started.

"I'm her stepfather," Tex mini-boomed to Smithie.

"I don't give a shit," Smithie returned to Tex.

Tex's face started getting red.

Ah, hell.

"You got other daughters, *ones you made*," Tex shot back. "Give *them* away."

"I will," Smithie rejoined. "The ones of my blood *and* the ones who want me to who dance for me."

"Dance for you? *Dance for you?*" Tex was winding himself up and I knew he'd finished that endeavor when he put both hands to his head and then jerked them straight up, bellowing, "That's entirely *loco!*"

"What's loco about it?" Smithie retorted. "No one gets to say what family is."

He had a point there.

Tex stabbed a finger my way with his gaze still locked on Smithie. "I sleep beside her mother."

"I introduced her to her man," Smithie fired back.

He kinda did that too, just not for the reason that brought us to now.

Tex gave up on Smithie and looked at me.

"He is *not* hornin' in on my action."

I had to find a compromise.

Immediately.

"Are you gonna dance with me at the reception?" I asked, thinking Tex would balk at that for sure and I could give the walk-down-the-aisle part to Tex and the father-daughter dance to Smithie.

"Yes," Tex answered immediately.

I blinked.

"You are?" I queried.

"Fuck yes. The father dances with his girl after the wedding. Right?" Tex replied.

"Yes," I whispered, and did it feeling Mo's arm get tighter around me.

Tex nodded sharply and stated, "I've already picked the song. 'Not

While I'm Around.'"

Oh boy.

I knew that song.

Uh-oh.

I was going to cry.

While I fought that urge, I felt the room and knew Smithie knew that song too and Tex just won the argument.

"What's Ray gonna do in all this?" Smithie asked me quietly, giving in without saying the words.

Ray was my biological dad. Since he began his ongoing gambling recovery, our relationship had been somewhat repaired. Like Mo's oldest sister, for the sake of family, and because she had a generous heart, Jet had asked our dad to give her away at her wedding.

Then again, that hadn't worked out all that well and not because Dad was a dick. Because Eddie had taken one look at Jet in her wedding dress and broke ranks at the altar to prowl down the aisle and claim her before Dad got the shot to give her away.

It was hilarious.

It super sweet.

It was totally romantic.

And it was hot as fuck.

Sadly, the scars my father left me would never go away, so he wasn't going to get that honor from me mostly because I was grown up, and Tex still lived the words of the song he'd picked for our dance. On the other hand, Dad played a role in making me, and throughout my life, he'd never lived those words.

"He'll be invited," I told Smithie. "But I think he'll get why he won't play a bigger part."

"Right then," Smithie muttered, lifting a hand and rubbing it over the top of his head. He dropped his hand and went on, "So, guess I'll see you Tuesday next."

Current drama over.

It was good to be loved.

I just wished being that loved wasn't so loud and didn't interrupt bathroom-counter sex with my man.

I mean seriously, if this shit didn't stop, my neighbors were going to come over and complain *to me*.

"Yeah, Smithie," I replied.

Smithie studied my face, couldn't process the love I knew was shining there in company, so he turned his attention up to Mo.

"Hey, Mo."

"Yo," Mo grunted.

With that, Smithie took his leave, but not before I grabbed his hand as he tried to make by me and made him stop so I could give it a squeeze.

Smithie squeezed back.

Then he vamoosed.

When we heard the front door close, Tex asked me, "Am I gonna have to fight 'em all back with a club?"

He might mean Ray.

He might mean Mag, Auggie, Axl or Boone.

Hell, he might even mean Paul, Taylor or Rick.

My family was expanding, bonds were tightening, and it was just simply the manner of men I was fortunate enough to have in my life.

But for that role, there was only one for me.

The one who made my mother happy.

And the one who would pick that song to dance the father-daughter dance.

I smiled at my stepdad. "No, Tex, I think you've successfully staked your claim."

"I better," he muttered. Then he asked, "You healin'?"

"Almost good as new," I told him.

He turned to Mo. "What're you up to today?"

"Hopin' I can spend a quiet Saturday with my girl without my sisters, her sisters, my brothers, her brothers, or any other parental units like you fuckin' it up," Mo replied.

"Right, that's my get-the-fuck-out cue," Tex said, came to me, dropped a hand on the top of my head before he removed it and kissed me there, gave Mo an insane-looking grimace that I was pretty sure was a smile, then he took off.

Mo moved to the front door to lock it behind Tex and came back.

The instant he hit the living room, I asked, "Where were we?"

Then I cried out because I was over his shoulder in a fireman's hold.

Seconds later I was on my back in bed with Mo on top of me.

Oh yeah.

That was where we were.

* * * *

Some time later...

"Mag, listen to me, *it's gonna be okay*," I said into my phone.

"Lottie, I'm gonna—"

"Mag," I cut him off, "you're gonna get married tomorrow. The end."

Mag was silent.

I was silent.

He broke it first.

"Have I thanked you, darlin'?"

I smiled. "No."

"Thank you, Lottie," he said softly.

What he was thanking me for, it was my pleasure.

"Don't mention it. Glad you're happy. Glad you're making Evie happy. Now go get some rest. You don't need bags under your eyes in the photos tomorrow."

"Like that'll happen," he muttered.

"It happens, even to dudes," I told him. "You need to hydrate and get sleep, or you'll have puffy eyes."

"I meant resting, babe."

Oh.

He was excited to make it official.

I loved that for Evie.

I loved it more for Mag.

Though I didn't share that with Mag.

He already knew it.

"I gotta check on Mo and Pooks. Make sure he's got her down. You good?" I asked him.

"I'm good, darlin'. Say hey to Mo for me and remind him the time we're hooking up tomorrow and not to forget the ring."

"He won't forget the ring," I assured him. "Later, Mag."

"Later, Lottie."

"At least try to rest."

Soft and sweet came, "I will, darlin'," and I was again oh so glad Evie was getting a lifetime of that.

And glad Mag had Evie to give it to.

We hung up and I placed my phone on the charge pad before I moved through the kitchen, the living room and up the stairs.

I stopped at the top landing, my breath suddenly catching in my throat.

Mo was in the nursery with our baby girl.

I didn't know this because he'd taken her up there twenty minutes ago to put her down.

I didn't know it because I could see him.

I knew it because I could hear him.

"No one's gonna hurt you. No one's gonna dare," his deep voice sounded.

Oh my God.

He was sing-talking *à la* Bono to our little Pooks.

But better.

I pressed my back to the wall and closed my eyes.

Mo's voice came back.

"Whistle, I'll be there."

Oh God.

That was my baby's daddy.

My man.

He kept going.

"Nothing can harm you. Not while I'm around."

I had to swallow the sob that soared up my throat.

I opened my eyes and lifted my hand, staring at the big rock Mo had planted there during our first vacation together. The one we took in Hawaii.

It was nestled above a wide gold band that had a match, the one on Mo's finger.

Our wedding had been *the best*.

Even better than Jet's, and she'd had a hayride.

And my gown had kicked Roxie's gown's ass. Sheer bodice and long sleeves with a full sheer skirt, all covered in sparkling diamanté. Plunging neckline that nearly went down to my navel, slit in the skirt that went up to my left hip, all this stitched to a bodysuit that covered only the important bits.

Outside the pictures of me with Mo, the pic of Tex escorting me down the aisle with my skirt flying out behind me, my left leg exposed from the hip down in full stride, me smiling so big at Mo, even in a picture, it was blinding, and Tex wearing his lunatic grin was my favorite.

Jet had been my matron of honor.

Mag had been Mo's best man.

And Mom had sat between Tex and my dad in the front row after Tex gave me away, Dad smiling huge, fighting tears but not fighting that was the place he needed to be. Just happy he got the honor of being there at all.

By the way, Mo's dad wasn't invited.

But he did send us a wedding card with a hundred-dollar bill in it through the mail, writing that he hoped Mo was happy in a way that screamed it was tentatively…and hopefully.

Mo didn't grab that olive branch.

His father had hurt his mother, his sisters.

For a man like Mo, there was no coming back from that.

Not while he was around.

With that hundred bucks, he took Alex, Dante and Cesar to the batting cages.

As an aside, I'd lost my nephews to their big, badass, commando Uncle Mo. They worshipped him.

I didn't mind.

I totally got that he was way more fun to wrestle with.

Especially when he didn't let you win.

Leaning against the wall, after I pulled it together, and after Mo was done sing-talking, I moved into the hall then to the doorway to Pooks's room.

I rested a shoulder against the jamb.

My mound of hunkalicious husband was in the rocker, the long trunks of his legs stretched out, ankles crossed, using his heel to rock the little bundle in a pink polka-dot onesie held belly and cheek to his wide chest with his hand on her tiny diapered bootie.

Her eyes were closed.

I looked to my man.

"She's asleep," I whispered.

"I know," he whispered back.

Of course he knew.

I said not another word.

I simply smiled at my husband holding our little girl and experienced something I experienced a lot from the minute I met Mo Morrison.

Falling a little deeper in love with him.

Then I left Daddy with his princess, his moon and stars…

And walked to our room.

The End

Also from 1001 Dark Nights and Kristen Ashley, discover Rough Ride and Rock Chick Reawakening.

Sign up for the 1001 Dark Nights Newsletter
and be entered to win a Tiffany Key necklace.

There's a contest every month!

Go to www.1001DarkNights.com to subscribe.

As a bonus, all subscribers can download
FIVE FREE exclusive books!

Discover 1001 Dark Nights Collection Six

DRAGON CLAIMED by Donna Grant
A Dark Kings Novella

ASHES TO INK by Carrie Ann Ryan
A Montgomery Ink: Colorado Springs Novella

ENSNARED by Elisabeth Naughton
An Eternal Guardians Novella

EVERMORE by Corinne Michaels
A Salvation Series Novella

VENGEANCE by Rebecca Zanetti
A Dark Protectors/Rebels Novella

ELI'S TRIUMPH by Joanna Wylde
A Reapers MC Novella

CIPHER by Larissa Ione
A Demonica Underworld Novella

RESCUING MACIE by Susan Stoker
A Delta Force Heroes Novella

ENCHANTED by Lexi Blake
A Masters and Mercenaries Novella

TAKE THE BRIDE by Carly Phillips
A Knight Brothers Novella

INDULGE ME by J. Kenner
A Stark Ever After Novella

THE KING by Jennifer L. Armentrout
A Wicked Novella

QUIET MAN by Kristen Ashley
A Dream Man Novella

ABANDON by Rachel Van Dyken
A Seaside Pictures Novella

THE OPEN DOOR by Laurelin Paige
A Found Duet Novella

CLOSER by Kylie Scott
A Stage Dive Novella

SOMETHING JUST LIKE THIS by Jennifer Probst
A Stay Novella

BLOOD NIGHT by Heather Graham
A Krewe of Hunters Novella

TWIST OF FATE by Jill Shalvis
A Heartbreaker Bay Novella

MORE THAN PLEASURE YOU by Shayla Black
A More Than Words Novella

WONDER WITH ME by Kristen Proby
A With Me In Seattle Novella

THE DARKEST ASSASSIN by Gena Showalter
A Lords of the Underworld Novella

Also from 1001 Dark Nights:
DAMIEN by J. Kenner

About Kristen Ashley

Kristen Ashley is the *New York Times* bestselling author of over sixty romance novels including the *Rock Chick, Colorado Mountain, Dream Man, Chaos, Unfinished Heroes, The 'Burg, Magdalene, Fantasyland, The Three, Ghost and Reincarnation, Moonlight and Motor Oil* and *Honey* series along with several standalone novels. She's a hybrid author, publishing titles both independently and traditionally, her books have been translated in fourteen languages and she's sold over three million books.

Kristen's novel, *Law Man*, won the *RT Book Reviews* Reviewer's Choice Award for best Romantic Suspense. Her independently published title *Hold On* was nominated for *RT Book Reviews* best Independent Contemporary Romance and her traditionally published title *Breathe* was nominated for best Contemporary Romance. Kristen's titles *Motorcycle Man, The Will, Ride Steady* (which won the Reader's Choice award from *Romance Reviews*) and *The Hookup* all made the final rounds for Goodreads Choice Awards in the Romance category.

Kristen, born in Gary and raised in Brownsburg, Indiana, was a fourth-generation graduate of Purdue University. Since, she has lived in Denver, the West Country of England, and now she resides in Phoenix. She worked as a charity executive for eighteen years prior to beginning her independent publishing career. She currently writes full-time.

Although romance is her genre, the prevailing themes running through all of Kristen's novels are friendship, family and a strong sisterhood. To this end, and as a way to thank her readers for their support, Kristen has created the Rock Chick Nation, a series of programs that are designed to give back to her readers and promote a strong female community.

The mission of the Rock Chick Nation is to live your best life, be true to your true self, recognize your beauty and take your sister's back whether they're friends and family or if they're thousands of miles away and you don't know who they are. The programs of the RC Nation include: Rock Chick Rendezvous, weekends Kristen organizes full of parties and get-togethers to bring the sisterhood together; Rock Chick Recharges, evenings Kristen arranges for women who have been nominated to receive a special night; and Rock Chick Rewards, an ongoing program that raises funds for nonprofit women's organizations Kristen's readers nominate. Kristen's Rock Chick Rewards have donated nearly $130,000 to charity and this number continues to rise.

You can read more about Kristen, her titles and the Rock Chick Nation at KristenAshley.net.

Discover More Kristen Ashley

Rough Ride: A Chaos Novella
By Kristen Ashley

Rosalie Holloway put it all on the line for the Chaos Motorcycle Club.

Informing to Chaos on their rival club—her man's club, Bounty—Rosalie knows the stakes. And she pays them when her man, who she was hoping to scare straight, finds out she's betrayed him and he delivers her to his brothers to mete out their form of justice.

But really, Rosie has long been denying that, as she drifted away from her Bounty, she's been falling in love with Everett "Snapper" Kavanagh, a Chaos brother. Snap is the biker-boy-next door with the snowy blue eyes, quiet confidence and sweet disposition who was supposed to keep her safe…and fell down on that job.

For Snapper, it's always been Rosalie, from the first time he saw her at the Chaos Compound. He's just been waiting for a clear shot. But he didn't want to get it after his Rosie was left bleeding, beat down and broken by Bounty on a cement warehouse floor.

With Rosalie a casualty of an ongoing war, Snapper has to guide her to trust him, take a shot with him, build a them…

And fold his woman firmly in the family that is Chaos.

* * * *

Rock Chick Reawakening: A Rock Chick Novella
By Kristen Ashley

From *New York Times* bestselling author, Kristen Ashley, comes the long-awaited story of Daisy and Marcus, *Rock Chick Reawakening*. A prequel to Kristen's *Rock Chick* series, *Rock Chick Reawakening* shares the tale of the devastating event that nearly broke Daisy, an event that set Marcus Sloane—one of Denver's most respected businessmen and one of the Denver underground's most feared crime bosses—into finally making his move to win the heart of the woman who stole his.

Dream Maker

The Dream Series, Book 1
By Kristen Ashley
Coming May 26, 2020

From New York Times bestselling author Kristen Ashley comes the first sexy, contemporary romance in a brand-new, spin-off from the Rock Chick and Dream Man series, in which two broken hearts find love and healing in each other.

Evie is a bonafide nerd and a hyper-intelligent chick who has worked her whole life to get what she wants. Growing up, she had no support from her family and has only ever been able to rely on herself. So when Evie decides she wants to earn her engineering degree, she realizes she needs to take an alternative path to get there. She takes a job dancing at Smithie's club thinking this would be a quick side gig, where she can make the money she needs. But with her lack of dancing skills and an alpha bad boy who becomes overly protective, Evie realizes this might not be as easy as she thought.

Daniel "Mag" Magnusson knows a thing or two about pain, but the mask he wears is excellent. No one can tell that this good-looking, quick-witted, and roguish guy has deep-seated issues. Mag puts on a funny-guy routine so he can hide his broken heart and PTSD. But when Evie dances her way into Mag's life, he realizes that he needs to come face-to-face with the demons of his past if he wants a future with her.

* * * *

I did not have the time, or the inclination (that last was a bit of a lie) to be charmed by, become besotted with and put the effort into taming a brokenhearted manwhore who was so pretty, my heart wept just watching him laugh.

But in the end, that heart would just be broken.

Because he'd break it.

"What's funny?" I asked.

"You might have wanted to leave some of the stock of Urban Outfitters for the other nostalgics," he answered on a grin.

Did he…

Actually…

Say that?

"Some of it's from Anthropologie," I sniffed.

He busted out laughing again.

"And some of it is vintage," I snapped over his hilarity.

Now, he looked like he was fighting bending double with his amusement.

"What do you drive?" I queried.

"F-250," he answered, still chucking.

"Sorry?"

"Ford F-250. A truck. A big one. And no, it's not diesel and it absolutely does not plug into anything."

I felt my lips thin.

He grinned again.

"I see we're gonna discuss global warming over dinner," he noted.

"There's nothing to discuss. The globe is warming. Thus, we *all* should take some responsibility for turning that around. End of topic," I retorted.

He was *still* grinning when he said, "Chill, Evan. I'm teasing you. Your pad is tight. I like it. And cross my heart," and he did just this with a very long, well-shaped forefinger, "I put all my leftovers in those reusable Ziplocs Mac bought us, and as often as I can, I refuse a straw."

"The end of the world as we know it isn't funny," I informed him.

"I'm not kidding."

I studied his face in an attempt to ascertain if that was a lie.

He was apparently being honest.

Or he was a good liar.

He smiled at me again and said softly, "Your jewelry."

"Right," I muttered, turned and walked back to my bedroom.

My mind ran amuck (mostly with thoughts about how soft his hair might be, then trying to stop thoughts of how soft his hair might be) as I put my little gold ball studs in my ears and one midi-ring on my left forefinger that had a line of tiny emeralds across the font.

This completed my outfit of army green crop pants, gray scoop-necked, relax-fit tee (which I'd also given the French tuck), and the sand-colored blazer I was going to don when I got back to the kitchen.

I walked out and I did so carefully because Mag was still standing in my living room, he was watching me, and I'd been known to be a klutz and I did not want to date this guy, but I also did not want to make a fool of myself in front of him.

I went to the kitchen to shove my phone and lip gloss in my little bag and put on my blazer.

As my kitchen had a huge opening to the living room, Mag asked through it, "Did you put on your jewelry?"

"Yes."

There was a pause then, "Did good, babe. You as gorgeous as you are, you don't need much."

My fingers stilled.

I wanted to be offended he'd called me "babe" and thought I needed his approval of my accessorizing.

All I could hear was the word "gorgeous."

And this was the charm I needed to guard against.

The problem with that was it felt too nice aimed my way.

I didn't know what to do, or say, so I looked down to my bag, fumbled my lip gloss, it fell off the counter, I bent to retrieve it…

And then, typical, within minutes of meeting him, I gave him a massive dose of the real Evan Gardiner.

This being, I slammed my forehead into the edge of the counter.

And that hurt.

A lot.

"Shit. Evan," Mag called.

But I did not reply because I was in the midst of overcompensating the recovery. Staggering back, I slammed into the counter behind me, the edge of it digging painfully into the small of my back, and between the crack on my head making me dizzy and the sting in my back, I went down, flat on my ass.

Fabulous.

Mag was there in what seemed like half a second, crouching beside me, his long, strapping thighs splayed wide, his trousers molded to the curves and dips of his clearly muscular knees, his hand coming toward me.

I started to rear away from it, and he murmured, "Whoa," and again moved fast so I banged the back of my head into his palm which cracked against the cupboard.

I heard Nancy Kerrigan's plaintive cry in my head, but mine had to do with why I'd given into this date.

"Oh God, sorry," I muttered, totally mortified.

"Just…don't move," he ordered, taking control of my chin and lifting it slowly.

I forced my eyes to his face to see him examining my forehead, but that close, I could see how curly his eyelashes were.

Not good.

Because they were *awesome*.

"Smacked yourself a good one," he murmured.

Man.

This was just…

Humiliating.

"I think you need ice," he went on.

"I—"

I stopped speaking because he moved fast again, doing this to pick me up.

Pick me up.

One arm under my knees, one at my upper back.

I was so stunned by this maneuver, not only him doing it, but his being *able* to do it, I said not a word as he walked me to my couch, laid me down on it, then strode back to the kitchen.

I heard the ice machine grinding and then he returned with a bundled dishtowel.

"Lay back," he demanded.

I reclined against my fringed toss pillows and Mag gently set the bundle on my forehead.

"You need at least fifteen, twenty minutes of that which means we're gonna miss our reservation. I'll order a pizza," he declared. "Let me guess. Your half, veggie."

I was not thrilled (at all) that I'd blown this date the way I had.

But one could not say I wasn't thrilled I'd blown this date and now had a real excuse to get out of it.

In an effort to do that, I peered out from under the towel and started, "Danny—"

"Mag."

"Sorry."

"What?"

"What?" I parroted, because he wasn't close, but he was not far, and I could see how curly his eyelashes were again.

"You said my name."

"I did?"

His eyes narrowed and he stopped bending over me, holding the ice to my head, and bent *into* me, pulling the ice away and staring into my eyes.

"What day is it?" he asked.

"Tuesday."

"Who set us up?"

"Lottie."

He held three fingers up to my face. "How many fingers do you see?"

"Three, Mag, stop it. I'm okay. I just…"

I didn't finish.

"What?" he asked.

"Just…"

I again didn't finish.

"What, Evan?"

God, really, was he actually that handsome?

And right there, hovering over me, looking concerned, which made him even *more* handsome?

"Evan?" he called.

"Your eyelashes are very curly," I whispered.

That was when he did it.

His gaze changed, it was an amazing change I felt in amazing places, it shifted to my mouth, and I felt that too, it was also amazing, and last, he murmured, "Baby."

"I'm not your baby," I breathed.

His gaze shifted back to my eyes, and he rumbled, all sexy, hot and sweet, "Oh yeah, you are."

My toes curled.

"Danny—"

"Mag."

"Mag, I—"

My phone buzzed with a text.

He looked to the counter that delineated kitchen from living room, to me, put the ice back on and ordered, "Hold that."

I did as told, and he straightened and took the single step it took him with his long-ass legs to get to the counter.

"What the fuck?" he asked.

I kept the ice where it should be but tipped my head to look at him only to see him reading my screen.

Yes.

Reading my screen.

"What are you doing?"

His eyes dropped down to me. "Who you gonna meet at Storage and

Such on East Colfax at eleven fuckin' thirty, Evan?"

Uh-oh.

"*Why* you gonna meet someone at Storage and Such on East fuckin' Colfax at eleven fuckin' thirty?" he continued.

I pushed up and reached out a hand. "Give me my phone."

"Answer me," he demanded testily.

I twisted in the couch to put my feet on the floor, saying, "I've known you all of ten minutes. You can't read my texts and it's none of your business who I meet where."

"You got a situation?" he asked.

I didn't.

My brother obviously did.

"No," I semi-lied.

"You keep bad company?" he asked.

I didn't.

But my brother totally did.

"No," I did not lie, though I had a feeling, if I went to Storage and Such on East Colfax, I would be.

My phone chimed again with another text and his eyes went direct to it.

Now...

Really.

I stood, pulling the ice off my head and snapping, "Danny!"

He looked to me and growled, "It says meet outside unit six and come alone."

I slowly closed my eyes and let my head fall back.

"Evan."

He was still growling.

I said nothing.

Come alone.

Mick, what mess are you in now? I thought.

"*Evie*," Mag clipped.

I opened my eyes and righted my head.

"There's a favor I need to do for my brother."

"At eleven thirty on East Colfax?"

I tipped my head to the side and shrugged, but that was a sham seeing as a chill was racing up my spine.

"Lie down. Ice on," he bit out.

"Danny—"

"Lie your ass down and get that ice back to that bump, Evie, then we'll talk."

"We won't talk, you'll just go. Obviously, the date's off for this evening. We'll reschedule."

Or we would *not*.

"Mac says you're a genius," he announced, apropos of nothing.

I blinked and asked, "What?"

"Lottie. She says you're a genius."

Wow.

That was nice.

"She says you told her that you took apart a radio, and put it back together," he carried on. "When you were six."

I did do that.

My mother thought I was a freak.

My father bought every broken radio he could find at thrift shops, brought them home, made me fix them, then sold them at triple what he bought them for.

I didn't, incidentally, see a dime of those earnings.

I was six, but, you know, *allowance*.

Maybe?

Mag continued talking.

"So, genius, look at my face and tell me if I'm leaving."

Dream Man Box Set, Books 1-4

By Kristen Ashley
Now Available

Meet the intense and sexy men of the Dream Men series from the *New York Times* and *USA Today* bestselling author of the Rock Chick Series!

Mystery Man
Gwendolyn Kidd has met the man of her dreams. He's hot, he's sexy, and what started as a no-names-exchanged night of passion has blossomed into a year and a half-long pleasure fest. Hawk Delgado has demons that keep him from connecting with anyone. But when Gwen is threatened, Hawk's protective nature comes out in full force. The problem is, when Gwen gets a dose of Hawk's Alpha attitude in the daylight, she's not so sure he's the one anymore.

Wild Man
Tessa O'Hara never expected the man of her dreams to walk into her bakery. Within thirty seconds he asks her out for a beer. But when she discovers he's an undercover DEA agent-and he's investigating her possible role in her ex-husband's drug business, Tess declares their relationship is over. Brock disagrees. He's committed to his mission, but he's fallen in love with the beautiful woman who's as sweet as her cupcakes-and he'll do anything to win her back.

Law Man
Sweet, shy Mara Hanover is in love with her neighbor. For four years, she has secretly watched her dream man from afar. Handsome police detective Mitch Lawson is way out of her league. She's a girl from the wrong side of the tracks, and there's no way a guy like Mitch would want anything to do with her. But when Mara gets pulled back into the life she's tried so hard to leave behind, it's Mitch who comes to her rescue.

Motorcycle Man
Tyra Masters has had enough drama to last a lifetime. Now she's back on track and looking forward to her new quiet life. Until she meets the man of her dreams. The tattooed, muscled biker plies her with tequila-and the best sex of her life. She knows Kane "Tack" Allen is the kind of man she's always wanted. Unfortunately, he's also her new boss...

Discover 1001 Dark Nights

COLLECTION ONE
FOREVER WICKED by Shayla Black
CRIMSON TWILIGHT by Heather Graham
CAPTURED IN SURRENDER by Liliana Hart
SILENT BITE: A SCANGUARDS WEDDING by Tina Folsom
DUNGEON GAMES by Lexi Blake
AZAGOTH by Larissa Ione
NEED YOU NOW by Lisa Renee Jones
SHOW ME, BABY by Cherise Sinclair
ROPED IN by Lorelei James
TEMPTED BY MIDNIGHT by Lara Adrian
THE FLAME by Christopher Rice
CARESS OF DARKNESS by Julie Kenner

COLLECTION TWO
WICKED WOLF by Carrie Ann Ryan
WHEN IRISH EYES ARE HAUNTING by Heather Graham
EASY WITH YOU by Kristen Proby
MASTER OF FREEDOM by Cherise Sinclair
CARESS OF PLEASURE by Julie Kenner
ADORED by Lexi Blake
HADES by Larissa Ione
RAVAGED by Elisabeth Naughton
DREAM OF YOU by Jennifer L. Armentrout
STRIPPED DOWN by Lorelei James
RAGE/KILLIAN by Alexandra Ivy/Laura Wright
DRAGON KING by Donna Grant
PURE WICKED by Shayla Black
HARD AS STEEL by Laura Kaye
STROKE OF MIDNIGHT by Lara Adrian
ALL HALLOWS EVE by Heather Graham
KISS THE FLAME by Christopher Rice
DARING HER LOVE by Melissa Foster
TEASED by Rebecca Zanetti
THE PROMISE OF SURRENDER by Liliana Hart

COLLECTION THREE
HIDDEN INK by Carrie Ann Ryan
BLOOD ON THE BAYOU by Heather Graham
SEARCHING FOR MINE by Jennifer Probst
DANCE OF DESIRE by Christopher Rice
ROUGH RHYTHM by Tessa Bailey
DEVOTED by Lexi Blake
Z by Larissa Ione
FALLING UNDER YOU by Laurelin Paige
EASY FOR KEEPS by Kristen Proby
UNCHAINED by Elisabeth Naughton
HARD TO SERVE by Laura Kaye
DRAGON FEVER by Donna Grant
KAYDEN/SIMON by Alexandra Ivy/Laura Wright
STRUNG UP by Lorelei James
MIDNIGHT UNTAMED by Lara Adrian
TRICKED by Rebecca Zanetti
DIRTY WICKED by Shayla Black
THE ONLY ONE by Lauren Blakely
SWEET SURRENDER by Liliana Hart

COLLECTION FOUR
ROCK CHICK REAWAKENING by Kristen Ashley
ADORING INK by Carrie Ann Ryan
SWEET RIVALRY by K. Bromberg
SHADE'S LADY by Joanna Wylde
RAZR by Larissa Ione
ARRANGED by Lexi Blake
TANGLED by Rebecca Zanetti
HOLD ME by J. Kenner
SOMEHOW, SOME WAY by Jennifer Probst
TOO CLOSE TO CALL by Tessa Bailey
HUNTED by Elisabeth Naughton
EYES ON YOU by Laura Kaye
BLADE by Alexandra Ivy/Laura Wright
DRAGON BURN by Donna Grant
TRIPPED OUT by Lorelei James
STUD FINDER by Lauren Blakely
MIDNIGHT UNLEASHED by Lara Adrian

On behalf of 1001 Dark Nights,

Liz Berry and M.J. Rose would like to thank ~

Steve Berry
Doug Scofield
Kim Guidroz
Jillian Stein
InkSlinger PR
Dan Slater
Asha Hossain
Chris Graham
Fedora Chen
Kasi Alexander
Jessica Johns
Dylan Stockton
Richard Blake
and Simon Lipskar

Printed in Great Britain
by Amazon